BROKEN THINGS *to Mend*

BROKEN THINGS *to Mend*

Karey White

Orange Door Press

Broken Things to Mend

Cover Design by Rachael Anderson
Cover Photography by Natasha Kimball

ISBN: 978-1-941898-10-9

Published by Orange Door Press

For the lonely who are tempted to give up.

Don’t do it.
Hang on to hope.

Also by Karey White

My Own Mr. Darcy

The Husband Maker

The Match Maker

The Wife Maker

Maggie's Song
(found in The Timeless Romance Anthology)

Lost and Found

Gifted

For What It's Worth

Prologue

1982

"No, no, Mr. Toller. You missed the road." Pearl turned in the seat of Jack's classic International pickup and pointed back at the road they'd passed.

"Pearl, it's getting late and I've got almost a hundred math tests to grade tonight." Jack sounded impatient and Pearl could tell he'd had enough of this wild goose chase of a night. But that was too bad. She needed him to go back and turn down that road.

After tonight he'd be happy he had listened to the old Chinese lunch lady.

"Go back now. Turn down that road." Pearl's words sounded frantic, her accent more pronounced. Jack ignored her and kept driving. "I said go back. You must listen to me, young man. Go back now." She emphasized every word with a staccato swat on his arm. She may have been a tiny woman, but she wasn't afraid to give him orders.

Jack slowed the pickup and pulled onto the gravel

shoulder of the road. "We've been driving for more than an hour, and so far you haven't shown me anything remarkable. I don't even know what you're looking for. I have hours of work ahead of me, it's after nine, and I need to get home." Jack turned in his seat and studied Pearl's face. "Do you even know what you're looking for?"

Pearl ignored the question and turned in her seat to look back at the road they had missed. The antique comb that held up her dark hair caught the light of the dashboard. She slowly turned back around and lowered her voice. "You must trust me. Go back to that road."

She had doubted that Jack would listen to her in the first place. He had looked surprised when, a little after seven, he'd opened his front door to see the new lunch lady from Sisters High School. He'd only said a few words to her since school had started, and that had been when he arranged to pay for the lunch of a student whose father had lost his job. Standing there on his front porch, she had asked him to take her for a quick drive. There was something important she needed to show him. Had she not been a tiny, old, Chinese woman, he probably would have shut the door on her, but Pearl knew she seemed harmless, and she could tell he was curious. Now for almost ninety minutes Jack had been driving Pearl up and down the country roads between Bend and Sisters, while she waited for a warm tingling in her fingers and toes.

Now she had the feeling and Jack wanted to quit. Why was it so hard for some people to let her help them? Why did so many have to be dragged kicking and screaming to their good fortune?

When Pearl spoke again, her voice was calm and determined. "That's the road. Go back to that road, Mr. Toller. You'll see."

Jack sighed, put the pickup in gear, and completed a

three-point turn. "I told you to call me Jack. And this is the last road I'm driving down tonight. If whatever you're wanting to show me isn't on this road, you're out of luck."

Jack saw Pearl's satisfied smile in the lights from the dashboard. She nodded and patted his arm, gently now. "This is it. You'll see."

Jack turned down the road Pearl had pointed out. It was a narrow two-lane, its surface tar and gravel instead of the blacktop they'd just left. He wasn't sure where it led, but he was sure it was taking him farther away from Sisters and the algebra tests waiting for his attention.

Pearl leaned forward in her seat, peering out the windshield. The headlights illuminated the deserted road. Silhouettes of tall pines rose ominously on either side of them. Pearl shivered, in spite of the warmth in her hands and feet, and she knew she couldn't let Jack abandon this outing.

They followed a bend in the road, then Jack slowed the pickup. "What the devil?" he said under his breath. Pearl relaxed into the back of the seat, suddenly tired. An attractive woman stepped around the open hood of a Chrysler Cordoba. She held her hand over her eyes, trying to see beyond the glare of the pickup's headlights. "Did you know she was here?" Jack sounded incredulous.

"You should go help her," Pearl said and closed her eyes. "I'll wait here."

Every once in a while there was something about a match that stayed with Pearl and ate at her like a flat-headed borer beetle gnawing away at the leaves of a sycamore. Jack and

Sharon were one of those matches. Pearl had already moved to Lake Oswego when they married, but over the next few years, the Tollers often came to her mind.

Almost nine years after their wedding, she felt compelled to drive over five hours from Seattle, where she had successfully matched seven couples and was scheming to match a particularly stubborn woman with a wonderful, if slightly homely, man. Sharon had been thrilled that Pearl would stop by as she was "driving through." They went to lunch at BJ's and talked for over an hour. Sharon had told her they'd been trying for years to start a family and how desperately they hoped it would someday happen. Pearl didn't tell her it already had.

Eight and a half months later, Pearl went to the library and looked up the birth announcements for Sisters, Oregon. Sure enough, Jack and Sharon had welcomed a baby boy, Silas James Toller.

Seven years later, Pearl was walking through a park in Northern California, timing a fabricated fall so that the two kind souls who would be closest to help her would be Mindy and Chip. They didn't know each other—yet—but someday they'd tell their children they met helping a clumsy, old, Chinese woman when she sprained her ankle. A cloud passed over the sun, and a cold dread swirled around Pearl, blowing the images of Jack and Sharon's faces into her mind. Ten minutes later, she limped away from a chatting Mindy and Chip and found a quiet corner. A couple of phone calls later, she was on the road to Sisters.

Pearl sat in the back of the church as people walked by the two coffins. Her heart ached for the abbreviated lives of Jack and Sharon, but that wasn't why she was here. Before the service started, Jack's sister Nancy walked to the front of the chapel, holding the hand of a little, sandy-haired boy. They stood together as the coffins were closed, then turned to take their seats on the front row. Across the congregation of friends and family, Nancy caught sight of Pearl. She settled Silas beside another woman and walked back to where Pearl was sitting.

"Please don't leave when this is over," Nancy whispered to Pearl. "I'd like Silas to meet the woman who brought his parents together."

That was the day Silas met Pearl. Aunt Nancy would tell him the story many times but it would be seventeen years before Silas would meet the old Chinese woman again.

Chapter 1

When other passengers asked Celia what was taking her to Sisters, Oregon, she lied.

"I have family there," she told the grandmother who sat down beside her at a stop outside of Chicago.

"Oh good. I was hoping you weren't one of those free spirits who think this is a good way to see the country. Nuts if you ask me." She twirled the fingers of her wrinkled, blue-veined hand by her ear in the universal "crazy" sign. "It's not safe for a young lady to travel alone, especially if you don't have anyone waiting at the station for you. I'd hate for someone to take advantage of you."

Celia didn't tell her that someone already had.

The grandmother slept most of the way to Bloomington, her purse clutched tightly on her lap. When they pulled up to the bus stop, she leaned across Celia and waved out the window to a young mother with two small children. "That's my grandson's wife. She takes such good care of me when I visit her. You'd think I was her very own grandma."

Celia watched the young woman guide her children to

the front of the bus, envious of the excitement on everyone's faces. Before she stood to greet her family, the woman patted Celia's arm. "Be careful, dear, and don't talk to strangers."

A knot formed in Celia's throat as the old woman opened her arms to the waiting family.

To the bedraggled young mother who boarded the bus in Booneville, Missouri, Celia said, "I'm visiting a roommate from college." The mother, barely older than Celia's twenty years, looked wistful at the thought of carefree, college days. She bounced her fussy baby in her lap as the bus moved toward Salina, Kansas, where she would meet her husband who worked on an oil rig. Somewhere near St. Joseph, the young mother asked Celia to hold her baby while she went to the back of the bus to "take a leak." When she returned to her seat thirty-five minutes later, Celia had soothed the baby boy to sleep.

"How'd you do that?"

Celia shrugged.

"Maybe you should keep him. He likes you better'n he likes me."

"No, he really doesn't. I can't keep him," Celia said, as though the woman had been serious. She carefully handed the baby back to his mother and turned toward the window to discourage further conversation.

"Wave goodbye to your new friend," the young mother said, wagging her baby's hand as she moved to the front of the bus in Salina.

It was almost midnight when a man boarded the Greyhound in Denver and took the seat next to her. His caustic cologne fought valiantly to mask the smell of cigarettes and unbathed body. He waited until the city lights no longer illuminated the interior of the bus before he leaned across the armrest and suggested that with the low lights and sleeping passengers, they could have themselves a little fun.

"I'm going to visit my husband," Celia said, and edged closer to the window to put more space between them.

The man leaned far enough into Celia's seat for his arm to touch hers. "Husband, huh? Maybe he should put a ring on that pretty little finger of yours before he lets you outa his sight. Or maybe there ain't no ring after all."

"I lost it," Celia said, hoping her voice didn't betray her panic.

"Uh huh. I'll bet you did." His voice was no longer flirty and suggestive, but hard and mean.

Celia reached for her belongings beneath the seat in front of her and stood. "Could you excuse me?" Her voice shook as she clutched her backpack and stepped around him. She hated that her legs brushed against his knees. Celia took an empty seat closer to the driver. She remained awake throughout the night, afraid the man might follow her.

No one sat beside Celia from Laramie to Burley, Idaho, where a blonde woman with two-inch, dark roots boarded the bus. She surveyed the other passengers for several seconds then settled into the seat next to Celia. She turned her red-rimmed eyes and bruised cheek away and opened a book. When she hadn't turned a single page between Burley and Boise, Celia knew the book was an excuse not to engage in conversation.

The book hadn't been necessary.

Celia stared out at the sand-colored land dotted with sagebrush and thought of the framed Ten Commandments that had hung in the living room of Jed and Myra Hundley's house, her second foster home. Since she was lying about herself instead of bearing false witness against her neighbor, would God give her a pass? Probably not.

Celia had been sitting in the church youth circle when a

cute boy had leaned over and asked why she was staying with the Hundley's. "Myra's my aunt," Celia had lied. The boy's mom asked Myra about it in a phone call the next day, and in turn, Myra had asked Celia.

"I didn't want to tell him I was a foster kid."

Myra had put her arm around Celia's shoulders. "I can understand that, but God doesn't say 'tell the truth unless it's embarrassing.' He loves the truth and he hates a lie. It's important to him because he is the author of all truth. Do you understand?"

Celia had nodded, even though she wasn't sure she understood. Why would God care if she wasn't hurting anyone? Why would he want everyone to know what a freak she was?

Celia had been placed with the Hundley's a few weeks before she turned thirteen, and even though they were still getting acquainted, Myra had made Celia a birthday cake, the first one of her life. It had been covered with little blue forget-me-nots because "no one should be forgotten on their birthday."

The Hundley's attended church every week, and the first thing they bought Celia was a dress, so she wouldn't feel uncomfortable in the Lord's house. It was a yellow dress with tiny white flowers and a lace collar. It was the prettiest thing Celia had ever worn, and it was the reason Celia still loved the color yellow.

The second thing they bought her was her own Bible. It even had Celia Edwards engraved on the front in gold. Every evening, after supper, Jed led them in Bible study and family prayer. Myra taught Celia how to pray, so she could take her turn, reminding her to be grateful.

"You know you have a lot to be thankful for, don't you?" Myra asked.

Celia shrugged.

"Honey, you have a smart mind. I saw the report cards in your file. Almost all A's. And with so much going on in your life, too. And you should be thankful for your bravery. You've got all kinds of courage. Mrs. Dimper told me how you took care of your mom while she was sick, and how you called 9-1-1, and how you held your mother's hand so she wouldn't be afraid."

Why did everyone talk about her mother being sick? She wasn't sick. She was a junkie. If she was going to die, why couldn't it have been from a heart attack or cancer destroying her insides instead of a needle in her arm and her nose constantly bleeding? Why couldn't it have been some heartless disease that stole her away instead of her mother choosing drugs instead of her daughter?

Celia didn't like to think about that awful night—her mother's hand gripping hers so tightly she could feel the bones rubbing together, the red and blue lights making frantic patterns on the dingy walls, strangers poking more holes in her mother's arm and pounding her chest as they asked Celia what her mother had taken. Celia didn't know.

"Get the girl outta here," someone had said. At first an officer who was chomping loudly on her gum gently pulled her by the arm, but when Celia wouldn't let go of her mother's now flaccid hand, the woman gave her arm a painful yank.

"You've got to come with me. Don't worry. Everything will be okay," she said through gritted teeth. Celia could see the piece of gum wedged between her teeth at the corner of her mouth and knew everything would not be okay.

Maybe she had been brave, but it was difficult for Celia to be grateful for anything that happened that night.

Myra had taught Celia about gardening, and together they had cared for a little vegetable garden in the back yard because "planting a garden is a sure way to show God you have faith in him." She lived with the Hundley's for almost two years. They had treated Celia with kindness, and she had dreamed of someday becoming their real daughter. She imagined Jed and Myra giving her a new Bible. This time the name on the front would be Celia Hundley instead of Celia Edwards.

Celia had cried herself to sleep for weeks when they had tearfully told her Jed was being forced to transfer to Atlanta, and by law, they couldn't take her with them.

Celia continued to pray through four more families that didn't love her as much as the Hundley's had. Even now she still prayed, though she hadn't felt much of God's love over the past eight years, and she felt a prick of guilt with every lie she told. I'm sorry for lying, she silently prayed. I promise I'll tell the truth when I get there. I just can't explain it to all these strangers. They'll pity me or think I'm crazy.

She imagined the embarrassing conversation that the truth would require.

"Where you headed?" they'd ask.

"Sisters, Oregon."

"Sisters, huh? I've never heard of it. Where is Sisters?"

"North of Bend. In the middle of the state."

"Now *that* I've heard of. What takes you there?"

"A tear."

Chapter 2

Pearl could tell from Silas Toller's voice that he thought she was a strange old woman. Or maybe he thought she was certifiably crazy. Why else would she call him—a relative stranger—and ask him to drive her to Bend? Again. Pearl had been in Sisters only a week, and this was the third time she had called to ask Silas to give her a ride.

Unfortunately, her intuition was shorting out. The first time, Silas had dropped her off at a gift shop while he picked up seeds for his aunt at the garden supply store. While he was gone, she had walked around the streets near the bus terminal, but she hadn't found her. The second time, Pearl had pretended she needed to pick up a package at the Greyhound station. While Silas waited in his Jeep, she went inside, removed a small package she had wrapped herself from her handbag, searched the station for the girl then went back to the Jeep.

Now she was asking him again, and she needed to be right this time.

"I'll be going over to the B-Bend ranger station day after tomorrow. Is there something I can p-pick up for you then?

"Is this your way of saying you don't like my company?" Pearl asked.

She could hear his embarrassment through the phone line. "Oh no, m-ma'am. I'm trying to save you a trip. If you need to go, I can take you."

"I'm teasing you, Silas. But I do appreciate the ride. I'd drive myself if my car wasn't still at the shop." The truth was that her car had been fixed for three days, but it still sat at the garage, waiting for her to pay for the repairs. Having it available to drive herself would be counterproductive.

"Another p-package?" Silas asked.

"I'm afraid so. But I'm hoping this one will be my last."

"I'll take you. I have to drive out to the M-McKay Crossing campground this m-morning to check on snow levels. I can p-pick you up around three."

"Thank you, Silas." Pearl's voice softened. "You're a good boy."

Pearl hung up the phone then pulled on her sweater and walked across Main Street and down 3rd until the houses grew farther apart. It looked like spring, but there was still a winter chill in the air, and Pearl pulled her sweater around her tightly. It would be nice to have her car for little jaunts like this, but how could she ask Silas for a ride if she had her car?

Nancy Toller's house looked straight out of a fairy tale—white fence, arched gate with climbing hydrangea that would look lovely once the weather warmed, gingerbread details. It was a small, charming house with a large garden plot behind it.

"Pearl, come in."

"Thank you. I was hoping we could chat."

Nancy had changed since Pearl had seen her the day of

the funeral. But of course, almost everyone ages. She was fleshier and softer than she had been. Her hair was shorter and instead of the brown hair she'd had the day of the funeral, it was now nearly white.

"Can I get you something to drink?"

"No, no. I'm fine."

The two women looked at each other for several seconds. They each seemed hesitant to speak. Nancy looked confused.

"I'm sorry. I don't mean to stare," Nancy said. "But I can't get over how little you've changed."

This was why it was better to keep moving, why second-generation attachments were dangerous.

"Oh you're too kind."

"No, I'm not. You look the same. I look seventeen years older. Heck, I look about thirty years older, but you look like you haven't aged a day since the last time I saw you."

Pearl held her hand to her mouth and whispered, "Don't tell anyone, but I've had a little work done."

Nancy smiled and relaxed, happy to have an explanation she could accept. "I should get the name of your doctor."

They laughed politely. When the quiet became awkward, Pearl cleared her throat. "You know Jack and Sharon meant a great deal to me." Nancy nodded. "And I've thought of Silas many times over the years. I figured it was time I stopped by to see how he is."

Nancy's face softened and Pearl could tell how much she loved her nephew. "Silas has been a blessing in my life and he's turned into a wonderful man."

Nancy told Pearl about her years with Silas, his love of the Trailblazers, the mountains, and dogs. "He loved Jack's collie. Now he has Winston, a golden retriever. He was a quiet boy and he's a quiet man. I think it's because of the stutter."

"Was that always a problem?"

Nancy shook her head. "No. Before the accident, he was a normal, talkative little boy. He didn't talk at all for several days after they told him his parents had died. He nodded or shook his head or hid behind me. When he finally spoke again, he had the stutter. It used to be worse than it is now. My heart would break for him. Sometimes he'd try to say something and he couldn't get it out. He'd try and try, and finally he'd give up."

"No wonder he's quiet."

"I searched for help for him. One doctor I took him to told me about something called Camp Rock Ridge. It was expensive—three thousand dollars—but I knew he needed it, so I sold his dad's old pickup to pay for it. He spent three weeks at the camp in Washington, working with speech therapists and practicing. The things they taught him helped a lot. He still gets stuck sometimes when he's nervous or under stress, but he's never completely paralyzed by it now. And he almost never stutters around people he knows well."

"He's been lucky to have you," Pearl said.

"No. I'm the lucky one. I never had a chance to have children of my own. He's been a gift to me."

The women sat quietly, thinking.

"I'm happy to see Jack and Sharon's son has become a good man," Pearl said quietly.

"Thank you for checking in on him. I know his parents would be pleased that you cared so much."

The streets in Sisters were quiet, but the few people who drove past Pearl as she walked back to the bed and breakfast smiled and waved. She had lived many places over the years, some remarkable and some forgettable, but something about Sisters had stayed with her. She was sorry she would only be here a few more days.

Chapter 3

The internet had said the average daytime temperature in March was fifty degrees. This wasn't an average March day.

A bitter wind struck Celia in the face when she stepped off the bus in Bend. It felt too much like Chicago. It was a reminder she didn't want, and she zipped up her hoodie. In twenty minutes the bus would take her on the last leg of her journey. Sisters was only twenty-five miles away.

Celia shivered, whether from the chilly air or the uncertainty of her future, she wasn't sure.

Now that she was so close to her destination, she felt the first tugs of doubt. Sisters was a small town, nothing like Chicago. What if there was nowhere to live? What if she couldn't find a job? What if Cassidy figured out where she'd gone and told Damien?

Celia folded her arms tightly against the memories. She was in Oregon, the most beautiful place in the world, according to her mother. It was because of her mom that she was here. When Celia was a small child, before the addictions had stolen her mother's smile, she had told Celia stories about the summer she had spent in Oregon, waiting tables in a picturesque town by the ocean. She had promised that someday she would take Celia there and they'd live in a warm cabin where nothing could hurt them.

Maybe if they had moved here sooner, her mother would still be alive.

Celia's stomach growled, reminding her she hadn't had anything to eat since somewhere in Idaho the day before. The man at the ticket counter told her there was a Safeway around the corner. She had time to grab a snack if she hurried. She lifted her backpack onto her shoulders and hurried out into the blustery wind.

The Safeway wasn't like any grocery store she could remember. Instead of cramped and dirty and crowded, the aisles were wide and the floor sparkled. If she had more time, she would have enjoyed walking up and down each row, imagining hearty meals with fresh bread and real butter.

She bought two cheese sticks and a banana. She wanted to add a candy bar or a bottle of lemonade, but if she did, she would have less than ten dollars, and somehow, ten felt safer than seven or eight.

She wanted to ask the clerk if she knew anything about Sisters, but she didn't. It wouldn't matter what she said anyway. Celia had no choice but to make Sisters work, at least until she had enough money saved to move on.

Maybe she should have chosen Portland or Eugene. There were probably more jobs in a city, and a better chance to find a small apartment or a room for rent. Maybe even a shelter. It was doubtful a town the size of Sisters had a homeless shelter.

Celia shoved the food into her pockets and pulled her hoodie up onto her head. Little crystals of moisture in the air—not really snow, but definitely not rain—prickled her cheeks. She looked up at the overcast sky and shivered. She didn't have anywhere to sleep tonight and less than eleven dollars in her pocket. She had planned to sleep in a park or under a bush until she had found a job and could pay for a place. She hadn't planned on snow or sleet or whatever this was. Wasn't Oregon supposed to be much warmer than Chicago? Celia realized with a sense of panic that she was in trouble. But she'd been in trouble in Chicago, too, and if she had to face a kind of trouble, she'd rather freeze to death here than take the chance of Cassidy's friend, Damien, big and drunk and mean, sneaking into her room again. He'd covered her mouth and held her down. He'd taken everything from her that night—her innocence, her confidence, even her smile. He'd left her with fear and bruises and disgust.

"Now wasn't that special. We'll have to do that again sometime." His words slurred together and he bumped hard into the doorframe as he left the room. She spent most of the night huddled in the corner crying. Before the sun had even peeked through the closed blinds, she had shoved everything she could carry into a pillowcase and the ragged, flowered backpack she had used since she had lived with the Hundleys. She tiptoed past Cassidy and two of her friends who had crashed in the tiny front room. Thankfully, neither of them were Damien. Celia slipped out the door and walked to an all-night grocery store and wandered up and down the aisles until she realized a man with a buzz cut and a tightly cinched belt around his pudgy middle was keeping his eye on her. He was probably a security guard and thought she might steal something.

How ironic that he wanted to protect the store from Celia. It would have been nice if someone would have been around earlier in the night to protect Celia.

Celia walked to try to keep warm. At first the sidewalks were desolate, then a few shopkeepers unlocked their doors. Trucks made morning deliveries to stores and restaurants. A few busy people in suits and dresses stopped at coffee shops on their way to work. As the morning sun rose, the streets became more crowded and energetic and lively. Celia moved unnoticed among the people who moved toward work and opportunity and success. She seemed to be the only person who didn't know where they were going.

Across the street she saw a Barnes and Noble. The warm air in the bookstore thawed her frozen hands and cheeks and by the time she could feel her toes again, she had an idea.

It took a few minutes, but she found an atlas of the United States, and sat down at a low table in the children's section. Maybe she was crazy, but it didn't matter. She was never going back to that apartment, so she might as well figure out where she should go.

The pages were large and colorful with so many towns and cities, it boggled Celia's mind. Every dot on the page represented a place she could go, a place that she hoped would be safer than here.

She started with Georgia. Did the Hundley's still live in Atlanta? She couldn't remember the name of the suburb they'd moved to. She ran her finger back and forth across the state looking for a name that sounded familiar, but nothing rang a bell. It was probably best anyway. By now they probably had a new family, a lucky little girl or boy they'd saved from the foster system. Celia bit the sides of her mouth and tried not to hate a nameless child that had probably received the love she had wanted.

Disappointed that she couldn't remember where the Hundley's lived, Celia turned the page. Hawaii. Although a warm, tropical climate sounded appealing, Celia didn't have enough money for an airplane ticket.

She spent a few minutes looking over the map of Idaho. She skipped past the page of Illinois. Why look at it when it was Illinois she was trying to escape. Iowa was too close. Page by page, she eliminated towns and cities. And then she flipped from Oklahoma to Oregon. The page looked different, the colors more inviting.

Celia could hear her mother's voice as she lay beside her. "Someday I'll take you to Oregon. It's the prettiest place on earth. The trees are tall and straight and the ocean is brave and beautiful."

"How can the ocean be brave?" Celia had asked.

"Some places the ocean is soft and easy and warm, but in Oregon, it's rocky and brisk. The water there has to crash over big, black stones to get to shore. It isn't easy, but the sound it makes is beautiful. Like music. And the spray, when it crashes against the rocks, is like a dance. The bravest thing I ever did was set off by myself to see the Oregon coast. I should have stayed there."

"Why don't you go back?"

Her mother had sighed. "I will when I feel strong again. Oregon isn't for the weak."

Celia hadn't understood what her mother was talking about, but sitting at that little table in Barnes and Noble, looking at the green map of Oregon, she'd pulled courage from the page. It was the only place she knew her mother had loved, the only place her mother had felt brave and in control of her life. Maybe it would do the same for her.

She ran her finger over the map, looking at the names of the towns and cities. She didn't know where her mother had lived, but as long as it was Oregon, she thought it would be okay. She remembered her mother's long, brown hair, before it had turned limp and dirty. She remembered her warm hand when it was strong and didn't shake. She missed her.

The page became blurry, and a tear slid down her cheek and fell onto the map. She wiped her eyes on her sleeve and looked down at the darker green spot where her tear had soaked into the page. It had landed on Sisters.

It had felt perfect. It was only the name of a town, but it sounded friendly and loving, like a real family. Celia closed the atlas and hugged it to her. She would leave this cold, dangerous place. She would go to Sisters, Oregon.

She had transferred the contents of the pillowcase into a battered little suitcase she found at a thrift store for six dollars. She walked to the bus station, where she had purchased a ticket and slept the night on a hard bench close to the ticket counter, because the benches in the darker corners scared her.

That had been three days ago. Now her journey was almost over. She walked across the parking lot and the bus station came into view. A bus pulled out of the parking lot and drove down the street. It took a moment for Celia to realize it was the bus she'd been on. Her bus—the one that was supposed to take her to Sisters and a new start—was leaving without her. Celia ran down the road, flailing her arms in a desperate attempt to catch the driver's attention. She thought he might have seen her when the air brakes gasped and the lights on the back of the bus lit up, but it didn't even come to a complete stop before it turned right and disappeared behind a building. How could she have lost track of time? She had her backpack, but the little suitcase was still on the bus.

Celia staggered back a few steps and collapsed against the side of a parked car. A soft sob escaped her throat. If she had ever had the bravery of the Oregon ocean, or her mother, or the kind Myra Hundley had praised her for, it had just run out.

Chapter 4

Silas waited in the parking lot at the bus station. Icy particles landed on his windshield where the warmth from inside the Jeep melted them. It looked like it might snow, and he hoped Pearl would be ready to go home after she picked up her package. He was tired and still had some paperwork to finish up at the station before he could go home and watch a Trailblazers game with a bowl of reheated chili.

Pearl walked out of the bus station and looked around the parking lot with a curious expression. Could she really not remember where he'd parked? She was a strange woman. He could have sworn she looked right at him before she turned and started around the building. Silas opened the door and called out her name, but she kept walking, so he closed the door, turned on the ignition, and started to drive toward her.

Pearl moved quickly for a woman her age. She crossed the road and began walking toward the grocery store. If she needed to stop at Safeway, all she'd had to do was ask. He eased the Jeep across the road and into the other parking lot, but Pearl wasn't walking to the store. She was walking the opposite direction. He turned down a row of cars and craned his neck to see where she had gone. There she was, talking to someone.

Silas pulled even with Pearl and the woman. She looked young, couldn't be long out of high school, and she was crying. The girl flinched away when Pearl reached up to pat her cheek, so Pearl brought her hand back down. They spoke for a minute, and Silas didn't know if he should park or stay where he was. Pearl solved his dilemma a minute later by coming to the driver's window.

"Silas, dear, could you call your aunt and let me speak to her?"

Silas pulled out his phone and dialed his aunt. "Hi, Aunt Nancy. P-Pearl needs to talk to you."

"Nancy, would you mind going to the bus stop for me? In about fifteen minutes the Greyhound will get there and they have a suitcase that belongs to a girl who is no longer on the bus. She was supposed to get off at Sisters but missed the connection at Bend. I think they'll leave it with you if you tell them she's your grand-daughter. We'll be along shortly and we'll pick it up at your house."

Aunt Nancy must have agreed because Pearl handed Silas the phone. "Silas, this is Celia. She missed the bus to Sisters. We're going to give her a ride."

"I thought you were here for a p-package, not a p-p—" Silas's lips pursed tightly as the word caught in his mouth. He took a deep breath and let it out slowly. "Person," he finally said.

Pearl turned away as if she hadn't heard him. "Celia, we'll take you to Sisters, and Silas's aunt is picking up your bag."

It was difficult to read the girl's expression. There was something of relief there, but also a wariness, like she didn't know whether she should accept the help Pearl was offering.

"Come on, dear. How else will you get to where you're going?"

Celia shrugged off her backpack and put it on the back seat, then slid in beside it. Pearl climbed in beside Silas and buckled her seatbelt. "Shall we?" she asked and Silas put the car in gear.

The drive to Sisters was silent. Silas wished he had turned on the radio while he waited in the parking lot so it would have been on. Now it felt like turning it on would magnify the awkwardness of the quiet, reminding them all that no one had anything to say. He glanced at the girl in the rearview mirror, careful so she wouldn't see him looking at her. He needn't have worried. She stared out the window the entire trip. This made it easier to inspect her, and he found his eyes drawn toward her face repeatedly.

The girl had pretty features—smooth skin, large blue eyes, and shiny brown hair. Everything about her looked young except her eyes. There was something about the far-off gaze that spoke of loss and sadness and something else. Silas wasn't sure what it was, but her eyes triggered something inside him and he wanted to know what lived behind their sorrow.

Silas ran into Aunt Nancy's and picked up a small, battered bag before he parked behind Home Sweet Home Bed and Breakfast. "Thank you, Silas. You're a fine young man." Pearl patted his arm and turned around to face Celia. "Come in with me, dear. We'll get you all squared away."

Silas got out and picked up the backpack and suitcase

from the back seat.

"I can get those," Celia said.

"S-s-so can I," Silas said as the blood crept up his neck to his ears.

Celia's eyes met his, and if he hadn't looked quickly away in his embarrassment, he'd have realized she had looked away almost as quickly.

Pearl watched them both then barely shook her head and clucked her tongue. These two would not be easy.

Silas dropped the bags inside the front door and walked back out without another word. Pearl watched him go, but Celia didn't even glance in his direction.

Pearl leaned around the doorway into another room. "Jenny?" When no one answered, she took a few steps down the hall. "Jenny?"

"Pearl. Sorry, I didn't hear anyone come in." Jenny stepped out of a room at the end of the hall, wiping her hands on the apron she wore. She was a large-boned woman, probably in her forties, with a gray-blond, no-nonsense bob. There were many men who probably envied Jenny's height. She had to be over six feet tall, and standing next to Pearl, she looked like Goliath's sister. "And who do we have here?" she asked.

"This is Celia. I'm hoping you have an extra room available," Pearl said.

Celia shook her head. "I can't—"

"Yes, you can," Pearl said to Celia, then turned to Jenny. "If no one's in it, maybe you could put her in that pretty yellow room at the end of the hall. I think she likes yellow."

Celia turned to Pearl in stunned silence. How could this woman know her favorite color? And how was it possible that she had been there to rescue Celia when the bus pulled away without her? This wasn't the kind of luck Celia was used to.

"I don't have any money," Celia whispered.

"I know."

"You're in luck," Jenny said brightly, cutting through Celia's discomfort. "It so happens the yellow room is available. Come with me and we'll get you all settled."

"Go on now," Pearl said, gently touching her back to get her to follow Jenny. "Don't forget your bags. You look tired. Why don't you rest for a little while and then I'll stop by and pick you up for dinner." She must have seen Celia's look of concern. "I'm treating. Don't look so troubled. I've been eating alone for days and I want some company."

Pearl turned her back on Celia, effectively ending the conversation. It may have prevented further discussion at the moment, but Celia had some questions, and come dinner, she intended to get some answers.

Chapter 5

Pearl knocked on Celia's door, and the girl opened it about a foot. She eyed Pearl with suspicion. "Are you hungry? Shall we go eat?"

"You really don't have to take me out to dinner. You've already done a lot for me."

"Nonsense. We must eat, so we'll do it together. And we must talk."

Celia slipped sideways through the barely open door. It seemed she tried to disrupt the world around her as little as possible. She followed Pearl down the hall with quiet steps. The woman moved with ease and grace and although she was old, her hair was dark and smooth in the pretty antique comb that held it up. When they reached the sidewalk, Pearl fell into step beside Celia.

"Do you like Mexican food?"

Celia nodded.

"Good. Most people expect me to eat Chinese for every meal, but I like many things. Jenny told me Rio's is good, and we can probably find a quiet table to talk. Did you get a little nap?"

"I was thinking."

"I believe you think too much and sleep too little. You look tired. How many days were you on that bus?"

"Three."

"Did you sleep much?"

Celia shook her head. "Only a little."

"Well then, I think we should eat and talk a bit, and then you should stay in bed until you wake up on your own. I'll talk to Jenny about saving some breakfast for you. Maybe you'll sleep right through to Sunday."

A bald man with a handlebar mustache seated them at a table in the corner. Jenny had been right. Even though the place was busy, conversations were subdued and the food looked plentiful. Celia carefully ordered, searching for the most food for the least money. She rejoiced a little when the waiter brought a bowl of chips and salsa to the table.

Pearl sat with her hands folded in her lap and watched Celia eat. The girl was ravenous and she didn't want to interrupt her with questions until she was comfortable and her hungry tiger tamed.

"I think I know why you're here," Pearl said when only crumbs remained in the bowl of chips.

Celia looked up, alarmed.

"Don't be afraid, dear. I'm your friend. I'm here to help you."

Celia wiped her hands on her napkin. "Why?"

"Because you need it. You're alone and scared, and I want to help you. I've been alone and scared, too, and had it not been for a kind friend, I might have been lost."

A wayward tear escaped Celia's eye, and she quickly brushed it away, angry that she couldn't control her emotions.

"I'm glad you chose Sisters. People here are kind."

The waiter brought steaming plates of food. These were no ordinary tacos. They were juicy and delicious and garnished with vegetables Celia had never seen. She ate in silence while Pearl's mouth took turns eating and talking.

"You don't have to tell me where you came from. I can tell you're running away from something and that's okay. As long as you're willing to run toward something when you see it's good for you." She took a bite and chewed for a moment. "There are good things for you here. I can sense these things. If you're open to it, you'll find happiness here. And peace. I think you would enjoy peace, yes?"

Celia gave an almost imperceptible nod which made Pearl glad. She hoped her words would sink deep into Celia's heart.

"I don't live here. Did you know that?" Pearl asked.

Celia swallowed. "You don't?"

"No. I'm also a guest at the bed and breakfast. But I lived here many years ago. In a little house a few blocks south. But now I live in California. I'm here visiting for a little while. Don't worry. You'll be fine. You're a brave girl. I can see in your eyes that you're afraid, but you're here, starting new with almost nothing. That takes courage."

Celia was finished, but Pearl still had more than half her food. Now it was time to take what little bravery she felt and ask a few questions.

"How did you know I needed a ride?"

"It wasn't hard to tell. You chased that bus, didn't you? That was a clue."

"You saw that?"

Pearl shrugged and took another bite.

"What makes you think I'm running from something? Or that this is where I planned to come. Maybe I was going to Seattle or somewhere else. A big city would have more jobs, you know. How did you know where I was going?"

Pearl reached across the table and patted Celia's arm. "So many questions. Were you going to a big city?"

Celia shook her head.

"This is a good place for you, Celia. It's not like where you came from."

"You don't know where I came from."

"I know."

"Then how do you know this is better?" Her voice was angry.

"I'm an old woman, and old women sometimes know things."

Celia wanted a better answer than that, but Pearl motioned for the waiter, and Celia knew she wouldn't be getting any more answers. At least not tonight.

A feeling of shame settled on Celia as they walked back to Home Sweet Home. This woman had rescued her. She had provided her a place to sleep tonight and had fed her. She had been nothing but kind and Celia had lashed out at her.

"Thank you." Her voice was contrite. "For dinner and my room and, well, everything."

"That's better. Old Chinese women don't like to be yelled at. We prefer to do the yelling." She looked sternly at Celia, before her face broke into a smile. Celia couldn't help but smile back. "You should go to bed. You have many big things ahead of you and they'll be easier after you sleep."

Chapter 6

Silas climbed into the cab of the Tigercat feller. He loved this part of his job. Anyone could drive a truck through Deschutes National Forest and pick up fees at the trailheads or drive through campgrounds to be sure campfire regulations were being obeyed. He didn't mind those parts of the job. They allowed him to make a living without having to do much talking or interacting with people. But thinning the forest in this giant machine was his favorite part. He was one of only a handful of Oregon forest rangers who had been trained to operate all the hand controls and the foot pedals that looked more like a church organ. There was something exhilarating about sitting in the cab, the engine drowning out the outside world, and a tangled, messy clump of trees in front of you. It required finesse and skill to maneuver the long mechanical arm between the healthy trees and pull out the sick and dead ones.

There were four others on his crew. Dan and Rusty were strapping the logs he had piled into bundles and loading them onto the back of the trucks. Emmett and Garth drove the trucks that would haul it all out.

Silas's crew had been sent to the West Bend part of Deschutes National Forest to thin out the dead trees and clean up any fallen debris from last winter's heavy snowfall. Last summer had been a hard one for Central Oregon. Eleven forest fires in Deschutes alone. The more dead timber they cleared out, the less chance there would be that it would serve as tinder if there was another long, dry summer.

Silas guided the arm of the machine, grabbed a tree, sliced it off at the ground then turned it onto its side. Then the arm guided the tree through its clutches, stripping the branches and cutting the tree in twelve foot lengths. Quite a different operation than it would have been a hundred years ago.

This part of the West Bend forest hadn't been thinned in a few years.

"If a tree falls in the forest . . . " Rusty yelled. "What's the rest of it?"

"If a tree falls in the forest and no one's there to hear it, does it make a sound?" Dan shouted.

"Right. That's it. I can't ever remember those things. It's like a joke. I always mess up the punchline."

Silas dropped a length of log onto the pile, sending out an explosion of bark and pine needles.

"We're in the forest and it's definitely making a sound," Rusty shouted.

The men worked without a lot of talk as it was difficult to be heard above the machinery. It was hard work and the men sweated through their clothes in spite of the cool, March day.

A little before lunch, Emmett drove away with the second load of the day. Garth hadn't arrived back, so the men decided it was a good time to eat. Rusty dropped the tailgate on his truck, and he and Dan sat on it and opened their lunches. Silas turned off the Tigercat and retrieved his lunch from behind the seat of the truck.

"Want to join us?" Dan asked.

Silas held up a book—something about World War II—and said, "I think I'll catch up on s-s-some reading." He climbed back in the feller, propped his feet up on the dashboard and ate a sandwich while he read.

"He's a strange one," Rusty said.

"Has been for as long as I've known him."

"How long is that?"

"We went to school together," Dan said. "Clear back to grade school. He's a loner. Doesn't like to talk much. I don't think he really likes people. He'd probably be a hermit if he didn't have to make a living."

"Maybe it's 'cause of his stutter. I wouldn't want to talk either if I couldn't get a whole sentence out."

"His folks died when we were kids," Dan said around a full mouth of bologna sandwich. After he swallowed, he continued. "He never had any good friends. Only thing he did extra-curricular was play soccer. He was fast and could handle the ball real good."

"He looks like he'd be fast—all strong and wiry—but he looks too tall for soccer. Aren't most soccer players short?"

"I don't know about that." Dan lowered his voice a little even though no one but Rusty was close enough to hear him. "You know who Sheila Warnick is?"

"Is she the one who works at Mountain Coffee? Looks like a supermodel or a movie star?"

"Yeah. That's Sheila. She asked Silas to Preference our senior year. Why, I'll never know. She musta' had a thing for mutes or something."

"Or maybe she wanted to do all the talking," Rusty joked.

"Well, she did do that. She tried to make it a nice date.

Went to Portland for her dress, and let me tell you, that dress. Oowee. She was a knockout. Took him to Bend for a fancy dinner before they came back to the school. I think they were waiting in line for pictures, and she said something to him and he didn't answer. She folded her arms and said, 'If you're not going to talk to me, I might as well have come alone.' His face turned all red clear to his ears, but he didn't say a word. Sheila had enough. She took him by the arm and pulled him outa there. I guess she took him home right there on the spot. I don't think he's ever gone on another date."

"Bet he reads a lot of books," Rusty said.

"Some of us were going to bet whether or not he'd ever get married. Or be with a woman at all. Problem was, no one thought he would, so there was no one to bet."

"Too bad 'cause he's an okay looking guy, I guess."

"Sure, but ya gotta be able to talk, right?"

"Well, I'm not sure I'd care if Sheila talked or not."

Both guys laughed.

"Sometimes I feel kinda sorry for him," Dan said. "But mostly, I'm glad I'm not like him."

Chapter 7

Celia didn't sleep until Sunday, as Pearl had predicted. She awoke Saturday afternoon, sunshine lighting up her yellow room so it glowed. Since Pearl had been waiting for her last night so they could go to dinner, Celia had taken a quick shower. Now she bathed in the deep tub for so long she almost fell back asleep. How long had it been since she'd had a tub she could soak in? Her apartment with Cassidy had only a shower with mildew growing in the corner above her head. The last foster home she'd lived in had a tub, but it had rough, scratchy strips on the bottom, like a diving board, that rubbed her raw if she sat on it. She couldn't remember taking a long bath since the Hundley's.

When she finally left her room, she found Pearl and Jenny talking in the parlor.

"Good morning," Jenny said. "Or I guess I should say good afternoon."

Pearl motioned for Celia to sit down. "I'll bet you're starving."

Jenny rose and headed for the kitchen. "I saved you some

breakfast if you don't mind eating pancakes this late in the day. I've got extra Pearl, if you'd care to join her."

"I think I will. They were quite good."

Several tables were set up in a blue and white room with windows along two walls. The tables were covered with white lace cloths. A giant painting of a pig filled most of another wall. It was rendered in shades of blue and pink and was quite lovely, even though it was a pig.

Jenny made several trips between the kitchen and the table, bringing a pitcher of orange juice and plates of eggs and pancakes and bacon. The bacon seemed insensitive since they ate under the sad eyes of the pig on the wall.

Celia ate until she was almost sick. She wanted to store up as much food as she could since she didn't know when she'd have another good meal.

"I thought I'd walk over to The Stitchin' Station after we eat. Would you like to join me?" Pearl asked between bites.

"That's okay. I can stay here."

"I'd really enjoy your company, and it would do you good to get out and breathe some fresh air. Say you'll come with me."

Celia nodded.

"You were a hungry girl," Jenny said when she picked up Celia's empty plate.

"Thank you. It was very good."

"We're going over to The Stitchin' Station, Jenny. Would you like to join us?"

"Would I ever. Unfortunately, I have guests who will be showing up in the next couple of hours, and I need to be here to check them in."

"Do you need the room I'm staying in?" Celia asked. She hoped she could stay one more night but knew better than to expect it.

"No, you're fine. Pearl has asked if you can stay there until she leaves and that's fine by me."

Celia wondered when Pearl would be leaving but didn't dare ask.

"Come along, Celia. Let's go look at some quilts."

Main Street was busier than it had been the evening before. Cars and trucks drove down the narrow street in an almost steady line. A few people chatted on the sidewalk in front of BJ's Ice Cream, enjoying the mild weather. The Stitchin' Station sat on the corner, about four blocks from the bed and breakfast. The four windows at the front of the store each featured a flower painted by a student in town, their name and grade signed below it. Celia's favorite, the pink daisy, was signed "Cammie B, 3rd grade." A bell above the door rang as they entered.

Celia had never been in such a place before. Bright, colorful quilts lined the walls. Some were random patchwork, some were intricately appliqued and others looked more like artwork, depicting wildflowers or rivers. She stopped in front of one that looked almost like a painting. Three snowcapped mountains stood behind a field of wildflowers.

"Beautiful, isn't it?" a woman said and Celia nodded. "If you go outside and walk across the street, you can see these three mountains in the distance. They're called The Three Sisters."

"Like the town," Celia said.

"Yes. The town was named after them. They're like three sisters watching over us. We call them Faith, Hope, and Charity. You'll have to take a look at them when you leave. Beneva Clyde made this quilt. She's won several awards at the Sisters Quilt Festival. This is one of her best, I think."

"Ah, you've met," Pearl said, stepping up beside Celia and the woman.

Celia looked more closely at the gray-haired woman who had been talking to her. She had a pleasant face.

"Not really," the woman said. "I've been telling her a little about this quilt."

"Then I should introduce you. Celia, this is Nancy. She's the one who picked up your bag at the bus stop yesterday. She's Silas's aunt."

"Thank you," Celia said. "For getting my bag."

"Of course. It was no problem." Celia liked Nancy's voice. It was warm and friendly.

"Nancy works here a few days a week."

"I should have retired years ago, but I like the perks. I get a discount on fabric, and I get first shot at all the new patterns. And best of all, I get to help with the Sisters Quilt Show. It's my favorite week of the year."

"Can you look around for a few minutes, Celia? Nancy and I have some catching up to do."

Celia didn't notice the confused look on Nancy's face.

The store felt more like an art museum to Celia. So many patterns and colors. Her hand bumped along the bolts of fabric and stopped to feel the thick skeins of yarn. There were three round racks of greeting cards, but these weren't the kind of cards Celia had seen in grocery stores. These were beautiful, quirky pictures with unpronounceable foreign names on the backs. Celia wandered through a section of art supplies and wondered what it would be like to be talented and artistic.

And then she stopped and looked across the room. How could she have missed the starburst quilt block hanging above the bolts of yellow material? The center was a school bus gold and each ray that extended from the center was a different yellow pattern. Celia smiled as she walked across the store and examined it more closely. At the end of the aisle was a basket that held the starburst pattern.

The only thing Celia had ever sewn was a pillowcase in school. It had been an ugly thing because Gina, her foster mother at the time, had refused to go spend good money on fabric for something that probably wouldn't turn out anyway. The morning that she was supposed to take fabric to school, Gina had brought out a dingy crib sheet that had been in storage for years. The fabric was rough and was covered with red and blue racecars. "You must be making your pillowcase for your brother," her teacher said when she walked by to check Celia's work. Celia had turned her back so the teacher wouldn't see her tears. She had no brother. She had no one.

"Isn't that a lovely one," Pearl said. "Your favorite color, too."

"We made that in quilt class a few months ago," Nancy said. "I think I've got a kit already put together in the back room if you're interested. Let me go look."

Nancy left and Pearl studied the instructions. A couple of minutes later, Nancy returned. "You're in luck. I have one more kit. The pieces are already cut and ready to assemble. All you need is that pattern to show you how to lay them out."

Celia had already looked at the price tag. It would take all her money to buy it. She wouldn't have any left for the cute stack of fabric tied with a white bow that Nancy held out to her.

"I can't. Thank you though."

"I'm sure you can do it. It's really easy to put together. The pattern has great instructions."

"It's not that. I don't have a sewing machine."

"You can hand sew them. A sewing machine is faster, but we've got a few purists who do all their work by hand. I can get you a needle and thread, too."

"Thank you, but . . . I don't have enough money."

"Oh, of course." Nancy looked uncomfortable and Celia

felt miserable.

"I'll bet Nancy can put it in the back room so no one else takes it, if you want to get it another time, dear," Pearl said. "If you like it, that is. Maybe we're encouraging you to buy it and you don't even like it."

"I love it." Celia said softly.

The women were quiet for a moment before Nancy's cheerful voice broke the silence. "Well, I have a better idea than hiding it back in the storage room. If you aren't busy, you could stay and help me put together kits for Monday's quilting class. We're making Amish Star blocks and each one has forty-one pieces of fabric. I'll be here all night if I don't have help. What do you say? Help me put together the kits and that pattern and fabric is yours."

Celia looked at Pearl.

"You don't need my permission, but I think it's a great idea."

Celia looked at the sunburst quilt block and her answer was easy. "Thank you. I'd be happy to help you."

"I've got a couple of letters to write," Pearl said, "so I'll see you back at Home Sweet Home when you're finished."

Celia followed Nancy into a large workroom set up with long tables for cutting and three rows of five sewing machines. "This is where we hold our classes. We limit each class to thirty people so we only have two people sharing a sewing machine. Otherwise they'd be here all night. Have you ever quilted before?"

Celia shook her head. "No, I've barely even sewn anything."

"You'll like making that sunburst. It's a pretty one and not nearly as complicated as it looks. I can help you, too, if you have any trouble, but I'm sure you'll do fine."

Nancy had already cut all the pieces for the Amish Star

blocks, and stacks of fabric cut in squares and triangles were laid out on the table next to a box of freezer bags. “I’ve got these all labeled so you know how many of each one goes in each kit. Try to make them look nice and orderly when you put them in the bag and then seal it. The last thing you’ll do is staple this instruction sheet to the top of the bag.” The bell on the front door rang. “Any questions?”

“I think I’ve got it,” Celia said as she picked up one of the bags.

“Wonderful. Then I’ll go take care of business up front. Come get me if you need me.” Nancy smiled as she walked to the front of the store.

Celia’s thoughts drifted to where she had been the last few days. It hadn’t even been a week since Damien had stumbled into her room in Chicago and now here she was in Sisters, Oregon. It surprised her that she was here. Would she love this place the way her mother had? One thing she knew for certain. She would never go back to Chicago. She’d had enough of sorrow and disappointment and rejection and brutality. In one day she’d been shown more kindness than she’d experienced since the Hundleys.

The sun was setting when she stepped out of The Stitchin’ Station carrying a bag with the Sunburst quilt pieces, the pattern, and a package of needles and thread. She hurried across the street and looked back at the mountains Nancy had told her about. There they were, rising up in the distance, purple in the evening dusk, their peaks still capped with snow that glowed pink in the waning light. The Three Sisters. Faith, Hope and Charity. The names were perfect and for a brief moment, Celia felt she was right where she belonged.

Chapter 8

When Pearl walked into the parlor Sunday afternoon, Celia was sitting by the unlit fireplace painstakingly sewing together the quilt block.

"Let me see what you're working on." Pearl leaned over Celia's handiwork.

"I haven't got much done yet. I'm not very good at this."

Pearl held up her work. There were only six pieces sewn together, but the stitches were small and even. "I think this looks very good. What a pleasant way to spend a Sunday afternoon."

"Thank you." Celia took back the handiwork and weaved the needle through the fabric.

Pearl sat down in the chair opposite Celia and watched her work. Celia must have felt her gaze because she looked up. "Is something wrong?"

"No. I'm only thinking." Pearl said.

They sat in silence for several minutes before Pearl spoke again.

"Celia, I must be getting back to California."

If Pearl hadn't been watching Celia's face, she would have missed the brief expression of panic that was quickly replaced by the dispassionate look Pearl now recognized. It was the face Celia showed the world when she was building up walls to protect herself, and the look hurt Pearl's heart.

"I talked to Nancy this morning. She's making a lemon meringue pie this afternoon and invited us over to have a piece." She paused for a moment, but when she got no reaction from Celia, she continued. "I can't be certain what kind of cook Nancy is—maybe the pie will be terrible—but she seems to me to be the type of woman who could make a delicious pie, so I thought we should give it a try. Would you like to go with me?"

Celia shrugged. "If you want me to go with you, I will."

"I'm not the one asking you to go. Nancy is. I think she quite likes you. You could show her the progress you've already made."

"I guess so."

It wasn't the enthusiastic response Pearl had been hoping for, but it would have to do. The important thing was to get her to Nancy's house.

"I'm tired," Pearl said, standing. "I'm going to take a nap and leave you to your sewing. Jenny left some sandwiches in the kitchen, so have one when you get hungry."

"Thank you."

Pearl paused on the stairs. "I don't suppose Jenny would care if you turned on the television while you work."

"That's okay. I've got some thinking to do." Celia sounded sad, but she looked up at Pearl and offered a weary smile.

Poor girl. Sometimes it seems God requires too much suffering of his children. Pearl reached up and touched the pearl comb in her hair. She knew something of pain herself.

She offered a silent plea that Celia would leave Nancy's tonight with a little more hope.

A golden retriever slept on the front porch. It lazily lifted its head and offered a half-hearted bark when Pearl and Celia stepped out of the Toyota Pearl had picked up from the garage yesterday. "I thought your dog was black," Pearl said when Nancy opened the front door.

"He is. Winston is Silas's dog." When he heard his name, Winston lifted his head off the porch for another moment before going back to sleep. "Come on in."

The scent of warm lemons made Celia's mouth water when they stepped into the cozy house. An old black lab moved slowly across the room and stopped beside her. Celia knelt down and rubbed behind the dog's ears.

"That's Nubia," Nancy said.

"As in the ancient civilization?" Pearl asked.

"No. After a variety of eggplant."

Pearl laughed. "I love eggplant."

"You'd have loved my gardens over the years. I've kind of got a reputation for growing the best eggplants around. I've grown at least twenty varieties."

"Twenty? I didn't know there were that many."

"Oh yes. There are even more than that, but not all of them survive in our climate here. I've had some eggplant triumphs and some eggplant disasters. I'm going to miss growing them." Nancy and Pearl exchanged a look Celia didn't understand. "Going to miss meeting so many nice people at the farmers markets, too."

Celia listened to the women talk about the farmers markets in Bend and The Dalles and about the various ways eggplant can be prepared. She sat on the floor and Nubia had snuggled in beside her, her head resting on Celia's lap, enjoying the attention, and thumping her tail softly on the floor.

The women were in the middle of discussing a particularly delicious eggplant sandwich Pearl had eaten in Boston when the front door opened. Nubia jumped to her feet and hurried to meet Silas, wagging her tail.

"I wondered when you'd come looking for your Winston. He's been sitting on my porch most of the afternoon."

"I had to go out to . . . "

When he stopped speaking mid-sentence, Celia looked up at him. His lips were pinched together tightly and his face had turned a deep red. He opened his mouth and pressed his lips together again. Celia wasn't sure what was happening. She glanced at Nancy to see if she was concerned, but she looked calm as she watched Silas.

Silas relaxed his still-red face and took a deep breath. His words were slower when he spoke again. "I had to go out to Pringle Falls campground. There were comp . . . laints." He seemed to get hung up on the "p" but this time it hadn't stopped him completely. He glanced down at Celia and she quickly looked away from his embarrassed expression.

"Got it all taken care of?" Nancy asked and Silas nodded. "As long as you're here, you should stay and have a piece of pie with us."

"I need to get home," Silas said, glancing at Celia again.

"Don't be ridiculous. It's lemon meringue and it will only take you a few minutes to have a piece. I'm cutting it now."

"I'll help you," Pearl said, and suddenly Celia and Silas

were alone in the pretty, mismatched living room.

Silas sat down on a worn leather chair and rubbed Nubia's head. Celia felt a pang of jealousy that his hands had something to do, while she had no idea what to do with hers. She occupied herself by picking at the strings in a small hole in her jeans. She risked a glance his direction but kept her eyes low, resting on Nubia, which gave her a good look at Silas's hands. His fingers were long, the knuckles a little knobby and the veins raised over their surface like a mountain range on a map. Above his hands was a blue and green plaid shirt and gray, down-filled vest. But Celia didn't dare look beyond that, in case he was looking at her.

She was glad when Nancy and Pearl returned, each carrying two plates of pie. Celia moved from the floor to a blue, stuffed chair and Pearl handed her the plate. It looked beautiful and bright and after one bite, she knew it would require effort not to look like a pig. It was one of the best things Celia had ever tasted, like sunshine in her mouth.

"Pearl says you brought your quilt block over," Nancy said.

"I've only done a little of it."

"I'd love to see it."

Celia reluctantly placed her pie on a little table beside her chair and took the quilt block out of her jacket pocket. She smoothed the pieces of fabric out against her leg then handed it to Pearl, who handed it to Nancy.

"You were right, Pearl, the stitching is remarkable." She turned to Celia. "You sure you haven't sewn before?"

"I made a pillowcase in school. On a sewing machine."

"Well this is lovely, and your stitches look like you've been doing this forever."

"I'm being really careful." She glanced at Silas and he quickly looked at his plate. "That's why it takes so long."

"Practice makes perfect," Pearl said. "Keep working at it and you'll get faster."

Celia nodded and Nancy handed the quilt block back. She had barely taken another bite of pie when Silas stood and walked to the kitchen with his empty plate.

When he returned to the room, he leaned down and gave his aunt a quick hug. "Thanks. That was good." He ruffled Nubia's ears and left without looking Celia's direction. She felt a strange mix of relief and disappointment as she heard him start his pickup and pull out.

"He must live close if his dog comes over," Pearl said.

"He lives down that lane beside my house. This house used to be my parents' and when Jack married Sharon—" Nancy turned to look at Celia— "Jack was my brother and Silas's dad, they built a house back there. Funny thing how here we are all these years later and we're both living in our parents' houses. It sat empty for a long time after Jack and Sharon died and Silas moved in here with me. Then we rented it out for a few years, and it helped pay for Silas's college. After he graduated and started working for the forest service, he moved back into it."

Celia and Pearl nodded as Nancy spoke, even though it seemed like she was almost talking to herself. She shook her head, as if to pull her back to the present.

"How long are you staying in town, Pearl?"

"I don't plan to stay too long. Just until I can be sure Celia is settled somewhere safe and proper."

Celia shook her head. "You don't have to stay for me. I'll figure something out," she said, even as she thought about the ten dollars in her wallet.

"Nonsense, young lady. You don't think I'm going to bring you here and leave you homeless, do you?"

"You didn't bring me here. You're not responsible to find

me a place to live."

Pearl waved her off. "It doesn't matter who brought you here. You, me, Silas or the Wizard of Oz, I don't feel comfortable leaving you homeless."

"She should stay here with me," Nancy said. "I've got a spare bedroom."

"I don't have any money to pay for a room until after I find a job," Celia said. It was an almost impossible situation. No money until she got a job. No job until she had time to look for one. No time because she needed to figure out where to live.

"We can work something out." Nancy held up her hand to stop all conversation while she thought for a minute. "I have a brilliant idea, if I do say so myself. I'm an old woman with more than an acre of garden. I decided last year would be my last since it wore me right out trying to take care of it, but I've got a lot of people who will miss my eggplant if I retire. You could help me with the garden and handle the farmers markets in exchange for a place to live and some of the money from the markets."

"I don't know how to grow plants." Celia wasn't sure how much an acre was, but she knew one summer in the tiny plot of ground in Myra's back yard hadn't prepared her for this kind of gardening.

"I'll teach you. I've got a green enough thumb to share with you. I quite like the idea of passing on my know-how to someone new."

"I think that's a wonderful idea," Pearl said.

It occurred to Celia that this conversation seemed somehow rehearsed and contrived. A part of her wanted to escape like Silas had and tell these two nosy women she wasn't their responsibility, and she didn't want their sympathy. The thought of being a charity case made her think of the Three

Sisters, looking down on the little town. Charity. And Hope. She needed some hope. She needed to have faith that she was doing the right thing by coming here. And if she was being honest, she could use a little charity, too. If she had to accept some help from anyone, wouldn't it be better to accept it from these two kind ladies?

"Are you sure?" she asked, almost afraid Nancy would change her mind and realize she'd made a terrible mistake making the offer.

"I'm sure. I think it will help us both out."

Pearl reached over and patted Celia's arm. "And I can go home knowing you're in good hands."

The two older women wore satisfied expressions and Celia couldn't help but smile. "Let's have another piece of pie," Nancy said. "And then I'll show you your room."

Chapter 9

Only two cars were parked behind Home Sweet Home Bed and Breakfast—Jenny's Subaru Outback and a black Mercedes with West Virginia plates. The silver Toyota Camry that belonged to Pearl was gone.

Silas pulled around the block but still didn't see it. Would she have left without saying goodbye?

Silas shook his head at the thought. Pearl didn't owe him a goodbye, especially after his rude behavior the day before. He hadn't said a word to Pearl or the girl she'd taken under her wing. He'd said goodbye to Aunt Nancy and practically run from her house. So Pearl had known his parents. So what. That didn't mean she had to track him down before she left town. She hardly knew him, after all.

It had been a long day. Most days he didn't mind the solitude of his job—preferred it, in fact—but today the quiet had felt tangible, and his thoughts had turned melancholy. If having Pearl around brought back the longing for his parents, it would be a good thing for her to leave. It had been a long time since he'd felt this emptiness, this hole in his life like something vital was missing.

It didn't take long to drive through Sisters to his house. He was disappointed to see Aunt Nancy's car behind The Stitchin' Station. He had hoped some dinner and a crime drama or two with his aunt would help lift his dark mood.

He drove down the lane south of his aunt's house and around the stand of trees. What was Pearl's car doing here? She opened her door, and by the time he had parked his Jeep, she was standing in the driveway.

"How are you, Silas?" she greeted him.

"Fine, thanks."

"Very good. I hoped I could speak with you for a minute. Before I leave town."

Something about not being forgotten warmed him.

"Come in."

He led Pearl up the steps of the ranch house his parents had built before he was born. He turned on the light in the front room and motioned for her to sit down. The interior of the house was sparsely decorated, tidy and masculine.

"This is very nice," Pearl said.

"I had to do s-some work after the last renters m-moved out. It was a m-mess."

"You did a good job."

"Thanks."

Pearl sat down on the edge of the leather sofa, her posture perfect, her hands folded in her lap. Silas sat in a straight-backed chair. "I'm leaving," she said and Silas nodded. "I have things to attend to in California. It has been good to see you again. You've grown into a fine young man."

A smile lifted the corner of Silas's mouth. Why was Pearl suddenly so formal?

"Silas, I almost left without speaking to you, because what I need to say will most assuredly make you think of me as a doddering old fool, but I'm afraid if I don't speak my mind, you will miss what is right before you."

Silas's amusement changed to confusion then curiosity. "Say what's on your m-mind," he said.

"There are changes coming and how you respond to them could very well determine your future happiness." Silas waited for her to continue. "Don't run away from something good, no matter how much trouble it might be. The future holds much promise if you step up and take it. Be the man you were meant to be."

She sounded like she was rattling off the fortunes from several cookies, and Silas had no idea what she was babbling about. He had stepped up. He had a good job and he looked after his aunt.

Pearl's expression softened and her eyes twinkled. "Good things will come to you when you step up to the plate."

The American euphemism delivered with Pearl's accent almost made Silas laugh.

"What changes are coming?" he asked.

She shook her head. "You'll know them when you see them."

Pearl stood, so Silas rose, as well. She reached up and patted his cheek. "Be happy, Silas, and don't be afraid."

Silas walked her to the door. "B-be safe."

"I certainly will."

He watched as she slowly drove away. What was she talking about? Don't run away from duty. Don't be afraid. There are changes coming. Step up to the plate. He wanted to laugh off the words of the strange, old woman, but a warmth settled over him, and he felt certain Pearl knew something of the future.

Three days had passed since Pearl had driven Celia to Nancy Toller's house, spoken a few crazy words, and returned to California. Two cold, miserable days that had left two inches of snow on the ground. There could be no gardening in weather like this, so while Nancy worked at The Stitchin' Station, Celia stayed at home, sewing her quilt block and trying to stay out of the way.

Since Celia had no money to contribute to groceries, she ate as little as possible, only venturing into the kitchen when hunger drove her there. Then she would eat small portions of several things, hoping Nancy wouldn't notice what was missing. It was a trick that had usually served her well in foster care.

"Celia, could you come in here?" Nancy said when she returned from work.

Celia had a sinking feeling in her stomach as she walked to the kitchen.

"Is something wrong?" she asked.

"Yes. If you're going to live with me, you have to eat."

"I did eat."

"Not enough to sustain yourself." She shook her head as she looked in the almost unchanged refrigerator and whispered under her breath. "Pearl was right."

Celia knew Nancy hadn't meant for her to hear that, but with all the strange things Pearl had said before she left, she wanted to know what Nancy was talking about.

"Right about what?"

Nancy sighed and considered for a moment what she

should say. "Pearl told me you would consider yourself a burden and that I'd have to insist that you behave like a normal person around here."

Celia lowered her eyes, not sure how to respond.

"Listen to me, Celia. I'm a kind person, but I've never invited a stranger to live in my home before, and if I didn't feel we could help each other out equally, I wouldn't have done it now either. But if I'm to keep up a garden this year, which I'd very much like to do, I can't do it alone. So you don't need to worry that you're taking advantage of me. You're not. The agreement was that you would work hard for me and I would provide a place for you to live and food for you to eat. If you're not going to eat, the deal will have to be off."

Celia could hear a smile in Nancy's voice and she looked up, relieved. "But there's no gardening to be done right now."

"There will be plenty, so eat up so when you're putting in long days, you won't resent me."

Celia smiled back. "Thank you."

Nancy took some noodles out of the cupboard. "Does spaghetti sound good?"

"Yes. Can I help?"

Together Nancy and Celia made spaghetti and salad. Celia ate two full plates.

Chapter 10

"You got enough firewood?" Silas asked, as he came through the front door. He stopped, his stunned eyes on Celia, who sat at a jigsaw puzzle at the card table set up in the corner of the living room. Cold air blew into the room as he stood there.

"Get in here and close the door or no amount of firewood will help me," Nancy said.

Silas closed the door and looked back and forth between Celia and Nancy, waiting for an explanation.

"I think you've already met, but in case you haven't, let me introduce you to my new boarder," Nancy said. "This is Celia."

"What?"

"She has moved in. I've given her the room that used to be yours."

Celia looked uncomfortable and wouldn't look at him.

Nancy continued, ignoring the awkwardness that filled the room. "I need help with the garden this summer, and Celia needed a place to stay. Two problems solved."

"B-but you said you weren't doing a garden this year."

"I changed my mind."

"I told you last year that I'd help you. You didn't need to . . ."

"You have a job. Now so does Celia."

After a long, uncomfortable silence, Silas nodded. He was surprised. Except for him, Aunt Nancy had lived alone all her adult life, so welcoming in a stray girl was unexpected. But she was stubborn and would do what she wanted. Still, a seed of concern planted itself in his mind, and he hoped Celia really was just a girl in a bind and not a con artist. Or worse.

"Do you need me to b-b— get you any firewood?" He was embarrassed at his obvious change of words, but it was something he did instinctively when he got caught on a sound. There was almost always another way to say something—a way that wouldn't get him stuck on bs and ps and ms—if he took the time to think it through. He didn't look over to see if Celia had noticed.

"We could use a load or two. Why don't you bring some in and I'll warm you up some dinner."

No one spoke a short time later as Silas ate his spaghetti and they watched a talent show on television. Celia barely looked their direction as she worked on the puzzle, and it might have been easy to forget she was even there, except that he was unsettled by her presence and suddenly aware of how pretty she was, and he didn't want to stutter in front of her.

When the show ended, Nancy took his plate. "You should go help Celia with that puzzle. I'd like to get that table out of the way."

Silas smiled. He knew this tactic. His aunt would lobby for his help on a puzzle, saying the puzzle was making her crazy, or that she wanted to put the table away, or that she was bored with it, only to have a new puzzle started on the same table the next time Silas stopped by.

The last time he had seen Celia, he had rudely left in a hurry. He didn't want to be rude again, so he pulled a chair up to the table and picked up the box lid to examine the picture—a folk artist's painting of Montreal. He wanted to say something, to crack a joke or ease the tension he felt between them, but he had never been good at cracking jokes. His stuttering always caused him to mess up the timing and instead of laughing, he could see that others were uncomfortable, or worse, that they pitied him. So he sat quietly, acquainting himself with the picture and the pieces until he picked up one that had the head of a dog and found the piece that showed the body and put them together.

Aunt Nancy didn't return for a long time. They heard her loading the dishwasher, then several minutes of silence, and finally, they heard her talking on the phone. All the while, Silas and Celia worked on the puzzle, neither of them speaking. Every minute that passed without words felt like a strand of twine being added to a rope, growing stronger and stronger and harder to cut through, until it seemed they had both been muzzled and were unable to speak.

Silas's discomfort reminded him of a ninth grade oral report on the Watergate break-in. He never referred to it as a break-in, just called it a scandal, because he thought it would be easier to say since he more easily got hung up on letters that started with his lips together. He could still remember the first line. He had planned to say "The Nixon Whitehouse was destroyed by the Watergate scandal," but it was the smallest word in the sentence that had killed him. He had stood in front of the class and started, "The Nixon Whitehouse was destroyed b-b-b—"

His lips had pursed tightly. That was the worst part of his stutter. It was like every muscle in his face pushed his lips together and it was difficult to pry them apart. He had felt his face get hot. Two girls giggled from the right side of the room and Silas knew without looking at them that they were laughing at him. The report should have taken two or three minutes. It took fourteen.

"Making any progress?" Aunt Nancy interrupted Silas's unpleasant memory.

"A little," Celia said. Her voice was as pretty as she was, quiet and sweet.

"Let me grab a chair and I'll help you," Nancy said.

"No." Silas stood up so quickly, he nearly knocked his chair over. Celia stopped working on the puzzle and both women looked up at him. "Here," he said moving around behind the chair. Aunt Nancy sat down. "I need to go."

He noticed Aunt Nancy's baffled expression, but he didn't dare look at Celia.

"Thanks for the wood," Aunt Nancy said as he closed the door behind him.

Hours later, unable to fall asleep, he listened to Winston snoring in the corner. Why was he always running when Celia was around?

He was almost asleep when he remembered Pearl's words. "Don't run away when something good is in front of you."

He drifted off before he could decide if Celia was a good thing or not.

Chapter 11

"We have two new quilters with us tonight. Jane, could you tell us who your guest is?" Everyone laughed and Celia decided Jane's guest probably didn't need an introduction.

A slim brunette stood and pulled the woman next to her to her feet. "This is my daughter, Francis. She's visiting from Eugene."

Several women said hello and expressed their delight that Francis was back.

"And this is Celia." Nancy held both hands out toward Celia as if she were presenting the group with a gift. "Celia is living with me for the summer and helping me with my garden."

"Does she know what she's gotten herself into?" an older woman asked from the corner.

"Now Cathy, don't be trying to scare her off. If she leaves, I won't have a garden this year and you'll be missing my eggplant."

"Where are you from?" asked a voice to her right.

"I'm from Illinois."

"My sister lives there," said another woman. "Were you anywhere near Champaign?"

"Not really." Celia didn't want to talk about where in Illinois she was from. She didn't even want to think about Chicago and the people she had left. Nancy noticed her noncommittal answer and directed the conversation away from Celia.

"We'd better get started, or we won't get this square finished tonight. Lisa, would you mind working over here with Celia so Jane and Francis can use the same machine? We don't want to interrupt their mother/daughter time."

Lisa moved to the table and sewing machine they would share. Lisa was pretty in the way of many young mothers who have become softer and rounder after having children. Celia thought she was close to her own age until she mentioned her three children at home.

"My husband signed me up for this class so I could get out of the house and talk to some grownups," she said as they experimented with different color patterns for their block. "He didn't have to tell me twice."

"Were you raised here?" Celia asked.

"I grew up in Medford. That's south of here. James—that's my husband—he's from here." She switched a blue strip of fabric with a yellow one. "I love it here though. Feels like home to me. What made you come to Sisters? Are you related to Nancy or something?"

"No, I met her after I got here. I thought it sounded like a nice place." She didn't tell her about the tear, or about how much her mother had loved Oregon, or about the night that had driven her out of Chicago.

"Well, welcome to town. It's a great place to live. Don't let them scare you about Nancy's garden. She's been doing it herself for longer than I've been here, so I'm sure between the two of you, you'll be fine."

Nancy was talkative as they drove home after the class.

"I'm glad you came with me tonight. You should plan on coming from now on. If you don't mind helping me put the kits together, we'll count that as your class fees."

"I enjoyed it. It was a lot faster using a sewing machine," Celia said.

Nancy laughed. "I'm sure it was. And it'll be good for you to get to know some of the other folks in town. There are some real fine people here."

"Lisa was nice."

"She's a sweet girl. James did all right for himself. She loves coming to class and getting a little break from those three wild boys of hers."

The light on the front porch glowed as they pulled into the driveway.

"Well look at that," Nancy said. "Silas must have come by and changed out that lightbulb. Wouldn't ya know, he'd come when we're gone."

Celia had been living with Nancy for three weeks now, and Silas hadn't been by since the night they had worked on the puzzle together. She couldn't help but wonder if it was because he didn't like her. Was she causing Nancy not to be able to see her nephew?

"Does he come over very often?" Celia asked.

"More than he has lately. I guess things have been busy for him at work."

"Are you sure it's not because of me?"

"Oh, I don't think it's that at all. Adam—that's his boss—probably has him running around on some project. Don't you worry. You watch. He'll start coming around all the time and you'll wish he'd stay away."

Celia wasn't sure she believed Nancy, but she let it go.

"I used to think I wanted more than an acre," Nancy said as they walked across what would soon be the garden. "I even asked Grant if he'd sell me part of his place." She pointed to a small farm adjacent to hers. "Thank goodness he said no. An acre is enough. I can rotate the plants enough to keep the soil healthy, and I have all I want to eat and enough to sell. It's plenty big."

Celia hadn't known how big an acre was, so Nancy had suggested they take a walk and map it out for planting.

"I grew a garden one year when I was a kid," Celia said. "But it was a little, back-yard thing. A couple of tomatoes and some zucchini. Nothing like this."

"Did you like it?"

Celia nodded. "I liked watching things grow."

"There's something wonderful about raising your own garden—getting your hands dirty and watching those plants change from seeds to food on the table. We'll start planting in the next week or two. I'll have Silas come and rototill for me. I used to do it myself, but a few years ago, I turned it over to him. It's a hard thing to admit you're too old to do something you love."

Celia had gone to bed when she heard Nancy say her name. Thinking she was calling for her, she opened the door, then stopped when she realized Nancy was speaking to someone on the phone.

"Say you'll come to dinner. You haven't been by in weeks,

and she's starting to think it's because of her." Nancy waited for an answer. It had to be Silas. "We'll plan on you Thursday. Oh, by the way, do you think you have time to rototill the garden for me? It's about that time."

Celia quietly moved back into her room. She didn't want Nancy to think she'd been eavesdropping.

"Thank you. Saturday is great. I know you're busy, and I really do appreciate it."

Celia held the handle and silently closed the door. Silas was coming to dinner on Thursday, and she wanted to make him comfortable. She felt certain he had stayed away because of her, and that wasn't fair to Nancy. Nancy had been so kind to her. Somehow she had to figure out a way to keep Silas from running away.

Chapter 12

Celia found the key to the shed on a hook by the back door. The key stuck in the padlock and for a brief moment, she was afraid it might break, but then it clicked and slid open. She let her eyes adjust to the dim interior before she started exploring. She had watched a YouTube video about rototilling on Nancy's computer this morning, so she had an idea what one looked like and felt confident she could figure out how to use it.

Behind the lawn mower and a snow blower, she found it. There was even a can of gasoline on the shelf.

Celia wrestled the tiller out the door, moving it from side to side inching it forward. It was heavier than she thought it would be. Once out of the shed, it was easier to lift it up on its wheels and move it to the corner of the garden.

Nancy had filled the crock pot before she went to work this morning, so there was nothing to do for dinner. Celia had straightened the house and vacuumed the floors, but by noon, she was bored, and the sunshine was calling her outside. The rototilling tutorials left Celia feeling confident she could plow the garden herself.

If only she could get the machine started.

She pulled the starting cord as hard as she could and almost tipped the tiller over. After several tries, she went back to the shed and brought out the gas can. The cap was on so tight it took a few minutes of work to get it open, but when she finally did, she poured the fuel into the rototiller. It took more than she expected it would, which made her hopeful that now it would be easier to start.

It only took two tries to start it up after she had added fuel. She pushed the bar down and the tines digging into the ground jolted the machine, startling her. She held the handle tightly and began to slowly move forward, trying to match her moves to those of the overall-clad YouTube teacher she had watched. Don't bury the tines too deeply. Move slowly to dig the soil evenly.

The roar of the engine drowned out the world and Celia was left with the vibrations of the tiller and the thoughts in her head. It had been a crazy five weeks, but here she was, in Sisters, Oregon.

I came to Oregon, Mom. I'm really here. She wondered what her mother would think about Sisters. The people she had met were so kind. No one knew about her past here. To them she was a normal girl working for Nancy.

A normal girl. It had been a long, long time since Celia had felt like she was something more than the freak foster kid whose junkie mom had overdosed.

Celia reached the end of the long row. The words from the tutorial ran through her mind as she made the turn. Lift the tines out of the soil and turn it around, then start again.

The sun slipped behind a cloud and the wind picked up, chilling her cheeks and fingers, but she felt strong as she pushed the tiller through the dirt. A peace she hadn't known since she was a little girl came over her.

Suddenly tears were streaming down her face. Why was she crying? Sure, she felt grateful to be here, in Oregon, where kind people had given her a chance to work. But tears? Was it because she felt tired? Was there pollen in the air? She knew it was neither of those things. She tried to wipe the tears onto her shoulder as she moved up the row, but they kept coming and finally she gave up.

With her back to the road and the engine filling her ears, she didn't hear Silas until he was beside her. She jumped and let go of the rototiller. Untethered to the ground, it jerked and swayed until Silas grabbed it and turned it off.

He opened his mouth to say something then saw her wet cheeks and stopped. "Are you okay?"

Embarrassed for him to see her like this, Celia wiped the tears away with her now freed hands. "I'm fine."

"Why are you crying?"

"I'm not."

"You are," he said, nodding and trying not to show his amusement at her denial.

Celia shook her head. "You're right. I was crying. Maybe it's because you scared me to death. I don't like it when people sneak up on me." How had she not noticed what a good face he had? It was hard to pull her gaze from the little smile that played hide and seek on his lips.

"I wasn't sneaking." He pointed to the lane at the Jeep Celia would have heard if the engine hadn't been so loud. "What are you doing, anyway?"

"I'm rototilling."

"You know how?"

"I watched a YouTube video."

Silas laughed. "You did?"

"Yes." Celia's back stiffened. "You can learn a lot on YouTube."

"B-but why? Aunt Nancy asked m—" His lips pursed and his face turned red. She could tell he was embarrassed so she looked back at the wide strip of dark earth so he wouldn't feel so uncomfortable. It took a few seconds but finally he finished. "—me to do it."

"I was bored. And I think I'm doing a good job." Celia swept her hand to take in the rows she had tilled.

"You are."

"Why aren't you at work?"

"I just got off."

"What time is it?"

Silas pulled his phone from his shirt pocket and held it up for Celia to see. It was after five. She had been working for more than three hours.

"I didn't know it was so late. I need to go in and make a salad."

"Go ahead. I'll p-put it away."

"Thanks," Celia said.

Inside, she washed her face and changed her clothes. She had planned to shower, but that was now out of the question. She knew she had told Nancy she would make the salad, but her arms ached and she felt like all her energy had abandoned her. She curled up on the bed until she heard the screen door bang shut. Then she pulled herself up and headed to the kitchen.

"Got ambitious, huh?" Nancy said, smiling.

"I figured I should get to work."

"You did a good job," Nancy said. "Nice even rows."

"And she wasn't even crying," Silas said. Celia turned on him with a glare, but he was smiling, and she realized there was no cruelty in his words, so she smiled back.

Nancy studied them and was about to say something when the crock pot began beeping. "I'll bet you're hungry."

"Starving." Celia said.

They ate shredded pork sandwiches and salad and talked about The Stitchin' Station and the forest thinning Silas and his crew had finished by Camp Sherman. Exhaustion seeped into her bones and she sank into the back of her chair.

"You should see the machines they use for thinning," Nancy said. "They make that rototiller look like a toy."

"Too m-much for you," Silas said.

Celia gave him a tired smile. "I don't know. Once I get that field tilled, I might be ready to move on to bigger and better things."

"One afternoon and you're already cocky," Silas teased.

"I watched some rototilling races on YouTube," said Celia, making Silas and Nancy laugh. "Those people are crazy."

Silas loaded up another sandwich, but Celia shook her head when Nancy offered her seconds. Something wasn't settling well and she began feeling a little sick. She swallowed and held still, trying to calm her stomach.

"You feeling okay?" Nancy asked.

"Yeah. I'm fine," Celia said, but a few seconds later, she excused herself and went to the bathroom.

She splashed water on her clammy face and sat down on the edge of the tub, taking several deep breaths to quell the nausea. It didn't work and soon she was kneeling in front of the toilet, retching.

When the violent spasms in her stomach settled, she

rinsed her mouth. Looking at herself in the mirror, she was surprised at the dark circles under her eyes. She'd been getting plenty of sleep, even taking naps some days, so why was she so weary? She had always felt a little more tired during that time of the month. Maybe . . .

What was the date? Why hadn't . . .

And then a panic seized her.

No, no, no. Please no.

The peace and strength she had felt working in the garden were gone, and in their place was a fear unlike any she had ever felt.

Chapter 13

An order of Amy Butler fabrics had arrived this morning, and Nancy was putting out bolts of the new cloth when the bell on the front door rang. It was Celia.

"Ooh, these are pretty," she said, and touched a bolt of orange and turquoise paisley.

"Some good pieces came in. You should pick out something new to work on."

Celia nodded and opened her mouth to say something, but closed it again. Lately, it had seemed like Celia had a lot on her mind, but she was so reserved that Nancy had no idea what was bothering her.

"Did you need me for something, or did you want to look around?"

Celia took a deep breath and tried again. "Do you think I could get a job for a few hours a week? I could work here, or if you don't need me, I could look for a job somewhere else. I need to have a little spending money. You know, for little things that come up."

Of course. Celia surely needed things an old woman wouldn't have sitting around her house. Why hadn't she thought of this? The poor girl.

Celia looked uncomfortable, but continued. “Of course I wouldn’t let it interfere with the garden. I’ll make sure I take care of that. I—”

Nancy held up her hand. “Say no more. Of course you need to have a little spending money. I know Val’s not hiring, but I have book club tomorrow night. I’ll ask around there. I can give you a few dollars to tide you over in the meantime.

“No,” Celia said, shaking her head. “Thank you, but I don’t want to take your money. You’re already feeding me and giving me a place to live.”

Not for the first time, Nancy wanted to pull the girl into her arms and hug her, but Celia held herself apart, and Nancy felt she’d be crossing a line Celia wasn’t comfortable with. But even though Celia was a determined girl, she seemed broken and fragile, like a china cup that’s been dropped and repaired too many times.

Nancy nodded. “I’ll ask around.”

“Thank you.” Celia looked relieved.

Nancy didn’t wait for book club. She mentioned Celia’s desire to work a few hours a week to Val, who told her she thought Ellis was looking for a part-time girl at the Sisters Gallery. A phone call later, Celia had an interview arranged for the next afternoon. Nancy was eager to get home after work to see how the interview had gone.

A happy Celia surprised Nancy with grilled cheese sandwiches and tomato soup for dinner. “I got the job.”

"That's wonderful."

"I hope you don't mind that I fixed dinner." Celia didn't explain that she'd prepared grilled cheese sandwiches because it was the only thing that sounded like it might settle well on her unpredictable stomach.

"Of course not. Let's sit down and eat and you can tell me all about it."

They ate at the kitchen table, and Celia told Nancy about her interview. "Ellis said he'd like to go have lunch with his mother at a care center in Bend twice a week, so I'm going to work Tuesday and Thursday from eleven to two."

"Sounds like a good arrangement. Ellis is a good man. You'll enjoy working for him. And if you're lucky, you'll get to see his little grandsons. Their mom sometimes leaves them there while she runs errands. They're a mischievous little pair, but too cute to get mad at."

"Thank you for talking to Ellis. I doubt he'd have hired me if it weren't for you."

"I only got your foot in the door. Ellis is a picky man. He wouldn't have hired you if he hadn't liked you."

"He said good things about you, too. I'm sure living with you didn't hurt." Celia paused. "I don't want you to worry about me being too busy. I won't let anything interfere with my work for you."

Nancy put her spoon back in her bowl. "There's something we need to talk about."

A brief look of panic passed over Celia's face. "Okay."

"I know you're a good worker. You didn't even wait for Silas to do the tilling, and every day I've worked, I've come home to a spotless house. But this arrangement doesn't mean you're my indentured servant. It doesn't mean you have to ask permission to do things. If you want to eat something, eat it. If you want to go to a movie, go to a movie. I like having you here and I want you to be happy."

Celia looked relieved and nodded.

"If I would have known it meant coming home to a clean bathroom and dinner already made, I would have taken in a boarder a long time ago," Nancy said and took another bite of her sandwich.

"But then you might not have had room for me."

"You've got a point there."

The mood was lighter than it had been for several days.

"So if I want to make cookies with those chocolate chips in the pantry, I don't have to ask?"

Nancy laughed. "You're catching on. When you make them, be sure to make enough for Silas or I'll never hear the end of it."

After dinner, Nancy and Celia worked on a cupcake puzzle while Nancy told Celia about the Sisters Quilt Festival.

"It's later this summer." Nancy gave Celia a serious look. "You will be here for it, right?"

"The garden will still be growing, so of course I'll be here for it."

"Good. You'll enjoy it. It's the largest outdoor quilt show in the world. Last year we had over a thousand quilts exhibited around town."

"Sisters hardly seems big enough to display that many quilts."

"For a small town, we manage to have a lot of fun. Did you say you lived in the city?"

Celia had never said exactly where she came from. Every question about her past was met with short, evasive answers.

"Yes. I definitely like the small town better."

"Illinois, right?"

Celia nodded.

"I went to St. Louis many years ago. It was nice, but I

don't think I could live there. Were you close to St. Louis?"

Celia picked up the box lid and found the cupcake with the pink sprinkles. "A suburb of Chicago."

Nancy wanted to clap her hands and let out a whoop. This wasn't terribly specific, but it was the first time Celia had willingly shared some of her history, and Nancy wasn't sure whether to be satisfied for the time being or keep digging for more of Celia's past.

Curiosity bludgeoned caution.

"Is your family still there?"

Nancy kept her eyes focused on the puzzle, trying to give the impression that this was a casual question.

Celia didn't answer immediately but when she did, her voice was barely audible. "I don't have any family." Despite the softness of the words, they grabbed Nancy's attention as if Celia had screamed the sentence at the top of her lungs.

A stillness settled between them, and Nancy hesitated to disrupt the quiet. "No one?" Her voice was barely above a whisper, but the pain her question could inflict made her feel terrible, as if by merely asking, she was twisting a knife in a deep, internal wound.

Celia smiled too brightly and her voice sounded falsely upbeat. "There's just me."

Neither of them spoke for several minutes. A newscaster droned quietly in the background about a breaking political scandal in Washington, D.C.

Finally, Nancy reached over and put her hand on Celia's arm. "Maybe I can be your family." Nancy was relieved when Celia didn't pull her arm away.

Celia swallowed hard and raised her shoulders. At first, Nancy felt rebuffed—wasn't she better than no family at all—but when she thought about it later, she realized how easy it would have been for Celia to reject the offer outright, but she hadn't. It hadn't played out like a scene in a movie, with Celia throwing her arms around Nancy and thanking her for her generosity. But this wasn't a movie. This was real life, and from what Nancy could tell, Celia's experiences had left her a skittish girl who would need time to open up. Nancy could give her that.

Chapter 14

Nancy didn't work the next day, so she and Celia spent the morning planting the garden. In a couple more days everything would be in.

The work was hard, but Celia loved the feel of the soft, loose soil in her hands and the cool gentle breeze on her sweaty face.

"If you're famous for your eggplant, why do you plant all these other things? Why not grow more eggplant?" Celia asked. She and Celia were working in side-by-side rows, dropping carrot seeds and brushing dirt over them.

"Have you heard of crop rotation? It's like that. Next year, I'll switch things up and I'll plant eggplant over here and carrots over there. That keeps the soil from getting depleted. And I do fine selling carrots and tomatoes and cucumbers, too."

Nancy left before noon to meet a friend in Bend for lunch and shopping. "You sure you won't come with me?" she asked Celia.

"I'm pretty tired. Maybe after I take a nap, I'll mix up some cookies."

Celia fell asleep within minutes of Nancy leaving and slept so soundly, a wrecking ball could have leveled the house around her and she probably wouldn't have awakened. Late afternoon light slanted through her window when she finally stirred.

Celia was glad they had put food in the crock pot this morning or she might have felt she needed to make dinner instead of cookies, but with the smell of chicken tortilla soup filling the kitchen, she began mixing the dough.

The sound of the mixer accompanied Celia's thoughts as she added the eggs to the bowl. When Celia had been nine, her Mom had called Grace Shipley's mother to see if Celia could go home with her after school. Celia had been excited. She didn't often get invited to play at other children's houses, and even if Mom had said she could invite a friend over, Celia would have been afraid to. What if they got home and Mom was stoned? Or had her own "friend" over?

The school secretary stopped by the classroom with two notes.

"Celia and Grace, I have a message here for each of you."

They exchanged worried glances and walked to the front of the room to pick up the little pink papers. After they had read them, they looked across the two rows of kids and smiled. Grace even gave Celia a thumbs up.

At the Shipley's, they played with Grace's Barbies and watched a rerun of The Brady Bunch.

"Girls, can you come down here?" Mrs. Shipley called up the stairs, and Celia's heart sank. She didn't want to go home yet.

"I was wondering," Mrs. Shipley said when they stepped in the kitchen, "if you'd like to help me make some cookies."

Celia was thrilled. She couldn't remember her mother ever making cookies, but it was clear after a few minutes that

Grace helped her mother regularly. With no prompting at all, Grace mixed together the dry ingredients while her mother beat the butter and sugar and eggs. They let Celia stir, and they gave her the most important part of the job—adding the chocolate chips. Celia beamed when they suggested that as the honored guest, she should be the one to taste the dough first.

When Mrs. Shipley drove her home later that night, she sent Celia with a paper plate of cookies to share with her mom. Celia waved to Mrs. Shipley before she walked through the front door, eager to show her mom the warm, gooey masterpiece.

But Mom wasn't there, so Celia locked the deadbolt, put the cookies on the coffee table to show her mother later, and began her math homework. Hours later, she woke up disoriented. Someone had turned off the lamps, but a streetlight lit up the coffee table. A ball of plastic wrap sat next to an empty paper plate. Who had eaten all her cookies? Was her mother home?

Celia tiptoed to her mother's room and looked inside. Sprawled out on the bed was her mom with a strange man beside her. Celia backed away quietly from the door and went to bed.

Celia didn't dwell on the last part of that memory. She focused on Mrs. Shipley and Grace and their sunny, yellow kitchen, and the warm chocolate chip cookies. Years later, when she made cookies with Myra Hundley, she made the connection. Real families bake chocolate chip cookies. For the first time in many years, here in Nancy's blue and white kitchen, she mixed in the chocolate chips. She hummed as she stirred.

The last pan of cookies were in the oven when Nancy returned.

"I was going to say you should have come with me, but these smell so good, I'm glad I left you home." She broke a cookie in half and took a bite. "Mmm, perfect."

Celia rinsed out the bowl and put it in the dishwasher. "Did you have a nice time?"

"It was lovely. I had the lemon ricotta pancakes with berries. And then the sales. I hope you don't mind, but when I saw this, I had to get it for you. It's the same color as your eyes."

Nancy pulled out a pretty blue wrap dress and handed it to Celia. It was soft and drapey and Celia held it up to her.

"It's beautiful."

"They had some beaded sandals I would have gotten to go with it, but I didn't know what size you wear, so you and I are going to Bend tomorrow right after you finish up at Ellis's."

"We don't need to do that," Celia said, thinking about her depleted funds.

"Nonsense. It's all on sale and I want to get it for you. We can call it an early birthday present, if you want. Or late. When is your birthday?"

Celia grinned. "October first."

"How old will you be?"

"Twenty-one."

"Ah, you're such a child. Anyway, I'm getting you those sandals, so you can either go with me and we'll get you the right size, or you can stay here, and if I end up with the wrong size, it will be a waste of money."

Celia surprised herself when she stepped forward and hugged Nancy. It was an awkward hug, barely more than a pat on the back, but it was the first real contact she'd had with anyone since . . . that night.

"I work in the morning, so you'll have some time to work on the garden and then we'll go when I get home. If I get off in time, maybe we'll go get more of those pancakes. They're heavenly."

Celia took the dress and hung it in the closet, letting the fabric spill over her fingers.

"Could you take these to Silas's?" Nancy asked, holding out a plate of cookies covered in plastic wrap.

The thought made Celia nervous, but of course she couldn't refuse.

"I don't think he's home, so take the key and leave them in the cupboard beside the fridge. Don't leave them on the counter or Winston will polish them off, including the plate."

Celia took the key off the nail by the back door and walked down the long, gravel lane that led back to Silas's house. The sun had barely gone down and the moon looked pale in the lavender sky. The garden stretched off to her left, the soil black furrows in the twilight. It was almost all planted and Celia felt an excitement that she would get to see her hard work grow into vegetables.

Silas's house was dark, save a dim light coming from a room in the back. When no one answered her knock, she used the key and let herself inside. Winston came forward from the lighted back room and gave a couple of impressive barks, but when he saw who it was, his tail wagged furiously.

"Hi there, Winston. It's just me."

She turned on a light switch and a lamp lit up on a table

to the right of the fireplace. Celia looked around. She was standing in a tidy, but masculine living room. The leather furniture looked almost new. A few books were scattered on the coffee table. She walked over to see what they were and saw a couple of thrillers, *East of Eden*, and a Bible.

Several family pictures lined the mantle. One caught her attention—a picture of a little boy and his parents building a sand castle on the beach. She walked over and took a closer look. She could tell the boy was Silas by the wavy, brown hair and the ears that stuck out a little.

She continued on to the kitchen and set the plate of cookies on the stack of plates in the cupboard. "That's so you won't eat them all," she said to Winston. The kitchen was a mismatched affair—older cabinets, new tile floor. A newer stainless steel refrigerator sat next to a white oven. It wasn't fancy, but it was clean. She opened the refrigerator, curious to see what kind of food a bachelor stocked.

"Hello?"

Celia jumped and bottles rattled as she slammed the fridge door. Silas sidled through the doorway around Winston and entered the kitchen.

"Oh, hi. Nancy asked me to bring you some cookies," Celia explained, embarrassed to have been caught looking around his kitchen. Not sure what to do with her hands, she shoved them into the pockets of her hoodie. Then, realizing it looked like she was hiding something, she took them out and folded her arms.

Silas looked from her hands to the counter to the refrigerator. "You p—" His lips pursed and Celia glanced at her feet, embarrassed for him. "You put the cookies in there?"

Celia's face flushed and she was glad she stood in the half-darkness. "No. They're in the cupboard. So Winston wouldn't eat them. Nancy said . . . "

Silas nodded. "Good thinking."

Silas and Winston stood silhouetted against the light of the back room, a man and his dog. She felt like an intruder as he stood facing her, and even though she couldn't see where he was looking, she felt his eyes on her.

"I should go." She was at the doorway to the living room when the kitchen light burst on, a spotlight behind her.

"Hey, why are you running?"

Celia glanced back at Silas and saw his smile.

"I'm not." She could hear the defensiveness in her voice. "I'm leaving now. Nancy said you weren't home."

"I wasn't."

"I don't want to bother you."

"You're not."

Celia shoved her hands in her pockets again. She should have hurried so she wouldn't have been caught in his house.

"It's just . . . I'm not . . . " She turned to the door. "I've got to go."

She hurried across the driveway and started down the lane.

"Thank you," Silas called from the front door.

"You're welcome," she said, but he probably hadn't heard her.

Chapter 15

Celia left Sisters Gallery with her first paycheck. It didn't add up to much—less than fifty dollars—but it would buy what she needed most right now. Confirmation.

After a stop at Oregon National Bank, Celia headed for the pharmacy. She didn't flinch when the bill came to more than a fourth of her paycheck. After all, it was the reason she had needed a job in the first place.

Celia walked by The Stitchin' Station, hoping Nancy was still working. When she saw Nancy's car parked on the side street east of the store, she hurried her step.

She patted Nubia's head when she walked in the house, but when the dog tried to follow her into the bathroom, she nudged her away and closed the door.

"Sorry girl, but this is private."

Celia locked the door, followed the instructions on the box, then sat on the edge of the tub, waiting and counting slowly to herself to keep track of the time. "One-one-thousand, two-one-thousand . . . "

She didn't look at the little window as she counted, afraid her scrutiny might alter the results. "Seventy-three-one-thousand, seventy-four-one-thousand." She felt a little sick to her stomach, a feeling she was growing accustomed to. She took a deep breath and slowed down, afraid she'd been counting too quickly. "One-hundred-seventy-seven-one-thousand, one-hundred-seventy-eight-one-thousand, one-hundred-seventy-nine-one-thousand."

She didn't say the last number. She pushed off her knees with her hands and looked down at the counter at the little, pink plus sign.

Instinctively, she rested her hand on her stomach, leaned back against the door, and slid to the floor as tears streamed down her cheeks.

Celia had known she was pregnant. She counted back in her head, careful not to think about the details of the night it had happened. She had been pregnant for over seven weeks.

Her breathing was quick and shallow and a sob escaped her throat. How could something like this have happened? Emotions warred within her—sadness, fear and anger. After a few minutes, rage overpowered everything else. She clenched her fists, and for the first time since she had left Chicago, she wanted to be back there. She wanted to find him and beat the smirk off his face. She wanted to kick him and pound him and demand that he suffer for what he had done to her. She wanted to call the police and watch them take him away in handcuffs.

For several minutes, Celia imagined the pain she wanted to inflict on Damien.

Nubia's whimpers on the other side of the door brought Celia back from her murderous Chicago rage and she concentrated on slowing her breathing. She didn't have enough money to go back to Chicago and exact her revenge, and even if she could afford it, she would never return there. She didn't want him to know his baby was inside her.

"No. It's not your baby," she said, refusing to let him own

something that was a part of her. He would never take anything from her again. It was her baby and she'd decide what to do with it.

It was still early. She could do whatever she chose. Even those most opposed to it, agreed abortion was acceptable in a case like hers. She shouldn't have to carry the burden of something she hadn't asked for, something that had been brutally forced on her.

But even as those thoughts scurried through her mind, she knew she would never do that. There was a baby growing inside her and she knew she could never intentionally hurt it. She would protect it from bad things the way she wished her parents had protected her.

Celia pulled herself up to the sink and looked at her reflection in the mirror. Her eyes were red and swollen, her skin splotchy. She rinsed her face with cold water and it helped, but she still looked a mess. Nancy would be home soon, and if she saw Celia like this, she'd have questions Celia wasn't ready to answer.

She put the pregnancy test back in the box and shoved it in her pocket. On her way through the kitchen, she scribbled a note on a piece of scratch paper. "Took Nubia for a walk. Be back soon."

Nubia wiggled with delight as Celia put the leash around her neck and led her out the back door. Two blocks away she came to a park. She walked across the lawn to a pavilion of picnic tables and buried the pregnancy test in the garbage can. Then she and Nubia started down a road that led out of Sisters, away from The Stitchin' Station and the Forest Service Office. Celia didn't want to run into Nancy or Silas.

"Did she tell you where she was going?" Silas said into the phone.

"No. She left a note on the table saying she was taking Nubia for a walk, but that was ages ago. I got home from work about four and she was already gone."

Silas looked at the clock on the stove. It was almost eight. "I'll take a drive around and look for them. Does she have any other friends?"

"Not that I know of. I'll come with you." Nancy sounded frantic.

"M-maybe you should stay here so you can call if they get back." Silas was already getting in his Jeep.

"I might go crazy waiting here, but you're probably right." Aunt Nancy's voice was filled with concern.

"Call if they come back," Silas said and pulled out of the driveway.

It bothered Silas that Celia would cause his aunt to worry. Aunt Nancy was too old to have to deal with someone taking off like this. He hadn't been comfortable with the plan Pearl and his aunt had cooked up, but in the last few weeks, he'd started to think having Celia around wasn't such a bad thing. Aunt Nancy seemed happy, and Celia had shown no signs of trying to take advantage of her. To the contrary, Celia had surprised everyone with her hard work and willingness to pitch in.

Silas drove down Main Street, then began to criss cross the side streets. He circled the park, but the only people there were Phil, who owned the Texaco station, and his son throwing a football. A few people ate at tables outside the Sno Cap, but none of them were Celia. Silas turned south and followed Elm Street until after it passed Logging Road then turned around, then cut across to Edgington until he came to the middle school.

How far could she go on foot with a dog? In addition to the main road that ran through town, there were many small roads that she could have taken. Would she know where she was or how to get back?

Silas's phone rang and the screen told him it was Aunt Nancy. "Did they get back?"

"No. I was hoping you'd found them."

"Not yet."

"Silas, it's dark now. What if she's lost? Would Nubia be able to find her way home?" Aunt Nancy's voice trembled.

Silas felt the same concern his aunt did, but he knew he had to remain calm. "We'll find them. Don't worry."

"It's getting cold."

"This would be a lot easier if she had a phone."

"You know she doesn't have any money. And she's been pretty stubborn about me not paying for anything extra."

"I know. I'll call you when I have news."

"Thank you, dear. I appreciate your help."

Silas circled back around and began canvassing the streets again, first the east to west streets, then the north and south streets, one after another, until he'd driven all over town. He had been out looking for almost an hour, and with every change in the digital clock on the dashboard, his anxiety grew. His thoughts were a tangle. One minute, he wanted to chew the girl out for worrying his aunt, the next he prayed she and Nubia were safe. A few times he decided when he found her, he'd haul her straight to the bus station and send her back where she came from, wherever that was. He'd even pay for the ticket to be rid of her. Then he realized he'd be sad not to see her again.

At the end of Main Street, instead of heading out of town, he turned onto the road that led to the high school.

There in his headlights were Celia and Nubia.

Silas let out a deep breath and pulled to the side of the road. Celia must have recognized his Jeep because she kept walking toward the headlights. Silas picked up the phone, and as he watched them approach, he called his aunt.

"I've got them."

"Oh good. Hurry home."

"We're on our way."

Celia opened the passenger door of the Jeep. "Are you here to give us a ride home?"

Silas wanted to shout at her and demand answers, but even in the dim light of the dashboard, he could see that Celia had been crying. He wouldn't add to whatever trouble she had faced tonight. At least not at the moment.

Silas moved a jacket and thermos from the seat next to him and motioned to the back. "You can p—" Silas slammed the steering wheel as his lips folded on the sound and started over. "Nubia can go in back."

He reached over and pulled the lever to move the seat forward, and Nubia scrambled into the back seat. He didn't immediately put the Jeep in gear when Celia closed the door. All the anger and frustration he had felt as he searched for her drained away as he looked at the sad girl beside him. Suddenly he felt compelled to protect her from whatever was causing her pain.

"Are you okay?" As he asked, he gently touched her arm. Celia flinched like she'd been snapped with an elastic band. Had she thought he would hit her? "Sorry," he said under his breath.

Celia turned toward the window as he put the Jeep in gear and headed to Aunt Nancy's.

Nancy was waiting on the porch when Silas pulled into the driveway. She hurried across the yard and opened Celia's door while Silas let Nubia out of the back.

"I was so worried about you," Aunt Nancy said and put her arm through Celia's, guiding her into the house.

Silas followed behind them and stood inside the door, twisting his beanie in his hands.

"You must be freezing," she said and led Celia to the couch where she covered her with a blanket. "Can I get you something? Are you hungry? I have some chili I can warm up."

Celia shook her head. "No thank you. I'm sorry I worried you. I didn't mean to be out so late."

Nancy noticed Celia's tear-streaked face and patted her leg. "Did something happen to you?"

Celia pulled the blanket tightly around her. "No, I needed to walk. But then I found a church."

"You've been at church?"

Celia nodded. "I'm sorry I was gone so long," she said again.

Nancy shook her head. "Don't be. I'm glad you're all right. I can tell you're upset about something. Can I help?"

Nancy saw Celia glance at Silas who still stood by the door before she answered.

"I don't think so."

Nancy could tell Celia didn't want to talk and wondered if it was because Silas was there. With a slight inclination of her head, she signaled that he should leave.

"Thank you for finding her, Silas."

"Yes, thank you," Celia said.

"Okay." Silas didn't look happy about being dismissed, but he pulled the beanie on and turned to the door. "Let m-me know if you need me," he said.

Nancy wasn't sure if he was talking to her or to Celia, but she answered anyway. "We will."

When the door had closed behind him, Nancy put her arm around Celia and was grateful when the girl melted into her shoulder. She rubbed her arm gently and waited for Celia to speak first.

A couple of minutes passed before Celia took a deep breath and began to talk. "I needed to think. And pray."

"Of course." When Celia didn't continue, Nancy asked, "Did it help?"

"I think so." Celia wiped a tear from her cheek.

"You know if you'd like to talk about it, I'm here."

"I know." Celia sighed. "Maybe sometime. But not yet."

Nancy swallowed her disappointment but held her tongue. Something told her it would be a mistake to push too hard.

"I'm really tired. I think I'll go to bed."

"Are you sure you don't want something to eat first?"

"Thanks, but my stomach's not feeling too great."

Nancy held the blanket that had covered Celia and watched her leave the room. Long after she'd disappeared into her bedroom, Nancy looked at the dark hall, feeling helpless.

Chapter 16

Celia noticed a change in Silas after the night he had spent looking for her. Even though she had rebuffed him when he had tried to comfort her, he came around more. He often came by after work and stayed for dinner. He usually lingered after the meal and worked on a puzzle or watched something on television with them. He didn't say much when she was around, but that was probably because when he did, he often struggled to get out his words.

But he was different with his aunt. One evening Celia stopped in the hall and listened as Silas and Nancy had a long conversation about how the unusually dry spring could affect the forest. She leaned against the wall and listened.

"Adam keeps calling to check on rainfall, like if he calls, it'll go up."

"It's been such a dry spring. I can understand why he's worried," Nancy said.

"He had two men nearly die in the Long Draw Fire. He doesn't want another year like that one."

"I know how he feels. I don't like it when you're out there

fighting fires. It's my least favorite part of your job."

"We've contracted a good crew from First Strike for this year. And m-maybe we'll get some good rain before it gets too hot. We have the forest in good shape though. We cleared out some of the old fire breaks while we were doing the thinning."

She was surprised at how easily he spoke. She had figured he stuttered around everyone, but he'd only stumbled on his words once during the entire conversation with his aunt.

"Stop eating that or there won't be enough left for dinner."

"Just making sure it's good."

"You know it's good."

Someone ran water in the sink. "Has she told you anything?" Silas asked. Celia held her breath as the conversation turned to her. "About what was wrong?"

Nancy's voice became quieter. "No. I keep hoping she'll confide in me, but whatever it is, she's keeping it to herself. She went to church last Sunday. Maybe she's talking to someone there."

A sadness filled Celia at Nancy's words. She wanted to trust her. But what if Nancy found out and thought less of her? She had once heard someone describe shame as a tangled blanket that you couldn't find your way out from under, but to Celia it felt more like a net trap. No matter how hard she searched for a way to free herself, she remained stuck. She would have preferred a blanket. At least then she wouldn't be able to see the scorn and disappointment from others.

She could hide under a blanket. A net left her exposed.

Why had she let this happen to her? Why hadn't she screamed or fought harder? Why hadn't she found somewhere else to live the first time she realized Cassidy's friends were losers? She shouldn't have allowed herself to be in this situation.

Nancy had been kind to her, wanted Celia to trust her, but would she feel that way if she knew? There was only one person Celia could trust, one confidante. God. But He had to love her no matter what. And He couldn't kick her out of Nancy's house.

Celia had enjoyed hearing Silas talk almost stutter-free when it was about his job. She didn't want to stand here and listen to them talk about her. She took a step around the corner.

"It smells great in here," she said. And it did. Celia hadn't felt like eating much all day and the biscuits in the oven were making her mouth water.

"Sloppy joe's on biscuits. That's how my mom always made them," Nancy said.

"They're the b—" Silas's lips collapsed on the sound. ". . . best," he said.

"Good. Cause I'm really hungry."

Celia ate three sloppy joes and might have gone for a fourth if no one would have known. She was eating for two, she thought and put her hand on her stomach, wondering again how big her baby was.

There was so much to think about. She knew she should think about seeing a doctor. She also knew she wouldn't be able to keep this a secret forever. Right now there were no visible signs, but a few months down the road, it would be impossible to hide. Would she have to leave? What would she do with the baby? She couldn't keep it. She was alone with nothing. She couldn't even support herself. How would she do right by a person who depended on her completely? And Damien. Would the baby have Damien's pointed nose? When it smiled would it look like Damien's sneer? Would she think about that horrible night every time she looked at it? That wouldn't be fair at all.

Maybe the doctor could help her arrange to give the baby up for adoption.

". . . won't you, Celia?"

Celia looked up to see Nancy and Silas looking at her. What had she missed?

"I'm sorry. What did you say?"

"You'll go with us to the rodeo and dance, won't you?"

Nancy must have been able to tell Celia had no idea what they were talking about. "The Sisters Rodeo. Next week. You'll go with us, right?"

"Um, I guess so."

Nancy laughed. "You didn't hear a word we said, did you?"

Silas was smiling and Celia laughed. "I'm afraid I didn't."

"The annual rodeo," Silas said. "There'll b-be things going on almost every day next week."

Nancy looked excited. "There's a bull-riding event—that's pretty wild—and the night before the main event there's a dance and barbecue. We can go to all of it. People come in from all over. And we get cowboys from just about everywhere."

"I've never been to a rodeo. I don't know if I've ever even seen one on television."

"Then you're in for a treat," Nancy said. "They're fun. Bucking broncos, bull-riding, barrel racing."

"Will you be in it?" Celia asked, looking at Silas.

Silas grinned and shook his head. "No way."

"The year before Silas's folks died, he was in a kiddie rodeo. Rode a sheep for more than eight seconds. His mom was cheering like crazy, but his dad stood there fiddling with his keys while he watched him. I teased them about that. It was like they'd switched roles."

Nancy had told Celia that Silas's parents had died in a car

accident, but they'd never talked about them. Celia watched Silas's face to see if it troubled him, but his expression was pleasant.

"Can you imagine how he'd have been if I'd been on a b-bull?" Silas was smiling even though he'd almost caught on every b.

"I've volunteered to help with the food at the dance," Nancy said.

"Can I sign up to help?" Celia asked.

"Sure. I'll give them your name. There'll be plenty of us helping so you won't be stuck putting out cookies or filling punch bowls all night. Silas? You want me to put your name down?"

Silas shook his head. "I'm already helping with the p-parade."

Sisters was different the next week. It was like her twangy boisterous cousin from the Southwest had swapped places with her and couldn't help talking loud, and showing off her new, boot-clad wardrobe. Silas didn't make it back from work in time, so Celia and Nancy sat together in the stands and watched an evening of barrel races without him. Horseback riding looked fun, but not the way these girls were flying and certainly not in her condition.

"Val's grandson is riding, so I told her I'd mind the store," Nancy said Wednesday morning. "I told Silas to stop by and pick you up about six."

"Oh, that's okay. If you can't go, maybe I'll stick around here and—"

"Don't be ridiculous, Celia. It's the most exciting night of the rodeo. Nothing but bull-riding. You don't want to miss that."

"I don't?" Celia didn't know why it would be so bad to miss bull-riding. Nancy laughed.

"No, you don't."

"Maybe Silas would rather go with someone else."

"I already talked to him. You don't really want me to tell him you'd rather stay home than go with him, do you?"

"No. I mean he might want to go with a friend or something. He shouldn't have to babysit me."

Nancy gave Celia a playfully stern look and shook her head. "Just be ready at six."

Celia knew it wasn't a date, but there was something about getting ready for an evening with just Silas that felt very different. For the first time since she'd arrived in Sisters, she wished she had something different to wear. Something pretty. This was ridiculous thinking, because she knew Silas certainly wasn't thinking of this as a date. He seemed to go back and forth between thinking of her as a kid that needed watched after and a potential threat to his aunt. Nancy was surely responsible for this arrangement.

Even though this wasn't a date, it was hard not to notice how nice Silas looked when he picked her up. His hair was still damp from an after-work shower and the light blue t-shirt made his eyes even bluer. He looked like a man instead of just a guy. And he smelled good. If he wouldn't have thought she was crazy, she would have leaned over and breathed in the pine and mountain air smell.

Celia spoke as Silas pulled out of the driveway. "I'm sorry Nancy roped you into this tonight."

Silas smiled. "Roped? Nice choice of words since we're going to a rodeo."

Celia laughed. “I’m serious. I’m sure you’d rather be going with your friends or something.”

Silas gave her a sideways look. “No. This was m-my idea.”

A surprising flutter of butterflies started in her stomach. “Oh.” She turned toward the window to hide the smile that forced itself onto her face. She needed to be careful not to read anything into this. He probably felt sorry for her since she knew so few people. But no matter how she tried to talk herself out of the idea that he might want to spend the evening with her, she realized that she hoped he did. He’d been kind to her, especially since the night she’d walked to the church. It had been years since she’d had a real friend and Celia realized she wanted one. She wanted someone to confide in, and although she didn’t feel anywhere near ready to share everything, it felt nice to spend an evening with someone who wanted to hang out with her.

As the sun neared the tops of the trees, the heat of the day began to cool. The parking lot of the fairgrounds was dusty, but inside the rodeo grounds, the dirt was a darker shade of brown and didn’t rise in puffs with every step the way it had everywhere else. They sat down on the bleachers and watched as people arrived and a couple of rodeo clowns carried on in front of them. A few people around them sang to the loud country music playing over the sound system.

“Too bad Nancy couldn’t come,” Celia said. “She said she likes bull riding the best.”

“I think Val takes advantage of her,” Silas said, “b-but she keeps saying yes.”

Celia’s reaction when Silas’s lips pushed together surprised her. She wanted to smooth them out and soften them and take away the pressure that held them there. She remembered the easy way he talked to his aunt and wanted him to talk to her in the same way. She was being ridiculous.

She couldn't reach out and touch him and they weren't anywhere near close enough for her to tell him what she was feeling.

What was she feeling? Certainly compassion for the difficulty he faced whenever he wanted to say something, but it was more. She wanted to take away his pain and embarrassment. She wanted to make him comfortable, to make their conversation easy. If it were ever going to happen, she knew it would take time. Would she be around long enough for him to feel at ease with her? She didn't know because of her own hidden shame.

The crowd attending for the bull-riding event was louder and rowdier than last night's barrel racing crowd. People yelled and cheered and gasped together. Eight riders were thrown off before finally a cowboy lasted eight seconds, and when he did, the crowd went crazy.

"That's Sp-Sp-Spencer," Silas said. "Val's grandson." He pointed to the chute where a cowboy in a green plaid shirt was getting situated on the bull.

Celia looked around the stands, but didn't see Val. Two men opened the gate and the bull raged into the arena, kicking and bucking with all his might. Spencer lasted about two seconds before he was thrown several feet from the angry animal. A clown in a loose red shirt and rainbow suspenders darted in front of the bull, zigzagging toward the opened exit gate, distracting its murderous gaze from Spencer. It charged toward the clown before seeing the gate and trotting away.

"Too bad," Celia said about the failed ride.

Silas shrugged. "If they don't get hurt, I think it's a successful ride."

"I guess that's true. But he probably doesn't feel the same way about it."

"He p-probably would if he got hurt."

The arena lights came on while the sky to the west turned gold and pink then indigo. They shared a popcorn and for a little while Celia forgot about her worries and secrets.

After the last cowboy had ridden and the country music started blaring through the speakers, they stood to leave. The crowd crushed around them and some teenagers squeezed between them. When Silas saw Celia was several steps behind him, he let the crowd move around him and put his hand on Celia's back. He kept it there until they were in the dark of the parking lot and the press of the crowd had lessened.

"Hey, Toller. I thought that was you."

A big man walked toward them, holding a little boy's hand. He was soft, the way a man who once was an athlete but now works at a desk is soft.

"Hi Alan."

The two men shook hands and Alan gave him a good-old-boy smack on the back.

"You gonna introduce me to your girlfriend?"

Silas glanced at Celia and gave a little shake of his head. "She's not . . . She m-moved in with m-my aunt."

Even though she knew he was right—she wasn't Silas's girlfriend—her heart sank a little at Silas's quick dismissal, then it hurt for him as he stammered.

"I'm Celia."

"Nice to meet you, Celia. I'm Alan Kilpatrick. Silas and I went to school together. And this is my little boy, Brock. Disappointing showing tonight, huh? Been a long time since only three riders hit eight seconds."

"Tough b-bulls, I guess," said Silas. "Are you still in P-P-Portland?"

"Yeah. Probably there for good. What are you doing now?"

"Still here. Working for the forest service. P-probably

there for good." Silas smiled but he looked self-conscious.

"Whatever happened to Paul? Do you know where he ended up?"

Silas and Alan talked for a few minutes about former classmates and changes around town. Silas seemed to like Alan, but he looked uncomfortable and Celia wondered if he'd have felt more at ease reminiscing with an old acquaintance if she hadn't been there.

By the time they finished talking, the parking lot was nearly empty.

"Why does he talk like that?" they heard the little boy say as he and his father walked away. Celia felt Silas stiffen beside her.

"Shh, that's bad manners."

"What? I only asked why he talks funny."

Silas didn't turn around and they walked in silence to the Jeep. What had been a fun evening had taken a very bad turn, and she watched as Silas clenched and unclenched his jaw. The five minute drive from the rodeo grounds to Nancy's house felt endless. Celia wanted to make him feel better, but she was afraid that anything she said would make it worse.

The headlights lit up the small shed at the back of Nancy's driveway. Silas left the car running and stared out the windshield. It was like he'd forgotten Celia was there.

"Thank you," Celia said. "Tonight was really fun."

Silas snapped out of his reverie and turned to look at her. It took him a moment to replay what she'd said in his mind. "Yeah." He paused. "Thanks for coming with me."

At first Celia felt relieved that he hadn't stuttered, but then she felt a twinge of guilt that she was paying such close attention to what he said.

"I guess I'll see you tomorrow?" Silas's face looked like a question. "At the barbecue."

"Oh, right. I'll see you then."

Light from the television illuminated Nancy, who sat sleeping in her recliner when Celia entered the house. She stirred when she heard the door close.

"You're home. Is Silas with you?" She glanced at the door behind Celia.

"He headed home."

"Oh, I guess you'll have to fill me in."

Silas pulled out of Nancy's driveway, and turned down the lane to his house, but instead of parking and going inside, he walked through the back yard and through a field that stretched out behind their property. Beyond the grassy expanse was a line of trees beside a small, bubbling creek. The creek had been a favorite place to play as a child, but after his parents' accident, it had become a refuge, a place to disappear. The rocks on the bank had been the victims of his varied moods over the years. Small pebbles had been his carefree toys as he'd thrown them at trees on the opposite side of the water. Later, after his parents died, he had sat on the banks, wishing the water was deeper and faster and could carry him away. When he'd tried to give a report at school and made a fool of himself, he'd picked up larger rocks and hurled them against the stones in the water, happy when one would split apart and shards would fly through the air like shrapnel.

It had been a while since he'd been back here, but the moon was high and he found his favorite spot—a fallen log that extended across the water—with ease.

He let his mind drift back over the events of the

evening—Celia, walking out in clothes he'd seen many times, but somehow tonight she looked different. She'd rolled up the cuffs of her jeans and tucked in the front of her loose-fitting t-shirt. Instead of torn sneakers, she'd worn sandals and her toenails were a soft shade of orange. Her hair was down instead of in the ponytail he was so used to seeing and it made her look less like a scared girl. She had turned to the window when he had told her it was his idea to go to the bull-riding together, but he'd caught her small smile and it had made his breath a little too shallow. As the crowd had filled in around them, they'd been forced to sit closer on the bleachers and their arms had brushed against each other several times. Instead of flinching away from him the way she had the only other time they'd touched, she hadn't seemed to notice. But he'd noticed. It had put him on edge all night and made him want to scoot even closer.

If only they hadn't seen Alan. If only Silas hadn't stammered and stumbled his way through that awkward conversation. Celia had let him guide her through the crowd with his hand on her back. Her pale blue eyes had smiled up at him as they talked.

Silas thought about her expression when Alan had asked him to introduce his girlfriend. He didn't know what he should have said—Celia wasn't his girlfriend—but somehow he knew he'd said something wrong. He had felt the shift in her mood, in the ease of the evening. And then she'd heard the little boy ask why Silas talked funny. Even as he wanted to curse at the little boy, he knew Brock hadn't meant any harm. It was a childish curiosity that had led to the question. And why shouldn't the boy wonder? Silas had been wondering for many years.

He wouldn't have cared about the question a few weeks ago. He'd heard things like it before. He might have even laughed it all off and given it no further thought, except for one thing. Celia. It was time to admit the change he'd been feeling for a couple of weeks now. His wariness had changed to concern then the concern had changed to something more.

He liked her. She intrigued him and surprised him. He liked how her hair, unremarkable brown inside, had golden-red highlights in the sunshine. He liked how pieces always worked themselves free from her ponytail and how pink her cheeks turned when she worked in the garden. He liked that the frightened girl he'd met outside the bus station in Bend sometimes smiled now.

He thought with disgust about the end of the evening. Celia had smiled and thanked him, trying to recover the pleasantness they'd shared before Alan and his little boy's interruption. Why hadn't he gone with it? Why had he sat there stewing in his embarrassment instead of smiling back and walking her to the door? Maybe he could have gone inside and prolonged the enjoyable evening. Maybe Aunt Nancy would have been in bed and he could have sat beside Celia and watched television.

Silas had spent his life avoiding connections with people. It was easier to be a loner than to watch the discomfort and pity people felt when they were talking to him. If he steered clear of others, he could avoid most of the looks of curiosity or confusion or pity. But Celia had smiled at him and talked to him like he was a regular guy, and until the end of the evening, he'd felt almost normal. Maybe it was time to set aside his insecurities and go after something. Did he dare take a chance and see if a girl like Celia could overlook his flaws and like him back? Could he set aside his feelings of being a freak and the fear that had held him hostage for so long? Maybe he could ask her on a real date. The thought made him feel a little sick. Did he really want to shake up the quiet, steady life he'd built for himself?

Suddenly Silas didn't feel like licking his wounds by the stream. He pushed himself off the log and headed across the field. Tomorrow night was the barbecue and dance and Celia would be there. For the first time in many years, Silas felt something he hadn't allowed himself to feel. He felt eager and motivated.

He felt hopeful.

Chapter 17

"I'm not sure how many more years Ed will insist on cooking hamburgers and hotdogs," Nancy said as she and Celia walked past a long row of food trucks pulled along one side of the park. "Most everyone on the committee thought we should skip the hamburgers this year and save ourselves all the work, but Ed says we need to keep with tradition. I say let's relieve the guys at the grills and let everyone eat from the trucks. As long as there's food in the park, that's tradition enough."

"Where did they all come from?" Celia asked. She'd seen a taco wagon in the parking lot of the grocery store, but nothing like this delicious-smelling caravan.

"Some are from The Dalles and Eugene. Probably even a few from Portland." They walked by a gourmet grilled cheese truck. "Darn it, Ed. I'd rather have a grilled cheese sandwich or a bowl of those noodles than one of his undercooked hamburgers." She waved at a girl taking orders in front of the truck with a steaming bowl of noodles on the side. "I may be back shortly."

Four men stood under the park pavilion at huge grills

sporting aprons that said “Rope ‘em and Ride ‘em in Sisters” and wielding long barbecue tools. The whole park smelled like spices and bacon and warm cookies.

“How’s business?” Nancy asked a woman sitting at a table at the front of the line.

“Better than I wish it was,” the woman answered. “How are we ever going to get Ed to turn it all over to them”—she pointed at the row of vendors—“if we’ve got lines waiting for his burgers? I thought we could count on you to take your business to the trucks.”

“It’s tempting. I’m glad there are plenty of out-of-towners to keep ’em busy.”

“Don’t tell anyone, but as soon as I’m through here, I’m hitting up that mac and cheese truck.” The woman turned to Celia. “You must be Nancy’s new roommate.

“I keep forgetting not everyone’s met her,” Nancy said and introduced Celia to Julie. “We’ll take three of Ed’s cheeseburgers.”

“Look at him.” Julie waved the twenty dollar bill Nancy had handed her toward the second grill where a gray-haired man was flipping burgers and cracking jokes, a huge smile on his face. “He looks forward to this every year. I’m not sure we can force him into retirement.” She handed Nancy her change.

“It’s probably what’s keeping him alive, so I guess in the spirit of geriatric solidarity, I’ll buy a burger as long as he’s grilling. But once he lays down the barbecue tools, I’m headed for the food trucks.”

“Is this your sister?” Ed said to Nancy when they made it to the front of the line.

“Oh Ed, I know you’re not that blind yet, so cut the bull.”

Ed winked and spoke to Celia. “She’s been talking back to me for more than forty years. I hope she’s nicer to you than she is to me.”

Celia grinned at the old man.

"I'm here buying your raw burgers, aren't I? I'd say that's being pretty nice."

Ed had been about to place a hamburger patty on a bun, but he feigned a hurt expression and put it back on the grill. "You want well done, you'll get well done." He turned back to Celia. "You think she actually wants it well done or do you think maybe she just wants to stick around and talk to me." He pointed his spatula at Nancy. "I've got you figured out."

After a couple more minutes and some silly teasing back and forth, Celia and Nancy walked to a picnic table with cheeseburgers, bags of chips and bottled water for three.

Nancy scanned the crowd and finally spotted Silas at the back of the food line. She got his attention and waved him over. "We got yours for you. Figured we'd save you the wait in line." Nancy slid the third plate across the table from her, putting Silas beside Celia.

"Thanks," he said.

While they ate, Silas filled them in on a couple of late entries to tomorrow's parade, and Nancy and Celia compared schedules for the following day.

"If you have time in the morning, I was hoping you could look over the garden with me," Celia said. "There are all kinds of things sprouting up out there but I'm not sure which are vegetables and which are weeds. I was hoping you could help me tell the difference so I don't pull up the wrong things."

"Of course. I don't work tomorrow until afternoon, but I think it's supposed to be pretty hot, so let's get out there early."

Nancy sent Silas to an ice cream food truck—her little sign of rebellion—and when he returned they ate gourmet ice cream sandwiches.

Silas pushed himself up from the table and stepped over the bench. "I'm headed home to feed Winston. Want m-me to stop by and feed Nubia?"

"I already did. But could you make sure I left the light on for her?"

"Sure thing." Silas looked directly at Celia. "See ya at the dance."

Celia watched Silas walk across the park. His mood had improved since last night and it was nice to see his smile again. When she pulled her eyes away from his retreating figure, she realized Nancy was watching her, a curious look in her eyes. Hoping to avoid an embarrassing conversation, Celia asked, "Do you need any help setting up the refreshments?"

"That's being taken care of. I signed us up for a half-hour shift during the dance and then we'll help clean up a bit afterward." A couple with a little girl in pink cowboy boots and a sparkly hat wandered by looking for a place to sit. "We were just leaving," Nancy said and motioned for them to take the table. "Let's walk along Hood Street."

Celia and Nancy strolled the row of galleries and antique shops as the sun dipped behind the trees. While Nancy stopped in front of Chicken Little Antiques to chat with one of her friends, Celia wandered to the window and looked at an antique sewing machine and a tiny nightlight that looked like icing roses. She was about to turn away when she noticed her transparent image looking back at her. She lifted the hem of the peasant blouse she wore and swung a little as she let it go, watching it move like liquid in the glass, and she felt grateful Nancy had loaned it to her. She felt pretty.

There wasn't much Celia could do about her scarce wardrobe right now. It would be frivolous to go buy something new when the next several months would bring so many changes to her figure, so for now she was resigned to wearing the few things she'd brought with her or the blue dress Nancy had bought for her. The dress had felt too dressy for a dance in a field, so Celia had put on her only pair of nice jeans and another t-shirt.

Nancy had taken one look at Celia, snapped her fingers, and hurried to her room. When she returned, she held up a breezy, white peasant blouse with tiny blue flowers embroidered on the front. "I thought maybe you'd like to wear this."

"Oh, that's okay."

"What, you don't like it?"

Celia shook her head. "You don't have to share your clothes with me."

Nancy turned the blouse toward her and scrutinized it. "I may be an old woman, but I think I have pretty good style."

"It's beautiful. But what if I get it dirty or—"

"You worry too much. There's nothing wrong with what you've got on, but we're going to a dance. You want something that catches the boys' eyes."

"I'm not looking for any boys, Nancy."

"Well, they'll be looking for you. Go put this on."

So Celia had, and now as she eyed her reflection, the sleeves fluttering in the breeze, she was glad she had.

"Pretty, huh?" Nancy said over her shoulder. Celia started and felt the heat rush to her face until she looked over at Nancy and saw that she was looking at the little nightlight.

The car bounced over the rough ground as Nancy followed the cowboy with a handlebar mustache directing traffic. A large field had been transformed for the dance—part of it was now a parking lot, and beyond all the cars was a tent so large it looked like it could fit seven or eight of Nancy's houses underneath it. Hundreds of sparkling lights crisscrossed the ceiling. Lanterns hung from metal fence posts that had been driven into the ground to light the way from the parking area to the tent. The whole field had been transformed into a magical place.

On the far side of the tent, a band was setting up their equipment and to the right were the refreshments. Nancy and Celia made their way over to the two steel troughs filled with ice and drinks and the table where they would sell cookies and cupcakes.

"Nice of you to finally show up." The woman behind the table sounded angry, but her smile gave her away.

"I'll be feeling the same way about you later when you're snoring away in your bed and I'm over here cleaning up."

Celia felt conspicuous and out of place standing by while the two women visited.

"Nancy, could I borrow the car keys? I don't want to have to carry my bag around all evening."

Nancy gave her the keys and Celia made her way back to the car. The truth was, she wished she hadn't come. An evening alone at Nancy's house sounded vastly better than standing around with a crowd of strangers hoping not to be noticed and not knowing what to say. She tucked a couple of dollars into her pocket in case she decided to buy a cookie later on then slid the bag under the seat. Suddenly she felt very tired. Surely Nancy wouldn't miss her if she rested in the car for a little while and it would spare her a few minutes of standing around conspicuously. She pulled the door shut and locked it, then leaned her head against the headrest and let her eyes close.

The band began playing and Celia fell asleep to a country song about partying down by the river.

Chapter 18

Celia jumped when Silas knocked on the window.

"You okay?" he asked through the glass.

It took a few seconds for Celia to get her bearings, but then she opened the door of the car. "Oh, I'm so sorry. I was resting my eyes for a few minutes and I guess I fell asleep."

"It's okay. Nancy just wondered where you were."

Celia got out of the car and locked it. "I haven't been gone that long, have I?"

Silas fell into step beside her and pulled out his phone to look at the time. "It's almost ten."

"No. I slept more than an hour?"

Silas shrugged. "I don't know what time you came to the car."

"Too long ago. I hope I didn't miss my turn at the table." She was practically jogging to the tent.

Silas touched her arm. He seemed tentative. "Slow down. They're fine. You're going to turn your ankle out here." He let his arm drop back to his side.

Celia took a deep breath and slowed her pace.

The music was loud and the crowd spilled out beyond the edges of the tent. Celia had never seen a gathering quite like it. In high school, she'd gone to one school dance after a game. So many kids were moving provocatively and grabbing at each other that she'd spent most of the night in the bathroom, trying to avoid the whole scene. When she'd lived with her third, and last, foster family, they had taken her to the wedding of a cousin. At the reception, she had sat at a table and watched as the bride and groom danced together before the others joined in. The most memorable thing about that night was that the couple had danced to "Unforgettable" by Nat King Cole. Her mother had sung that song to her when she was a little girl, before the drugs made her forget she even had a little girl.

This was completely different. The band played mostly country songs and all ages were dancing together. There were old couples, young couples and even some parents on the floor with their children. Several teenagers jumped and swayed and laughed together in the corner, and it looked like a couple of people might have even been dancing alone. Those that weren't dancing were sitting in folding chairs clustered in groups or standing outside the perimeter of the tent. Everyone seemed to be having a good time.

"There you are," Nancy said when they approached a group of older women. "I thought maybe some cowboy had swept you off your feet."

"I fell asleep in the car."

"You must have been tired to be able to sleep through all this." She swept her hand, taking in the crowd.

"I guess so. I can take a turn now at the refreshment table."

"We're both signed up from ten to ten-thirty. We'll head over there in a minute."

Soon Nancy was refilling plates with goodies and Celia was putting cans of pop and beer and bottled water into the now slushy ice troughs. Out on the floor, people line danced to a song Celia had never heard. Most of them knew the routine pretty well, but when someone would make a mistake, teasing and laughter would follow.

Celia looked around for Silas, but after he'd brought her back from the car, he'd disappeared, and she couldn't find him in the throng.

"Go ahead and have something, if you want," Nancy said. When Celia dug into her pocket for her money, Nancy put up her hand. "Oh no. You get a drink and treat for working the table. Why do you think I volunteer every year?" She winked.

Celia picked a chocolate chip cookie with walnuts and a bottled water. There wasn't much to do at the table, but it gave her a good vantage point to watch people. She saw a woman about her age swing dancing, spinning and turning under the man's arms, her full skirt twisting around her legs as it tried to keep up. Her partner said something and she laughed. Celia felt a pang of jealousy. He was looking at her with such affection, and she looked like she didn't have a care in the world. What would it be like to be able to let loose and enjoy the moment like that? Celia couldn't remember ever feeling as carefree as they looked.

While Aunt Nancy and Celia took their turn at the refreshment table, Silas stood outside the tent in the shadows with a few of his coworkers, but he wasn't participating in the conversation. He couldn't have said what they were even talking about. He had looked for Celia when he arrived at the tent, ready to ask her to dance, but he couldn't find her. He could have asked Aunt Nancy, but he knew she'd want to meddle and he wasn't sure enough of his own feelings to put her on the case. He felt in his gut that if this was a good idea, he needed to make it happen on his own.

When more than an hour passed and he still hadn't seen a sign of Celia, he gave in and approached Aunt Nancy.

"Did Celia go home?"

Aunt Nancy looked surprised. "No. I haven't seen her for quite a while. I thought she might have been with you."

Silas scanned the tent again.

"I gave her the keys to my car. She didn't want to carry her bag around. Maybe—"

"I'll go look," Silas interrupted.

He'd felt a wave of relief when he'd found the car and Celia asleep. Now when he thought about asking her to dance, his courage felt a little shaky. He wanted to do it, had fallen asleep last night picturing the way he'd ask her. He had even practiced the words, saying them over and over until he managed to get them out without messing up, but now that time was running out he didn't feel so confident.

He looked at his watch. Their shift would end any minute. If he was going to make a move, he needed to do it soon. The dance ended in about an hour and he knew it could take him that long to get up his nerve. He left the guys without a word and headed back inside the tent.

Celia smiled at him as he walked toward the table. "Did you want something to eat? Or a drink? I had one of these chocolate chip cookies, and I highly recommend them."

She looked so pretty with her hair down, and when she looked at him, he felt flustered. Would he be able to get the words out? Saying them alone in his Jeep wasn't the same as saying them here, with her looking up at him, the twinkling lights reflecting in her eyes.

Silas looked over the food. The temptation to buy something was compelling, and he almost took the easy way out, but after several seconds, he looked back at Celia and shook his head. "I thought m—" he was stuck there for long enough that the muscles in his lips and jaw ached. He pulled them apart with effort and looked away, taking a deep breath before he tried again. "M-maybe, would you like to dance?"

Celia looked down for a moment, and Silas felt his heartbeat pounding in his ears. He looked past the people dancing and wanted to walk out of the tent and back to the safety of the darkness.

"Okay."

He looked back at her. "Okay."

The music was ending as Celia stepped around the table. A new song started as they walked onto the dance floor. It was a slow one, and as everyone around them came together to dance, he put his arm loosely around Celia's waist, took her hand and began moving to the music. His efforts were a little clumsy and they moved almost arm's length apart from each other.

"I'm not a very good dancer," he said.

"I'm sure you're better than me."

She glanced down at her feet, like she was concentrating on moving them the right way. She was so pretty and unsure and the familiar feeling of wanting to take care of her and make her happy swelled up in him and made him forget about his own worries.

"You're doing great." He lightly squeezed her hand. She looked up at his face and a smile touched the sides of her mouth.

"Thanks. This is the first time I've ever danced with

anyone."

"Ever?"

"Crazy, huh?"

Silas shrugged and pulled her a little closer. Their movements became smoother as they relaxed into the song, and as the last note faded away, Silas wished the song had lasted much longer.

"Let's keep it here for another one," the man at the microphone said.

Silas leaned his head back a little to look at Celia. "One m-more?"

She nodded. Her hand moved on his shoulder, and he had trouble taking a deep breath. Almost without realizing he was doing it, he moved his hand farther around her back. Her blouse was soft and silky. Her hair smelled like coconut, and she leaned her cheek against his shoulder. Would she be able to tell he was hardly breathing?

"You're where I'm supposed to be, you're my home sweet home," sang the man at the microphone. Silas had wished for this—Celia's hand in his, her head resting against him, her hair brushing against his cheek. This was what he'd fallen asleep thinking about last night, but suddenly it wasn't enough. He wanted more, and the ache of it made him want to hold her tighter and never let go.

"When I'm broken and need mended, when my hope is almost ended, you're right there where I'm supposed to be." The last cord faded out, and Celia slowly stepped away and looked up at him. He wanted her to be feeling what he was, but her face was hard to read. Was she surprised? Afraid? Finally, it settled into a reticent smile.

"I thought you said you didn't know how to dance."

Silas shrugged. "I don't really."

"I thought you were pretty good, but what do I know?"

Another song started, this one quick and lively and dancers began moving around them.

Celia motioned toward the chairs where Nancy was sitting. "I guess I'll go . . . "

"Yeah."

"You want to come?"

"No. I'll just . . . " He wasn't sure what to say, so he let his voice trail off.

"Okay, I'll see ya later."

As Silas watched her move between the dancers on the floor, he could almost feel the walls he'd built up crumbling, leaving his heart exposed and defenseless. He'd worked in the mountains alone. He'd fought fires that could have killed him. He had faced the loss of his family. But this was different. This was a new kind of terrifying.

Chapter 19

It was already light, but the air had a cold bite that the sun would overpower before long. Nancy and Celia were already in the garden when Silas drove by on his way to the station. He'd never minded working Saturdays before, but this morning, he wanted to be working in the garden. He wanted to be wherever Celia was.

Both women waved as he drove by, and as he turned the corner, he looked back and saw that Celia was still watching the Jeep, although it was hard to read her expression from so far away.

He thought he'd spend the day thinking about Celia as he drove to several trails and collected money from the fee boxes, but he'd hardly started his rounds when Jean radioed him.

"Hey Silas, where are you?"

"Tumalo Road."

"Good. We got a call that we had overnight campers at Tumalo Falls. Could you check it out?"

"Sure thing."

Tumalo Falls was a day use area without proper camping

facilities, but every year, there were at least a few who tried to get away with camping there.

Silas reached the picnic area and walked along the half-mile trail to the falls, keeping an eye out for signs of tents or a campfire. Shortly before he reached the overlook, he spotted two hammocks stretched between trees about thirty feet off the trail. When he reached them, he found a small propane stove with still-warm coffee in a pan on top of the single burner. Backpacks rested against the trees under the hammocks, but no one was in the little makeshift camp.

Silas walked back to the trail and continued toward the fenced lookout area. Water crashed over the falls, and Silas looked over the rail for a minute, admiring the majestic view. Behind him he heard someone yelling. He started back along the trail, looking for the voice. He wasn't far from the campground when someone came crashing onto the trail.

"We. Need. Your help." A woman was doubled over breathing hard and struggling to get the words out.

"What's wrong?" Silas asked, looking around to see if he could see what had her so upset.

The woman took a couple of deep breaths and looked up. "My husband. He's stuck on the rocks."

Silas followed the woman who led him through the trees toward the top of the falls. The sound of water grew louder as they approached a drop off. "He's down there."

Silas looked over the edge. About thirty feet down, clinging to the rocks as he crouched on a small ledge was a man.

"How long has he b-been there?"

"Since right after sunrise. I told him he didn't have enough experience, but he wouldn't listen to me. We've got to get him." The woman was frantic and started to cry. Silas knew he'd have to get help. The man was too far down to attempt it on his own.

"We will. Wait here."

Silas ran back down the trail, slowing only after he slid a couple of times and realized if he fell and couldn't get help, the man's life would be in danger.

He silently prayed as he ran. *Please don't let me get stuck on my words. Jean, there's a man stuck by Tumalo Falls.* No, he'd get stuck on the m. *Jean, I've got a man on the rock face at Tumalo Falls.* There was the m again. *There's a climber trapped on the rock face at Tumalo Falls.*

By the time Silas reached his truck, he had his wording worked out.

"Jean, there's a climber trapped on the rock face at Tum—" Silas slapped the side of his truck as his lips crushed the m. He hardly ever got hung up in the middle of a word. Why now? *Reset.* The advice of the counselors at Camp Rock Ridge ran through his mind. He took a deep breath and started over, slower. "There's a climber trapped on the rock face at Tumalo Falls."

The rest of the morning was spent working with rescuers as they pulled the man off the cliff. His only injuries were a few scratches and bruises, but he was pretty shaken up. Silas felt like a jerk when he cited them for camping and climbing outside the designated areas, but they were so relieved, they didn't seem to mind.

It had been a difficult morning, and when he finally pulled his truck out of the campground, all he wanted to do was tell Celia about it.

Nancy worked in the garden with Celia until almost eleven when she changed for work and headed to The Stitchin' Station. Celia knelt on the little knee pad and pulled the green sprigs next to what she hoped were the vegetables. Nancy had shown her what to remove, but once she'd left, Celia's confidence wavered. She worked her way down two more rows, hoping she wasn't destroying the garden.

When her empty stomach growled, she walked to the house on stiff and tired legs to scrounge up some lunch. She thought she might return to the garden after she ate her salad, but as she rinsed off her plate, her arms felt leaden and weariness pressed itself on her. Perhaps a short nap would give her enough energy to continue working. As soon as she curled up on her bed, she fell asleep.

"I don't understand what makes p-people do such stupid things," a man's voice said in her dreams. "He could have died."

"Anything you want to tell me?" someone else asked. The words didn't make sense as fragments of conversations wormed their way into her consciousness.

"I thought you liked her." Celia opened her eyes. How long had she been asleep?

"I do like her, but we don't know much about her. I don't want you to get hurt." It was Nancy's voice. Celia's sleep-muddled mind tried to make sense of what she had been hearing.

"Don't you want to know m-more?"

"I don't know if she'll ever tell us about her past. And since we don't know what that is, I want you to be careful."

"I've b-been careful my whole life and look at me." Celia noticed he was stuttering more with his aunt than he usually did. Was he angry?

Nancy raised her voice. "What about you? There's

nothing wrong with you, Silas."

"Shhh. She'll hear you." Quiet footsteps moved down the hall and stopped at the door to her bedroom. Celia closed her eyes, hoping they'd think she was still asleep. The door squeaked softly as it closed, and when the conversation continued, the voices were muffled. Celia slipped off the bed and moved to the door, opening it very slowly to avoid the usual creak.

Nancy gave a short laugh. "Not too long ago you were telling me I should be careful."

"You didn't listen. You even encouraged m-me to come around more and hang out with her."

"I figured you could both use a friend, but that's all I was encouraging. She has secrets, Silas. It's one thing to give her a place to live and have her work for me. It's quite another to start dating her. Hold off until we know more about her. 'Til we know if she's even going to stick around here."

"Has she said she's leaving?"

"No. But every day I wonder if she'll be gone when I get home."

Silence stretched out for a long time and Celia wondered if Silas had left.

Nancy finally spoke. "Don't be upset with me. It's my job to worry about you."

"I know. B-but I'm not a kid. I'm twenty-six years old. You should let m-me worry about myself."

Nancy sighed. "It doesn't work like that. Just take a step back until you know more about her." There was the sound of pans banging before she changed the subject. "Tell me more about the climber. Where was he from?"

Celia quietly closed the door and curled up facing the wall. After they had danced, she had wondered if Silas liked her. It hadn't been an unwelcome thought. Now she knew. She also knew Nancy didn't approve. That stung, but Nancy was right. He knew almost nothing about her, and if he did, Celia suspected his feelings would change.

They had been planning a full evening. The parade, the last night of the rodeo and the fireworks display following, but now Celia couldn't bear the thought. She had been looking forward to seeing Silas tonight, but not with Nancy scrutinizing their actions and worrying about Silas and probably wishing she hadn't allowed Celia into their lives.

After she heard Silas leave, she joined Nancy in the kitchen.

"We should leave for the parade in half an hour," Nancy said. She smiled, but there was a little tension behind her friendly tone.

"I think I'll stay home." Nancy looked surprised. "I'm not feeling too well tonight."

"Are you sick?" Nancy walked over and put her hand on Celia's forehead. She may be concerned about her nephew, but she was still behaving kindly toward Celia.

"I'm feeling a little tired and achy."

"Did we wake you earlier?" Nancy looked guilty.

"When?"

"Silas and I were talking earlier. Were we too loud?"

"No. I must have been out of it."

Nancy looked relieved. "I hate for you to miss tonight. The last night's always fun."

"Yeah. Too bad. You guys go have fun though. I'll just go to bed early."

Celia wasn't tired at all after they left so she watched some television. About eleven, she heard the explosions of the fireworks outside. She walked out on the porch and sat on the steps watching the tiny lights burst like millions of stars against the dark sky. She wanted to enjoy them, but all they did was make her feel lonely. An ache sprouted in her chest and grew until her throat was tight and tears escaped her eyes.

Nancy had been kind to her, and Silas might even think he liked her. But neither of them trusted her and neither of them knew her. No one did. In this entire world, there wasn't a single person who knew her and loved her.

Not one.

Chapter 20

Silas looked at the clock. Nine-forty-eight. He straightened his necktie and looked in the full-length mirror on the back of the closet door. The tie was much too long. It made him look like a little boy dressing up in his father's clothes. Technically this was his father's tie, but Silas wasn't a little boy. He yanked the knot loose around his neck and started over, knowing this was probably making him late.

He glanced at Aunt Nancy's house as he drove by. What would she think if she knew where Silas was going? Was he wasting his time this morning? Not that going to church was a waste of time, but he knew he wasn't going for the right reasons. He was going because, for at least the past two Sundays, Celia had gone to church. He should have asked her which church she attended, but he hadn't, so now he could only hope she had returned to the church she'd walked to the night he found her crying.

Silas parked his Jeep in the shade of a pine tree and walked to the door. He ran his hands through his hair as he looked at his reflection then walked inside.

The air felt cool in the foyer. An organ began playing "How Great Thou Art" and Silas moved toward the chapel. He stood at the back and scanned the room, looking for Celia's brown sugar hair. On the third row from the back he found her. She looked shocked when Silas slid past a couple at the end of the bench and sat down beside her.

She was wearing the blue dress and it occurred to Silas it was probably the only dress she owned. Part of her hair was pulled back off her face. She had pretty cheekbones. He turned toward the front of the room where the man leading the music cut off the last note with a flourish.

Silas hadn't been to church since Easter Sunday, and then it had been a different denomination. He'd never been to this one before, but as the minister began speaking about forgiveness, he found himself interested in the message and moved by the stories he told. He felt Celia's glance several times, but kept his gaze on the minister or the stained glass behind him, or the organ.

The meeting lasted more than an hour, but Silas didn't mind. He was sitting beside Celia. He had wanted to sit beside her at the rodeo and fireworks the night before. Despite Aunt Nancy's worries, Silas had thought of nothing but Celia as he stood at the beginning of the parade route, motioning each entry forward at forty-five second intervals. When the convertible with the mayor brought up the end of the parade, he'd worked his way down the street to The Stitchin' Station, where the employees always sat chairs out for their families. He had been disappointed when he realized Celia hadn't joined Aunt Nancy for the parade. It was difficult to be good company for the evening when his mind kept wandering to Celia.

It had taken Silas a long time to fall asleep after he arrived home from the fireworks. Aunt Nancy's concerns seemed valid. What did they really know about Celia? Pearl had picked her up in Bend, brought her to Sisters, and helped her find a place to live. But then Pearl had left. Had she even known Celia? Silas couldn't remember anything that would indicate that they were friends, or even acquaintances. So Pearl had pulled some strings, but that couldn't really be an endorsement of Celia's character or intentions, could it?

Celia had told Aunt Nancy she came from Chicago and didn't have any family. That's all they knew. It seemed like she wanted to leave the past behind her, but what was that past? At first Silas had thought she might be a con artist, but he didn't feel that way now. Maybe that proved she was pulling a really good scam. Or maybe she was running from the law.

As he tossed and turned, none of those things felt right, but it was true. They didn't know much about her. Despite that, Silas was interested. He felt drawn to her, protective of her. The logical solution was to find out more about her and the only way to do that would be to spend more time together.

He'd start the next day. Aunt Nancy had told him Celia had gone to church the last two Sundays. Would she make it a third? He didn't know, but if she did, he could be there. He wanted to spend time with her anyway, so why not?

Now, here he was in a church he'd never attended before, but the message was good—forgiveness was a good thing, right? The minister had charisma. A few times he cracked tasteful jokes and he seemed sincere. The building was peaceful and the morning light made the stained glass depiction of the Garden of Gethsemane beautiful. And Celia was beside him. He felt good.

He glanced over at Celia as she wiped away tears. Was she crying about something the minister had said? Silas thought over the last few sentences of the sermon. Something about needing to forgive others seventy times seven. Silas wondered what had prompted the tears. Did Celia need to forgive or did she need to be forgiven? He wanted to put his arm around her and offer some comfort but she turned away from him as she wiped her cheeks, and he could tell it would be better if she didn't know he'd seen her tears.

After the services were over, they sat on the bench as the organ played and others rose to leave.

"Do you go to this church?" Celia asked softly.

"First time at this one."

"Why?"

"I thought you m-might want some company."

She looked at him for a moment. "Thanks."

Silas nodded. "You want some lunch? I thought we could go to Bend. M-McKay's Cottage."

Celia hesitated. "Um, sure."

When they walked to Silas's Jeep, he walked with her to the passenger side and opened the door. It wasn't an easy vehicle to board, especially in a dress, so when Silas held out his hand to help her, she took it.

"Should we be inviting Nancy?" she asked when they drove past the road that led home.

Silas was glad he knew Aunt Nancy was scheduled at The Stitchin' Station. "She's working today. We'll get something for her."

They drove the same road they'd traveled with Pearl two months ago, but this time neither of them were silent. Silas pointed out the Three Sisters mountains. "That's Faith, that one's Hope and that's Charity."

"Appropriate names for a Sunday afternoon."

"There's a s-sermon in there somewhere."

"Do you know one? An old pioneer story or something? About how they got their names." Celia asked.

"I don't."

"It seems like there should be one. An old legend or something."

Silas looked at her sideways. "You should make one up."

She shook her head. "I'm not good at making up stories."

"You're giving up that easily? Come on. Those m-mountains deserve a story."

Celia shook her head again.

"You've really let them down. They've b-been waiting all these years for you to come to Sisters and give them a legend."

Celia smiled. "Really? It's my job? They've been here for thousands of years and no one's given them a legend? You old-timers should be ashamed." She turned toward the mountains. "Sorry Sisters, the people who have lived here enjoying your beauty for all these years have really let you down."

"And the one you've waited for for centuries is still letting you down."

The mood was light and Celia looked happy. "Oh no, you can't put this on me. But . . . " Celia turned toward Silas, and when he saw the playful way she was looking at him, something seized inside of him.

"What?" Silas gave her a suspicious sideways glance.

"We could create a legend together. Back and forth. Line by line." Silas looked doubtful. "Unless you're afraid your lines will stink."

Silas laughed and shrugged. "Okay. You first."

Celia looked thoughtful as she studied the mountains for a minute. "Thousands of years ago in a land of green trees and blue skies, a woman gave birth to three little girls."

Silas nodded. "Not bad."

"Not bad? It was great. Let's hear what you've got."

"Their parents named them M-Mary, Sherri, and . . . Larry."

Celia looked appalled. "I said three little girls. Larry?"

"I couldn't think of something that rhymed with M-Mary and Sherri."

"Let's see. Carrie. Jeri. Terri."

"Yeah. Those are better. You should have named them with your line, I guess."

"I guess so." Celia folded her arms. "Ah ha. After a few days, the parents realized life would be very confusing if the girls had rhyming names, and they didn't much like the name Larry anyway, so they renamed the girls Mary, Elizabeth and Gertrude."

"Gertrude is better than Larry?" Silas was laughing.

"For a girl, yes."

"Okay." Silas needed to come up with a good line. "The girls were p-pretty and grew to be very tall. Over ten thousand feet to be exact."

"It's a legend. Not literal. What am I supposed to do with ten thousand foot tall girls?"

"Hmm." He rubbed his chin. "That's your p-problem."

They drove at least a mile before Celia offered the next sentence. "One year, heavy snows came and covered the three sisters with beautiful, white dresses."

"P-people came from all over the world to climb up the sisters and s-ski down their skirts."

"Were there skiers thousands of years ago?" Celia asked.

"There were in m-my legend. And don't I get a little acknowledgement for that line? Ski down their skirts? It's a good line."

Celia rocked her hand back and forth in a so-so way. Back and forth they went, adding to their story.

"The sisters shouted to each other across the cold, winter air."

"'I have more skiers than you,' Gertrude said."

"'But I'm more beautiful than you,' said Elizabeth."

"'I think we should stop fighting,' M-M-Mary said."

"The sisters decided they should be best friends instead of rivals."

Silas looked at Celia. "I have nowhere to go with this."

They laughed, and Celia said, "Get creative."

It took a couple of minutes before Silas continued. "Since M-M-Mary was so wise, the three sisters decided they would stay together forever."

Celia nodded and got a teasing look on her face. "And then the sisters looked far into the future and saw that a kind man named Silas, who would someday work in their forests and write a long-overdue legend for them, had trouble saying Mary's name, so they changed their names to Faith, Hope and Charity." For a moment, Celia looked nervous, but relief filled her eyes when Silas started laughing, a real, joyful laugh.

"And Faith, Hope, and Charity lived happily ever after," he said without a stutter.

They grinned at each other as Silas reached over and, for just a second, he squeezed Celia's hand.

Many people had teased Silas about his stutter. Every other time it had felt hurtful and had left him feeling insecure. He wondered how it was possible for it to feel so different this time.

Chapter 21

McKay's Cottage was a craftsman-style home converted into a restaurant. Sunday brunch was a busy time and even though they were seating people inside and had more than a dozen tables set up around the yard, Silas and Celia still had to wait at the bottom of the stairs for twenty minutes. Servers in khakis and McKay's Cottage t-shirts worked quickly and cheerfully.

"This must be a fun place to work," Celia said. "Everyone's smiling."

"They p-probably get to eat while they work."

Celia hadn't eaten breakfast, and as the servers walked by them carrying beautiful plates of food to the tables on the lawn, her mouth watered. It looked delicious. And expensive. She had a twenty dollar bill in her bag, but now she worried that might not be enough. A few minutes ago, the idea of spending it all on a meal at a restaurant would have horrified her, but the food looked so good and she was so hungry, all thoughts of frugality vanished, and she couldn't wait to eat.

When the hostess finally seated them, Celia opened the

menu and couldn't contain her smile. She could order whatever she wanted, and what she wanted was the meal she remembered Nancy raving about—the lemon ricotta pancakes with fresh berries.

Had she ever had a nicer day? The peacefulness of church had calmed her turbulent feelings, and in spite of his conversation with Nancy, Silas had surprised her. She could tell he liked her. He had laughed at her teasing, had even touched her.

A light breeze rustled in the trees and the umbrellas that shielded the tables from the sunshine flapped lightly. It carried the fragrance of the flowers that lined the front of the yard. Celia looked around at the people seated near them. There were some that looked like they'd come from church. A table of six not far from theirs talked about their morning hike. It was a cheerful setting, and she didn't feel like an outsider looking in at others' happiness. It felt like she fit in. Was it because of church or because of Silas? She didn't really know, but for a few moments she felt contented and peaceful.

When she took her first bite of pancakes, she sighed and Silas laughed. "That good, huh?" He was eating a salmon and potato hash.

"This might be the best thing I've ever eaten."

They didn't talk much as they ate—just occasional comments about the food. Mostly, Celia savored each bite and did her best to push aside thoughts that threatened to ruin this perfect day. *This will bother Nancy. He wouldn't be here with you if he knew you were pregnant. You'll have to tell them some time. You won't be able to hide it in a couple more months.* As each thought crowded in, she beat it back. Didn't she deserve a perfect day just once?

She looked across the table and saw that Silas was sweeping crumbs from his scone into a little pile, his expression thoughtful. Was he thinking about what his aunt had said? Or maybe it was their conversation in the car. Why had she teased him about his stutter? He had seemed okay with it, but when she thought back on the things she'd said, it scared her that she had been so forward. Maybe he regretted following her to church and wished he were somewhere else.

"Is everything okay?" She braced herself for his answer.

Silas met her gaze then leaned forward.

"Tell m-me about you." His mouth stalled on the "m" long enough that she knew this wasn't a casual question.

Celia had prepared herself for whatever Silas had to say about himself or his feelings, but she hadn't prepared herself for this. She didn't like talking about herself. Her life made people uncomfortable and she didn't want to spoil the day with stories of drug addicted parents and disappointing foster homes. Or worse.

Celia tried to laugh. "There's not much to tell, really."

"Celia. Don't. P-please. I want to know more about you."

He was so earnest, she knew she couldn't joke or squirm her way out of an answer. She gave up and sighed. "What do you want to know?"

"Tell me about your family."

Celia watched the perfect day slide over the horizon, and even though it was midday, she suddenly felt overcome by the coldness and darkness of her past. She blew out a deep breath and slumped back in her chair. She picked at a thread on her napkin and her voice was unemotional as she recited the bullet points of her life. "My dad left when I was a baby. I never knew him. My mom died when I was eleven. I lived in four foster homes after that. I got out of the system a little more than two years ago." She lifted her eyes to his. "Not very exciting."

Silas didn't answer immediately and Celia could see she had surprised him. "You have no family?"

Celia shook her head.

"No aunts or uncles?"

"I have an uncle. I think he lives in Wisconsin, but his wife didn't want to deal with a kid whose mom died in front of her of an overdose. Too much baggage to have me around their daughter. I never saw them after the funeral."

"Are you ready for your bill?" a friendly server asked.

"I think so," Silas said.

"Could I get a scone and jam to go?" Celia asked the server. She turned to Silas. "We should take something to Nancy." Silas nodded as Celia turned back to talk to the girl. "You can put the scone on my bill."

"Oh, so you want separate checks?"

"No." Silas pulled out his wallet. "I'm p-paying."

"I don't mind—"

"I invited you."

"Don't fight him on it," the server said. "Just bring him back sometime and treat him. It's a win-win."

"Thanks, Silas. Those were the best pancakes ever."

Silas didn't speak while they waited for the server to bring back his change. The cheerful hikers were gone and the cool breeze had given way to the sun beating uncomfortably on Celia's back. She was tired and emotionally spent. She should have kept her history to herself or made something up. She felt exposed and afraid.

Silas opened the Jeep door for her. He stood between her and the open door after she pulled herself to the seat. He shoved his hands into his pockets and leaned against the door. "I hope m-my questions weren't too hard. I wasn't trying to p-pry."

"I know. It's why I don't talk about myself much."

Silas nodded. "I get it. I thought I had it bad."

"You did have it bad. You lost your parents."

"B-but I had Aunt Nancy."

They waited for a group of people to walk past them, and Celia leaned her head against the seat. "It isn't a contest to see whose life is harder. Everyone has hard things. I don't want you to feel sorry for me."

"Have you felt sorry for me? You know, 'cause I'm an orphan?"

Celia barely smiled. "I guess so."

"Then let me feel sorry for you."

Celia's smile widened. "Fine. But only until we get home. After that, no feeling sorry for each other because we're orphans or abandoned."

"How did she die?"

"My mom?"

"Yeah."

"It was a drug overdose. I was with her."

Silas took his hands out of his pockets and folded his arms. "That deserves m-more sympathy than the ride home. It's gotta be good for at least a day."

The corner of his mouth curled up in an almost-smile and Celia laughed. She'd have wanted to punch most people for making light of such serious things, but because Silas had lived through so much pain himself, it didn't feel like joking. It felt like commiserating, and even though she had secrets that would eventually be more than he could handle, she would allow herself to feel this breathless connection. At least for today.

Chapter 22

"I saw your nephew at church this morning. I didn't know he belonged to our congregation," Ann-Marie Wheeler said as she purchased fabric for the back of a quilt top she'd finished.

Nancy retrieved new bags under the counter to hide her surprise. "That's nice. You probably saw my boarder, too?" she asked while she finished the transaction.

"Yes. I can't remember her name."

"Celia."

"Right. She's a pretty girl."

"Yes, she is."

Ann-Marie's voice became excited. "Are they dating? Oh my, they would make an adorable couple. Ah, and how nice for Silas."

Something about Ann-Marie's tone grated on Nancy's nerves. Did she think Silas wasn't worthy of a pretty girl? Nancy chided herself after Ann-Marie left. She was a kind woman and had always liked Silas. Why would she be anything but pleased to think Silas was dating Celia?

Why wasn't Nancy happy with the idea? Maybe she was

behaving like an over-protective parent, one who thinks no one is good enough for their child. Celia was a lovely girl and a hard worker. She was thoughtful and quiet and Silas liked her. In truth, Silas had been a lonely boy and was now a lonely man. Nancy should be hoping he'd find a good woman to share his life with. Nancy wouldn't be around forever.

No matter how she tried to convince herself she should be encouraging Silas, the uneasy feeling remained. She was sure Celia was hiding something. She guarded herself more than Nancy felt comfortable with. Maybe Silas and Celia would be a good fit, but until Nancy knew more, it would be difficult for her to give her blessing.

Celia stood at the counter chopping cucumbers when Nancy walked through the back door. "It smells good in here. What are you making?"

"A salad. I've got baked spaghetti in the oven."

"You should have waited. I could have helped."

"That's okay. I'm going to a get-together at the church tonight, so I was hoping we could eat before I go."

"Of course." Nancy stole a slice of cucumber and popped it in her mouth. "Is Silas going with you?"

She tried to sound casual, but she saw Celia's back stiffen.

"I don't think so. He said something about watching that fishing show with you."

"What's this?" Nancy held up a Styrofoam box.

"That's a scone from McKay's Cottage. For you."

Nancy lifted the lid. "And jam. Here's my dessert for

tonight. Did you go to McKay's Cottage today?"

"Silas and I went after church."

Nancy wanted to pry, but didn't want Celia to feel defensive. "What did you have?"

Celia smiled. "Lemon ricotta pancakes with berries. They were unreal."

"I know. That's my favorite place to eat. Thank you for the scone."

"Sure."

Nancy was glad to see Celia relax. Nancy wanted to ask her about her past, what her feelings were about Silas, what secrets she was keeping from them, but instead they talked about a quilt Nancy was planning for the quilt show, the food at McKay's Cottage, and the garden.

"You can drive my car to the church if you'd like. I don't know how late you'll be, but I don't want you walking home in the dark."

"If you're sure you don't need it, that would be great."

"I'm not going anywhere else tonight. I'm ready to kick my feet up and stay put."

Celia left before Silas arrived. Nancy changed into a housedress then called him. "Have you had dinner?"

"Not yet."

"Come on over and have some spaghetti and salad before the show. We've got plenty."

"Great. I'll head over."

Silas arrived a few minutes later. Nancy felt a tug at her heart as she watched him look around for Celia. "She went to a social at the church."

Silas looked embarrassed that he had been so easy to read. "That's good."

Nancy led Silas into the kitchen and dished up a plate of spaghetti. She sat across from him while he ate.

"Church, huh?" She smiled to soften the question.

Silas grinned around a bite of food.

"How did you choose which congregation to attend?"

Silas swallowed. "I went with Celia."

"I know. Ann-Marie came into the store and told me she saw you. Thinks you and Celia make an adorable couple." Silas looked pleased but kept eating.

"Please tell me you learned more about her. I can live with you two seeing each other if it isn't just mooning about how pretty she is. You need to know more about her. About her past. Be sure you like who she really is, not only what she looks like or how good she kisses."

"We haven't kissed." Silas poured dressing on his salad. "And I did ask questions."

"And?"

"She doesn't talk about things b-because she's had a hard life and I don't think she likes to complain or feel sorry for herself."

"Hard life how?"

"Her dad left when she was a baby and her m-mom died of an overdose when she was eleven. She lived in foster homes."

Nancy was quiet for a moment, letting the information sink in. It was terrible to think of Celia as a little girl going through that. She felt a swelling in her heart for the broken child who had become the young lady she knew.

"Didn't she have any other family that could take her in?" It had gone without question that she would take care of Silas when Jack and Sharon died.

"She has an uncle. He didn't want her."

Nancy's heart ached. It was difficult to imagine family leaving one of their own to be cared for by strangers.

"She doesn't want us to feel sorry for her. So she doesn't

talk about it."

Relief washed over Nancy. She didn't need to worry about Silas's interest in Celia. Then relief was filled with shame for doubting the poor girl.

Nancy scooted her chair back from the table. "Did you have a nice time today?"

Silas nodded. "Did you get your scone?"

"I did. Thank you."

"It was Celia's idea."

Nancy patted Silas's arm as she walked by him to go to the living room. She wanted to say something but didn't know if she could speak over the lump in her throat.

Chapter 23

A woman in a pink pantsuit unlocked the door of the Sisters Family Health Clinic and disappeared inside. Celia had tried the door ten minutes earlier and had been waiting on a bench across the street since then.

A bell rang as she opened the door and the pant suited woman turned to her in surprise. “Did you have an appointment?”

“No. Not yet.”

“We’re not actually open until nine.”

Celia’s palms were sweating and she could hear the blood pounding against her ears. “I was hoping I could talk to someone before it got busy.” She lowered her voice as if she didn’t want the empty waiting room to hear of her shame. “I need to see a doctor who delivers babies.”

The woman’s eyes traveled to Celia’s stomach but since it wasn’t yet giving away her secret, she looked back up at Celia’s face.

The bell above the door rang again and a man entered. Everything about him was square—gray hair was combed over his box-shaped head and he had a stocky, cube-shaped body. "Good morning, Lacy."

"Hi, Doctor Vernon. You're here bright and early."

"Didn't get a chance to finish up yesterday's paperwork." He headed down a hallway.

When he was gone, Lacy turned back to Celia. "Have you seen a doctor about this yet?"

Celia shook her head. She had known this was going to be hard, but the reality of standing here in this doctor's office, knowing she was going to have a baby, knowing she would have to answer questions she didn't want to answer and have her body examined in ways she didn't want to think about became too much to handle. She hugged her arms tighter around herself.

"What insurance do you have?"

The question pushed Celia over the edge and a tear slid down her cheek. "I don't have insurance."

"There are a couple of places in Bend that might be able to help you. There's a Planned Parenthood . . . " Celia shook her head and took a step back. "Or if you don't want that, there's a Volunteers Clinic that charges on a scale depending on your income. I can write down their information for you."

"I don't have a car."

Lacy sighed. "I'm not sure we can—"

"Is there a problem here?" Dr. Vernon was about the same height as Celia, but his girth filled the doorway to her right.

Lacy answered before Celia had a chance. "She thinks she's pregnant and wants to see a doctor, but she doesn't have insurance and says she doesn't have a way to get to Bend."

The way Lacy spoke made Celia sound like a difficult child and a first-class loser.

Dr. Vernon's face was kind, his voice gentle. "Come on back here and let's have a talk." He turned to Lacy. "Have

Karen start with my first appointment if I'm still busy."

"Of course, doctor."

Celia followed Doctor Vernon down the narrow hall and into his dated teal and brass office. He motioned to a chair across the desk from his. "Please, have a seat." He picked up a box of tissues from the credenza and handed them to Celia before he sat down. Then he, wheeled himself forward, and folded his hands on his desk. "I'm Doctor Vernon, and you are?"

"Celia Edwards."

"Nice to meet you, Celia." Celia wiped her eyes with a tissue. "Don't mind Lacy. She doesn't have the best bedside manner, but she keeps the place running, and I'd be lost without her. But sometimes it's not about appointments and insurance. It's about helping people, and no offense, but you look like you could use some help. Am I right?"

Celia nodded.

"So tell me what's going on."

Celia breathed deeply and let it out slowly, determined to keep her voice from shaking. "I'm pregnant."

"Most of the time, that would be cause for congratulations, but I get the feeling that's not the case with you."

Celia shrugged and shook her head at the same time.

"So this was unplanned?"

"Yes."

"Do you mind if I ask about the father?"

"He doesn't live here and he's not involved."

"Should he be involved? Would he want to help you through this? Financially, at least?"

"No." Celia's voice was firm. "He shouldn't be involved."

"Does he know?"

Celia shook her head again.

Dr. Vernon leaned back in his chair and made a church and steeple with his hands as he thought. "I certainly won't tell you what you should do, but in most cases, it's reasonable to think that the father should be made aware of the situation."

"Not in this case."

"All right. There are definitely exceptions. In which case, I should ask if the circumstances are such that you should consider speaking with the authorities."

A sob escaped Celia's throat, and Dr. Vernon came around his desk and took the seat beside her.

"I'm sorry, Celia. I didn't mean to scare you."

"It's okay."

His voice was gentle. "Were you raped?"

Celia nodded.

"The authorities that handle rape cases are usually very kind. I know someone I could call."

Celia couldn't speak but she shook her head.

"All right." He patted Celia's arm. "Give it some thought, and if you decide you want that name, you can let me know."

"It wouldn't matter. He doesn't live here, and I'm not going back."

"Back to . . . "

"Chicago."

Dr. Vernon nodded, but Celia could tell he didn't like the idea of a rapist going unpunished. Celia felt sick. She hadn't intended to tell the doctor what had happened. All she wanted was to figure out how to get the medical care she needed.

"I'm a family doctor, Celia, and I can deliver babies, so you don't need to worry about that. Let's get a little information, and then we'll set you a regular appointment and get you taken care of."

He asked her a few questions then stepped out to talk to Lacy. He returned with forms for her to fill out for Medicaid and an Oregon Healthy Baby program.

"Let's figure out when this baby is due." He pulled up a program on his computer. "Do you know when you had your last period?"

"No. But I know what day it happened." Celia told him the day and he entered the information.

"Your baby is due on the eleventh of December."

Right before Christmas. Somehow knowing a date made it all more real, more terrifying.

"Celia, do you need some information about alternatives? Especially in circumstances like this. You're early enough in your pregnancy that you have options."

"You mean abortion?"

"That's one option. Most people don't consider it a sin for a woman who has been raped."

"I could never do that."

"Very well. Other options like whether you keep the baby or give it up for adoption can be discussed later. Let's go make you an appointment and then you can take these papers home and fill them out. If you want to bring them back in, I'll have Lacy submit them for you."

Celia and Dr. Vernon walked to the door. If she were braver, she would have hugged him for his kindness to her. Instead she said, "Thank you."

"I'm sorry about this hard thing you're having to face. Please remember you're not alone. We'll help you through this." He patted her on the back then opened the door. "Lacy, we need to make this young lady a formal appointment, and when she brings back these forms, I need you to get them submitted as soon as possible."

There was something different in Lacy's demeanor and she agreed with no hesitation.

Dr. Vernon returned to his office and Celia stepped up to

the counter.

"Can you bring those back in the next couple of days?" Celia agreed. "Then let's get you in here sometime next week." She smiled at Celia when she handed her an appointment card. "Let me know if you need anything."

Celia knew she looked a mess when she left the clinic. Her eyes were as puffy as the clouds that hung lazily above her, but she didn't care. Her heart felt grateful as she walked toward Nancy's house—grateful for Dr. Vernon and even for Lacy. She was glad she had decided to come to Sisters. She looked at the mountains in the distance. Three Sisters. Faith, Hope and Charity. Maybe they really were looking out for her.

The phone was ringing when Celia walked through the back door and there was no sign of Nancy. She almost didn't answer it, but what if it was Nancy trying to reach her?

"Hello."

"Celia. It's Silas."

"Hi, Silas. I don't think Nancy's here right now."

"That's okay. I was calling you."

Celia couldn't help but smile. "Oh. What's up?"

"If you're not busy tonight, I thought we could go to a movie in B-Bend. I'm not sure what's p-playing, but you can choose."

"That sounds fun."

"Good. Let's go early and eat." They decided on a time and said goodbye.

This was like a real date with a boy Celia liked. The

confusion of the day muddled her head. Was she a girl going on a date with a boy she liked, or was she a scared, soon-to-be single mother with a baby who would have to rely on her to find it a happy, safe home?

She was both of those things, but she knew there might come a time when those things wouldn't be able to coexist.

She grabbed a pen out of the drawer and went to her room to fill out the forms. She'd take care of the Celia she didn't want to be this afternoon, and tonight, she'd do her best to be the young Celia that was developing a crush on a good-looking forest ranger.

Chapter 24

The best thing about her date with Silas was the normalness of it. Silas picked her up, they ate tacos at a little restaurant in downtown Bend, and they saw a pretty forgettable movie starring Tom Cruise. They talked about Silas's job and the climber who had to be rescued, and when Celia said she'd like to see the spot, Silas suggested they hike there the following weekend. Celia told him she had come to Oregon because her mother had said it was her favorite place. She didn't tell him how she'd come to choose Sisters. They didn't hold hands and there was no goodnight kiss.

It was a perfect date.

Celia hadn't dated much in Chicago. She changed high schools three times and it wasn't easy to get to know people. A guy named Bralon had invited her to a place called Monkey Island to play arcade games and eat hot dogs with him and a group of friends. She had been so terrible at the arcade games that she had ended up being the butt of most of their jokes. After high school, her roommate, Cassidy, had insisted on setting her up with a friend of whatever boy she was dating at the time, but after two or three evenings with handsy guys who'd had too much to drink, she told Cassidy she wasn't interested in any more arranged dates.

It didn't even cross her mind that perhaps Silas didn't like her in the way she had thought he did until she was going to bed that night. It had felt so pleasant to be with someone comfortable, someone she didn't have to fight off. She refused to worry about how he might feel. If he only wanted friendship, that was okay with her. She could use a friend, and she suspected Silas could too.

"Busy afternoon?" Ellis walked into the gallery from the hallway that led to the parking lot in back.

"Not too many people," Celia said with a grin. "But quality over quantity, right?"

Ellis grinned back and looked around the room, trying to figure out what had sold. His eyes rested on an empty spot on the wall. "You sold the 'Spirited Appaloosa'?"

"They didn't even ask for a discount."

When Celia had started working for Ellis, he had instructed her that the prices were set so there was wiggle room if people wanted to negotiate. He was always willing to come down fifteen percent in order to make a sale.

"You got over eighteen hundred dollars for it?"

"Yep." Celia was proud of herself. She had made sales before, but up until today, they had never been more than a few hundred dollars.

"Good work, young lady. I think I might need to give you more hours, which reminds me. My wife's heading back to

South Carolina to see her sister for a couple of weeks. I was thinking I might fly out and meet her for a few days. If you think you could handle the hours and Nancy's garden. I don't want to steal away her help."

"If it's only a few days, we could work it out. I can take care of the garden before I come in at ten."

"It'd be a few long days for you, but I haven't gone with her for years. And I thought maybe you could use the extra money."

He was right about that. She wasn't sure if it was the baby, the good food she ate at Nancy's, or a combination of the two, but her jeans were definitely snugger than they had been when she'd arrived in Oregon.

"That would be great." Celia retrieved her bag from under the counter. "I would have hung another picture, but I wasn't sure what you'd want there."

"I'll probably give Nick a call and see if he has another piece he'd like to bring in." Nicolas Heggerty was the artist who had painted "Spirited Appaloosa." His paintings were of landscapes and animals, but they were a little abstract and done in unexpected colors. Suddenly Celia made a connection.

"Did he paint the pig at the bed and breakfast?"

Ellis looked pleased. "He did. You have a good eye."

"I really liked that one."

"Listen, Celia. Since you got full price, I'm going to give you a bonus for that sale."

"You don't have to—"

He held up his hand to stop her protest. "We'll call it a commission." Ellis opened the cash register, pulled out some bills, and stuffed them into an envelope. "I'm sure you can figure out something to do with this."

Celia took the envelope, and Ellis walked with her to the

door and held it open for her. "I'll let you know next week what days I'll need you."

"Thank you, Ellis."

Celia forced herself to wait until she was at home before she opened the envelope. Inside was two-hundred dollars. She fell to the bed and held the bills to her chest. She could buy some much-needed clothes.

Sisters was a lovely little town, but one thing it was short on was clothing stores. Maternity clothes were nonexistent. She would need to go to Bend, but how could she get there? Nancy would probably be thrilled to take her, but how would she explain her need for large, loose clothing?

Celia thought as she pulled weeds. Nancy's garden had become one of her favorite places in the world. The plants were big and leafy and evidence that she had done a good job picking out the weeds and leaving the vegetables. Nancy had taught her how to use a digging fork to keep the dirt around the plants from becoming too packed down and hard. This let the plants breathe and made pulling the weeds easier. Celia looked at the even rows. Except for a small patch of string beans that had come up with sparse, yellow leaves, the garden looked good and Celia felt a sense of pride.

"Have you noticed the beans?" Celia asked as she scrubbed the dirt out from under her nails.

Nancy was sitting at the table paying bills. "Yes. They don't look too good. I asked Jim about that and he said we probably need a crop rotation there."

"They look like they're dying. Do you think we'll get any beans from them?"

"Probably not. He suggested we pull them out so they don't leach any more nutrients out of the soil. I was going to pick up a couple of bags of compost from Organic Nation next time I'm in Bend. We can work that into the soil after we pull out the beans. Hopefully get it ready for next year."

"I can go pick it up if you'd like me to. And I'll get started clearing out that section," Celia said as she dried her hands.

"Oh, Celia. I hate to pile extra work on you."

"What extra work?" Silas asked as the back screen door slammed shut.

Nancy told him what they were talking about.

"I can help her clear it out."

"And I can go get the compost while you two are at work tomorrow," Celia said. "I need to pick up a few things anyway. If you don't mind me taking your car, that is."

"Take the Jeep. I'll b-b—" Silas sighed and slowed down. "I'll have my work truck anyway."

Nancy still looked uncertain. "You don't mind picking it up? They'll help you load it."

"I don't mind. Just tell me where it is." Celia tried to keep her voice sounding willing, but not too eager.

"I'll draw you a map."

And just like that, Celia had an opening to go to Bend on her own and buy clothes for her soon-to-be expanding figure.

Chapter 25

Baby Bump Boutique was bursting right out of its maternity pants with adorableness. Portraits of beautiful mothers—either pregnant or holding new babies—were scattered around the boutique. Elegant dresses, stylish jeans, and casual workout wear filled racks. Mannequins with various sizes of stomachs displayed perfectly accessorized outfits. It even smelled like baby powder.

"Welcome to Baby Bump. Can I help you find anything?" The woman was a waif. Even with high heels, she only came to Celia's shoulder and there was no way she could weigh in triple digits. Celia felt like a giant oaf. Was this really a good way to sell clothes to women whose girth would be expanding over the next nine months?

Celia looked around, overwhelmed. "I'm not sure what I'm even looking for."

"Are you here for yourself or someone else?"

Suddenly Celia was very aware of her ringless finger and her worn clothes. She hated what people would think of her. At best it would look like she was careless and irresponsible, but some would see her growing belly and think she was immoral or promiscuous. It made her angry all over again, but what could she do? She couldn't announce the rape to everyone who looked at her. Her reputation was one more thing Damien had taken from her that night. She wanted to be the kind of person who could forgive him, but all she ever felt when she thought of him was hatred. "I'm here for me."

"Congratulations. How far along are you?"

"A little more than thirteen weeks."

"No wonder you're so tiny." The woman seemed very sweet, but calling Celia tiny from somewhere down around her knees didn't feel very sincere. "We have a great promotion we're running right now. It's called Eating for Two and it gets you two of everything—two dresses, two tops, two pair of jeans, two bras and two panties. All for six-hundred ninety-nine dollars." The clerk didn't notice Celia's stunned face as she continued to talk. "Of course, everyone needs more than two of these things, so we're throwing in a second two-fer for six hundred more. It's a great deal and you can choose from everything in the store except those formal dresses along that wall."

Celia wasn't sure what to do. She thought about the two hundred dollars in her bag. She had hoped to keep some in case of an emergency.

"Do you have any sales racks?"

The woman looked disappointed. "Of course. Back there in the corner is our clearance rack. Everything on it is fifty percent off."

"Thank you."

Celia continued on to the discounted clothing, and the clerk went back to the sales counter. It may have been that she knew she wouldn't make much off Celia, so why bother, or perhaps she was kind and was giving her some privacy. Celia didn't care what the reason was. She was happy to be left alone. If only someone else would come into the shop so it wouldn't just be Celia and the pixie.

It didn't take long for Celia to realize that even at the clearance price, she couldn't afford to shop here. Maybe she should have googled "how to get out of an expensive store and save face" instead of "maternity clothes Bend Oregon."

Celia started toward the front door.

"Ma'am?" Celia had never been called ma'am before. She stopped and looked at the pretty, heart-shaped face of the miniature woman. Her expression looked sympathetic, and Celia subconsciously stiffened her back.

"Yes?"

"There's a Walmart on Pinebrook and a really good thrift store on Second Street. Good luck with your new baby."

Celia relaxed. How could she possibly be defensive with a woman who was trying to help her?

"Thank you."

Three hours later, Celia drove back to Sisters with three forty-pound bags of compost, a loose-fitting, knit dress, a long, stretchy skirt, four shirts, one pair of jeans, roomy sweats, and new underwear. And she still had almost thirty dollars in her bag.

Nancy was standing by the back door when Celia came to the kitchen for breakfast Saturday morning. She poured herself a bowl of Frosted Mini Wheats and milk.

"What are you looking at?" she asked as she stepped up

to the door.

"I'm watching Silas."

Celia looked across the yard to the garden and saw Silas pulling up bean plants.

"Why didn't he wait for me?"

"Guess he was being thoughtful."

"Well, that's nice of him, but I'm the one getting my board here for taking care of the garden." Celia stepped past Nancy and out onto the porch. "Hey, Silas," she yelled.

Silas looked up and lifted a bean-plant-filled hand in greeting.

"What are you doing?"

Silas grinned and called back to her. "Killing b-beans."

Celia turned around and saw Nancy smirking. "Has he had breakfast?"

Nancy shrugged. "I don't know. He doesn't usually keep me posted on his breakfast."

Celia turned back around. "Have you eaten?"

Silas put his hand to his ear and Celia shouted louder. "Have you eaten?"

Silas nodded and pulled up another bean plant.

Celia headed back in the house and banged her bowl onto the counter. "What's he doing? He should have waited for me," she said under her breath.

"Celia, stop." Nancy had followed her across the kitchen and put her hand on Celia's arm. "He probably wanted to help you. Let him. You sit down and eat your breakfast and then you can go help him."

"He'll probably be finished."

"Then you can help him with the compost. But eat first. I promise I won't evict you because Silas pulled more bean plants than you." Celia sighed and took her bowl to the table. "And don't go being all women's libber on him when he comes in. He was being thoughtful, so all you have to say is thank you."

Celia was tying her shoes when Silas walked through the door. "You should have come and got me. I would have helped you."

"It was a surprise. You weren't supposed to catch me."

Celia glanced at Nancy. "Thanks. It was a nice surprise." Silas looked pleased. "But I want to help with the compost."

"Whenever you're ready."

Nancy knocked on Celia's door. "The phone's for you."

It was Silas. "I can't go to Tumalo Falls today. I'm taking M-Mark's shift. They had a b-baby last night. I'm sorry."

Celia was surprised how disappointed she felt. "That's okay. Maybe we can do it another time."

"How about Wednesday?"

"Sure. Wednesday's good."

"Great. M-maybe I'll see you after work."

Silas hadn't said he would come to church with her before their hike, but she had hoped he would. Now the hike was off and if she went to church, she would go alone.

Celia took a deep breath and went to her room to change. Sure, it was a letdown that their plans were off, but on the scale of her life's disappointments, this was barely a blip.

So why did she feel like it bleached all the color from the day?

Chapter 26

Today was the day. Silas had been gearing himself up since he and Celia had composted the bean patch on Saturday. When they hiked to Tumalo Falls, he would hold her hand and when he took her home, he would hug her goodbye. Maybe, if the stars aligned, he would even try for a kiss. He had spent the last few days planning and plotting. About halfway to the falls, there was a steep, rocky area. He'd lead out then casually reach back and take Celia's hand to pull her up. Once he had made that initial contact, it would be easy to do it again, like at the spot where they'd leave the trail so he could show her where he had found the little campground the rescued couple had set up.

All he had to do was man up. He could do this. He had fought deadly forest fires. He had helped on search and rescue assignments. He had even come face to face with a bull moose during mating season. He wasn't a coward.

So why did this feel so much scarier?

When Mark had called to see if he could take his shift, Silas had been both frustrated and relieved. But all the extra time had done was make him more determined. And more nervous.

Silas glanced at Celia sitting in the passenger seat. How was it possible to look so good when you weren't even trying? She wore no makeup, her hair was in a ponytail and she had on a too-big pair of sweatpants and a t-shirt. And still she looked pretty. Celia caught him looking at her and smiled. He needed to keep his eyes on the road.

"So you get to drive through this every day?"

Silas nodded. "It's a good job."

"What made you decide to be a forest ranger?"

He never told people the real reason. He usually said it was because of how much he loved nature and how beautiful it was, but something about Celia made him want to tell the truth. The whole truth.

"I get to b-be alone most of the time and I don't have to talk very m-much."

Celia nodded like she understood then she gave him a teasing smile. "You can take me home if you'd rather be alone."

Silas looked thoughtful. "Hmm. Tempting."

"I mean, I've really been looking forward to seeing some of Oregon besides Sisters and Bend, but I don't want to spoil your solitude."

"Maybe I should drop you off. You could m-make it home by dark. I think."

"If you're going to do that, please pull over and do it now."

Silas slowed the Jeep and pulled off the road. Before he came to a complete stop, he shook his head and pulled back onto the road. "Whatever. I guess I can deal with you for long enough to see the falls."

"You're a generous man, Silas. I'm very grateful."

Silas felt proud of his forest as they drove. He traveled

these roads so often, sometimes he forgot how beautiful it was, but as Celia pointed out distant peaks or the sun-dappled road that wound between sky-high trees, it was like he was seeing it through fresh eyes.

They parked at the Tumalo Falls trailhead and Silas grabbed the backpack he'd prepared with water and snacks.

"Do we need to pay?" Celia asked as they walked past the fee collection board.

"No. One of the perks of the job."

Mother Nature must be on Silas's side, because she gift-wrapped a perfect day for them. It would have been too hot, but a soft, cool breeze kept it comfortable. Birds serenaded them as they walked up the trail. White, fluffy clouds moved slowly across the sky. The forest was bright and vibrant, but peaceful at the same time.

They were almost to the spot Silas had pictured in his mind. The gentle slope of the trail became steep and what had been a mostly smooth path became uneven and rocky. "Watch your step," he told her and he looked up at the place they would have to climb up and around several large boulders. That's where he would do it. He'd climb around them then warn her of the rocks as he reached back and took her hand, helping her over the hazardous stretch.

Silas's heartrate increased as his nerves kicked in. He could do it. He could do it. He could do it.

"Do you mind if we stop for some water?" Celia asked, interrupting his silent pep talk.

"Sorry. I should have asked if you were thirsty."

"It's no big deal. Just feeling a little parched."

Silas pulled the water out of the backpack and handed her one. They each took a long drink then Celia handed hers back to him.

"Thanks."

As Silas put the bottles back in the pack, Celia moved out in front of him. He watched as she pulled herself over the boulders and around the difficult stretch of the trail. A few loose rocks gave way under their feet and slid down the hill, taking his perfect plan with them.

"Come this way and I'll show you where they set up camp." They left the trail and Silas led the way to what had been the campground. "They had two hammocks set up here." They retraced the steps Silas had taken when he'd followed the woman to the cliff to see where her husband was. They stood together at the top and Celia leaned in when he pointed to the ledge. "He was right there."

"He's lucky he didn't die," Celia said.

"He hung on there for almost three hours."

Celia shook her head. "I wonder if he's scared of heights now."

"He is if he's smart."

Silas knew of a good place to watch the falls—one that was close enough to feel the spray on their faces when the breeze blew toward them. They sat together on a rock and Silas handed Celia a banana.

"Thanks for bringing me here," Celia said after she ate a few bites. "I could sit here forever."

"Except this rock is p-pretty hard."

Celia bumped against him with her shoulder. "I'm serious. This is so nice."

"Do you ever miss Chicago?"

Celia shook her head. "There's nothing there to miss."

"I thought Chicago would be an interesting p-place." Usually Silas was aware of every stutter, every potential trap in his speech, but he barely noticed his impediment any more when he was with Celia. She made him think of other things.

"I guess it's an interesting place to visit if you've never been there. But I'll never go back."

"How long did you live there?"

"All my life." Celia's mood had turned serious. She leaned forward and rested her elbows on her knees. Silas wanted to ask more questions, but her faraway look stopped him. He let the peacefulness of the area settle around them before he spoke again.

"I'm glad you chose Sisters."

Celia tilted her head and looked at him, a smile on her face. Then she sat up straighter and linked her arm through his, resting her hand on his wrist as she leaned against him. "Me too."

Silas was so stunned he wasn't sure what to do, so at first he held very still, hoping she wouldn't pull away. He needed to do something to return the show of affection, but he was afraid he'd do the wrong thing. Finally, he lightly patted her hand with his then left it resting on hers.

They sat like that—listening to the water, feeling the spray, settling into the beauty of the setting. They weren't exactly holding hands, but it was close enough that Silas felt elated. The future was full of promise. He wanted to lift her chin and kiss her, right here in this perfect setting. But he wasn't a guy who could pull off a move like that, so instead, he rested his cheek against her hair and tried to breathe like a normal man would.

Chapter 27

Celia's right leg began to tingle as it fell asleep. Celia stretched it in front of her and turned her foot in a circle, trying to get rid of the sensation of needles poking it.

"If we sit here much longer, you might have to carry me down the hill."

Silas laughed. "I guess we'd better get moving."

Celia was sad to leave this peaceful spot, sad to no longer be so close to Silas, sorry his hand wasn't on hers. She liked his quiet steadiness, his willingness to be still. He didn't bombard her with questions and demand explanations. He asked enough to show he was curious and interested, but was willing to follow her lead. He seemed to sense when she couldn't say more.

When they reached a steep, rocky part of the trail, he held his hand up to help her over the rocks. She was disappointed that when the trail leveled out, he let go.

It was early afternoon when they arrived back in Sisters. Celia loved the picturesque street that led through town. It hadn't taken long to learn her way around and as they passed the small businesses and restaurants, she felt a calming familiarity. They saw Ellis as he headed into the bank. He waved and smiled and a hard lump settled in her throat. The feeling was probably irrational—she had read that emotions were intensified when you're pregnant, and she certainly believed it—but Celia felt an overpowering sense of belonging. This little town felt like home to her in a way nowhere else ever had.

She looked at Silas with a question when he drove past the street that led home.

"I'm hungry. I thought we could get a hamburger."

"Oh. Sure." It was a much better idea than going home and eating leftovers or a sandwich, and it would prolong their time together. Celia would have agreed even if she weren't hungry.

They ate cheeseburgers under a blue and white striped umbrella at Sno Cap. A woman named Irene that Celia had met at church stopped by to say hello. Two young children ate ice cream cones beside her.

"I told the kids if they would help me plant flowers this morning, we'd come get ice cream."

"Looks like your plan worked," Celia said.

"I should have thrown cleaning their bedrooms into the bargain. Anyway, hopefully we'll see you Sunday. They're having a potluck after services. You should stay for that."

"Maybe I will. Thanks."

When they returned to the car after lunch, Silas didn't turn on the Jeep immediately. He rested his hands on the steering wheel and looked out the windshield. Celia thought he might want to say something, so she waited. "Do you need to get home for anything?" he finally asked.

Celia tried to act nonchalant. Was it possible he wanted their time together to continue as much as she did? "I've got no other plans today."

"Have you ever been to Eugene?"

Celia laughed. "If it's not between Sisters and Bend, I haven't been there. Oh, except Tumalo Falls."

Silas started the Jeep. "Eugene has a good ice cream place."

Celia laughed and pointed at Sno Cap. "I think we already ate at a good ice cream place."

"True. B-but I was thinking of a road trip."

Celia buckled her seat belt. "I think I like road trips. Especially if we're not on a Greyhound bus."

"Good. Let's go."

Soon they were headed out of town on a road Celia had never seen.

"What is this road-trip worthy ice cream place called?"

Silas grinned. "You would ask that."

"What? You don't know the name?" Celia asked.

"Yes, I do. But it's not easy for me to say."

Celia wanted him to feel so relaxed with her that he could speak as easily as he did when he was with his aunt. Even though that hadn't happened yet, she was glad he seemed comfortable talking about it.

"You know you don't have to worry about that with me."

"I know." He sounded like he meant it.

"So you should tell me."

Silas pulled onto the road. "P-Prince P-P-Pucklers." The muscles in his face worked hard to push out the sounds.

Celia almost snort-laughed. "Prince Pucklers?"

Silas nodded. "Don't laugh. They have good ice cream."

"Good. They'd better have with that name. I don't think you were worried about having trouble saying the words. I think you were embarrassed to say the words 'Prince Pucklers.'"

Silas laughed. "That's it. You caught me. Speech camp

would say I should tell you the name over and over until I can say it right."

"Speech camp?"

Silas turned off the radio as the station was overtaken with static. "I went to a camp in Washington. For stutterers." He spoke slower, as if talking about it made him more careful.

"What was that like?"

Silas told her about the three weeks he had spent at Camp Rock Ridge. "It didn't cure me, b-but I think it helped. Gave me some tricks to use."

"What kind of tricks?"

"Slow down. Re-route. That's when you figure out a different way to say something so you can avoid your triggers."

"What are your triggers?"

"Hard consonants mostly." He was careful and deliberate as he spoke. "Ms and p-ps and bs. And sometimes s is hard. It's like my mouth gets stuck."

Celia nodded. "Are there other tricks?"

Silas glanced at her out of the corner of his eye. She didn't want him to be annoyed, so she softened her question with a smile.

"Think and plan ahead what you want to say."

Celia jabbed him lightly with her elbow. "So where are we going?"

Silas smiled and shook his head, but spoke slowly. "We're going to Eugene for ice cream at P-Prince P-Pucklers."

"I'm sorry, I missed that. Where are we going?"

Silas laughed. "We're going to Eugene for ice cream at Prince P-Pucklers."

Celia shook her head and pointed at her ear. "I must be hard of hearing. Could you say that one more time?"

"Jerk."

"I heard that."

"Good." Silas was in a good mood despite the name calling. "We're going to . . . Prince . . . Pucklers."

"Awesome. A friend of mine said they have really good ice cream." Celia turned slightly in her seat so she was facing him. "Seriously though, was it hard? I mean when you were growing up."

Silas shrugged. "Yeah. But everyone has hard things." He looked at Celia. "Like you and your mom."

Celia looked at her hands and nodded. "Yeah."

Silas reached over and covered her hand with his. "Tell me about her."

Celia turned her hand over in his and held it. Her eyes studied the scattered freckles and veins on the back of his hand. "There's not that much to tell. She chose drugs instead of me."

Silas was thoughtful for a minute before he asked, "What's your b-best memory?"

Celia thought. "Probably bedtime when I was really little, before she got messed up. She almost always read me a book—something about how many kisses it takes to say goodnight, or something like that. I loved that book. It said something about ears being like roses and I thought that was so cool. I'd always touch the ridges in my ear and imagine it was a rose, a yellow one. Then she'd kiss my ears and my eyes and my nose before she'd turn off the light."

"What else?"

Celia let her mind travel back through time. "She always told me I was smart. Even when she was a disaster. She said I'd never be screwed up and alone with a child to take care of because I was too smart to let that happen." Celia swallowed hard, willing herself not to cry as it hit her that she was more like her mother than she had ever wanted to be.

Silas asked more questions, and maybe because his voice was gentle and he held her hand, Celia answered. She told him about when her mom had dragged her all over town looking for "the man who had some medicine she needed." Celia had been so tired she could hardly put one foot in front of the other. When Celia had started to cry, her mother had shaken her shoulders and asked her why she didn't care about anyone but herself. When they finally found the man in a filthy apartment that smelled like rotten food, he had yelled at her mother for bringing her punk kid with her because he wanted the kind of payment she couldn't give with a kid there. Her mom had left her sitting in that terrifying, dirty kitchen while she had gone in the bedroom with the man. When they finally went home, her mom was happy and laughing and said that tomorrow Celia could skip school so they could sleep in and then play at the park, her way of trying to make up for the miserable night.

"I'm sorry," Silas said when she stopped talking.

"It could have been worse," Celia said.

"How?"

"It sounds awful, but I think it would have been worse if she had lived. At least when she died, I got to live for almost a whole year with the Hundleys. They were good, kind people. That makes me sound like a terrible person."

"No, it doesn't."

Celia looked at him, surprised. She had always felt so guilty about the relief she had felt when her mother finally died.

"It doesn't?"

"It m-makes you sound like a little girl who needed rescued."

"The Hundleys definitely rescued me." Celia told Silas about the Hundleys, especially Myra. "She was a good mother to me. It about killed me when they had to move, but at least I was there long enough to see what a real family was like. And to learn how to pray."

They settled into a pleasant quiet the last few miles before they got to Eugene. Celia had never shared so much about herself, and she suspected Silas had shared more than he usually did, as well. They had both been through terrible things. Even though their challenges had been different, they seemed to understand each other, and Celia wasn't sorry she had told him so much.

Without thinking about it, she rested her free hand on her stomach. Part of her wanted to tell Silas about the baby growing inside her. She longed for him to know what had happened to her. Would he be as kind and understanding about that? Would he hold her hand and try to make her feel better or would that be the wedge that would drive him away? It was one thing to overlook the damage inflicted on a neglected little girl. Would he feel differently about the damage that had been done to her by Damien? Someday soon he would find out, whether Celia told him or not. Maybe she should tell him and be done with it. If he couldn't handle it, she wanted to know so she wouldn't allow her feelings for him to grow any stronger.

She took a deep breath and squared her shoulders. "So-"

"Here we are," Silas said at the same time.

They pulled into Prince Puckler's and Silas squeezed her hand before he let go to turn off the Jeep.

Chapter 28

"How did you find this place?" Celia asked as they stood in line looking at the flavor board.

"Aunt Nancy brought me here after we went to a Ducks game."

"Ducks?"

"That's the m-mascot of The University of Oregon."

"Who picks a duck to be their mascot?"

"Careful. We like our ducks."

Celia held up her hands in surrender. "Hey, ducks are great. Nothing more intimidating than a duck waddling toward you." Celia turned back to the flavor board. "What do you think I should get?"

"Whatever sounds good." They stepped up to the counter.

"Have you tried the Mandarin chocolate?" Silas shook his head. "Have you?" Celia asked the girl behind the counter.

"It's one of my favorites."

"I'll get that," said Celia. "In a waffle cone."

The girl entered the order into the cash register and turned to Silas. "And you?"

"I'll take strawberry."

While the server rang up their order, Celia turned to Silas. "Tell me we didn't drive for two hours so you could order strawberry ice cream."

Silas laughed. "I like it."

"Is that what you had the day you came to the game?" There had to be an explanation for this generic selection after an ice cream road trip.

"No. I had mint Oreo that day."

"Well, mint Oreo sounds a little more worthy of coming this far. Doesn't BJ's have strawberry ice cream? Right there in Sisters?"

Silas pretended to be annoyed. "Yeah. I like theirs, too. B—but this is what I wanted, so enjoy your exotic flavor and I'll enjoy mine."

"Yours is hardly exotic." Celia licked her ice cream cone as they walked to a table by the window. "Mmm, this is fantastic."

"So is this. Want a bite?" Silas held out his cone filled with pale pink ice cream dotted with bright strawberries.

"No thanks." Celia eyed Silas suspiciously. "Are you asking me because you want some of mine? 'Cause I wouldn't blame you since I ordered better than you."

"I was trying to be nice. I don't want any of yours."

Celia raised an eyebrow. "You can have yours. If I want any strawberry ice cream, I'll get it in Sisters. Maybe at the grocery store."

Silas shook his head but he was smiling.

The restaurant had been busy, loud and cold, and the afternoon heat felt good when they walked out to the sidewalk. Instead of walking to the Jeep, they strolled down the street, stretching their legs and checking out the eclectic shops.

"It wasn't just about the ice cream," Silas said.

"What?"

"I like strawberry ice cream, b-but I didn't suggest we come to Eugene for the ice cream." Celia gave him a questioning look. "I wasn't ready to take you home yet."

Celia's lips curled into a smile and her insides began a fierce round of calisthenics. She felt him glancing at her and she found it hard to catch her breath, but a confession like that deserved some kind of response.

Celia caught his hand in hers and squeezed it. "It was a really good idea."

It was dark when Silas pulled into Aunt Nancy's driveway. Silas couldn't remember a day he had enjoyed more. The afternoon had flown by as they held hands and laughed and talked. Celia was different than any girl he'd known. She kept him on his toes because she constantly surprised him. One minute she'd be lost in her thoughts and serious and the next she'd crack a joke. She seemed reserved and shy but then she'd elbow him or take his hand. He liked so much about her.

But even more than that, he liked himself better when she was around. He almost forgot about his stutter when they were together, and when he did get hung up on a word, he didn't feel the usual embarrassment or humiliation. She treated it like it was just another trait. Silas has blue eyes and brown hair. He's tall and lanky. He has long fingers and big feet and a stutter. He liked how Celia teased him and made him laugh. It made his heart swell like an inflated balloon when she opened up and told him her secrets, because he knew she didn't share those things easily. He felt protective of her and wanted to assure her that the pain of her past was behind her and good things lay ahead of them.

He felt sure of that. It felt as natural to think of Celia in his life tomorrow as it did to think that the sun would come up the next morning or that Aunt Nancy would have black licorice in her purse. Silas liked her. This felt right to him, and he almost couldn't remember the loneliness he had felt for most of his life.

He didn't tell Celia the way he was feeling. He didn't want to scare her off with a hasty declaration, so he'd take it slow and let her feelings catch up to his.

They held hands as they walked to the front door. The light was on inside, and through an open window, they could hear the judges on a dancing show talking.

"Want to sit out here a few minutes?" Silas motioned to the swing on the other side of the porch.

Celia grinned. "Still not ready to call it a night?"

Silas held the swing still as she sat down and pulled her legs up on the seat beside her. "Maybe we should have kept driving."

"We could have driven on to Portland next," Celia said.

"I hear they have a good ice cream p-place there."

"Got a craving for some vanilla now?" Celia asked.

"I'll let you choose for m-me next time so you'll have nothing to criticize." Silas put his arm around her and she rested her hand on his leg. He reached over with his other hand and played with her fingers.

"If the only thing I can find to criticize is your ice cream choices, you're doing all right. Besides, I'm teasing, not criticizing." It was an effort to keep her breathing even as she watched their hands.

"Today was a good day," Silas said.

"Almost perfect."

Silas tilted his head away and looked at Celia. "Almost?"

She jostled him with her elbow. "If we say it was perfect, we've got nothing to look forward to. We'll just be looking back and talking about today."

"Hmm. I like that answer."

They sat quietly on the swing, their movement slow and hypnotizing as Silas gently pushed off with his foot. Inside the house the host announced that Jaz and Miguel would perform a waltz, and a song began playing. The melody floated out the window and danced across the porch.

"You might think the breeze is blowing just to make you colder, but darling don't you know that breeze is saying, man, just hold her. You might think the moon is glowing just to light the skies, but you'd be wrong 'cause girl that moon is there to light your eyes."

It was almost embarrassing how romantic the song was, and it reminded Silas of dancing with Celia a few weeks ago. It surprised him how much his feelings had changed. That night all he'd wanted was to gather enough courage to ask her to dance. Now he was a man thinking about a future with a woman who made him comfortable while lighting a fire in him. Not long ago, he had refused to look too far down the road because when he did, all he saw was an older, lonelier version of himself. Now he saw so much more. It was like she'd taken his black and white life and painted it with bright colors.

Aunt Nancy turned off the television, and the patch of living room light that had lit the far end of the porch disappeared. Earl Murphy's dog barked wildly for a couple of minutes—probably chasing a squirrel or a skunk—until Earl came out and called the dog inside.

Silas shifted in the swing so he was facing Celia. Her face

looked soft in the pale glow of the porch light. When she looked back at him, he didn't look away. Instead he held her gaze and moved closer until both of them shut their eyes at the same moment that their lips met. Her lips were soft and sweet and he let the kiss linger for several seconds. When he began to pull away, Celia moved her hand to his jaw and pulled him close, kissing him back. It was as if the gesture opened Silas's soul and he suddenly felt a longing for things he hadn't allowed himself to want. There, with his eyes closed, their lips moving together, a world of possibilities flourished. He felt brave and strong and worthy.

He wrapped his arm around her waist and pulled her closer, wanting to erase any distance between them, wanting the closeness to fuse them together so tightly, neither of them would ever again have to face the world alone.

He smiled to himself when Celia finally went inside and he walked back to his Jeep. If he had been falling for her before, today had sent him crashing down the hill like a skier in an avalanche.

Celia closed the door and gently turned the lock. The room was dark except for a glow from the porch light outside and the bathroom light down the hall. Nancy had gone to bed. Had she known Celia and Silas were outside? She felt her face redden as she thought of Nancy peeking through the curtains to see them kissing in the swing.

She leaned against the door and listened as the sound of Silas's Jeep faded away down the lane. She smiled and touched her just-kissed lips. Was it only this morning she had sat on the rock watching the water and wishing Silas would hold her hand. It had taken every speck of her courage to put her arm through his. Like an airplane taking off, the day felt like it had picked up speed, carrying her faster and faster toward the feelings she felt tonight.

Silas. She couldn't even think of his name without feeling like an embarrassing cliché. Her heart melted, her knees were weak, her pulse raced. He wasn't like any man she had ever met. He didn't bluster or brag. His actions weren't meant to impress. He quietly moved through his life, responsible and kind. He cared for his aunt and he worked hard.

After what Damien had done to her, Celia had thought she'd never trust another man, but without even knowing Celia needed her faith restored, Silas had shown her how different a man could be.

As Celia fell asleep, her mind drifted to the last few minutes of the drive to Eugene. At that moment—after sharing so many details about their pasts—Celia had wanted to tell him about the baby. He was so gentle, so wonderful, surely he would understand and not hold it against her. She imagined what his reaction would be. His kind eyes would recognize her pain and he would pull her into his arms. He would tell her he was sorry for what she had gone through, and he would promise to help her get through whatever was to come. He would hold her hand while she chose who should raise the child and he would let her cry on his shoulder when her heart was breaking.

All she needed to do was find the right time to tell him. She'd figure that out another time. She didn't want to dream about hard things tonight. She turned over and looked at the sliver of moon through the bedroom window. Tonight she wanted to dream about swings and love songs and almost perfect kisses.

Chapter 29

"Adam needs to see you before you head out today." Jean worked the front desk at the Deschutes Ranger Station. "He's in his office."

Silas knocked on the frame of Adam's open door. Adam, who was on the phone, motioned for Silas to come in and take a seat.

"Silas just got here, so I'll fill him in," Adam said into the phone. "He worked a few fires with First Strike last year, so he knows their protocol. Good luck up there."

Adam hung up the phone and turned to Silas. "How soon can you have things arranged to leave for a few days?"

Silas's heart fell. He'd never minded overnight assignments before—Aunt Nancy didn't mind taking care of Winston—but now it meant leaving Celia. "What's happening?"

"We've got a fire up at China Hat. First Strike is on their way there, but we need you there. I want to say it's only a day or two, but it's been so dry, I'm worried."

Silas put aside his disappointment. "I can be out of here in an hour."

"Good. I want to get this thing put out as fast as possible. I hope we don't get hit as hard as some forests. Salmon-Challis is battling four fires this morning."

"Is it Carlos's team or M-Manny's?"

"You've got Carlos on this one." Silas nodded and stood. "Be careful out there."

Aunt Nancy was sitting on the front porch drinking a cup of coffee when he drove by, so he stopped.

"Can I b-bring Winston over for a couple of days? There's a fire at China Hat."

Aunt Nancy met him at the steps. "Oh Silas, I was hoping you wouldn't get sent out this summer."

Silas laughed. "They didn't send m-me to training so I could stay home and watch the fires on the news."

"I know. But I hate it."

"Is Celia here?"

"She's back in the garden. Trying to beat the heat."

"Thanks." Silas kissed her cheek and jogged back to the pickup.

"Be careful. And call me when you're headed back."

Silas saluted and headed down the lane. Celia pulled a hoe beside a row of zucchini, clearing the shallow irrigation trench. At the sound of the pickup, she turned toward the lane. Silas pulled onto the grassy shoulder and turned off the engine.

Celia smiled as he walked toward her, and another surge of disappointment coursed through him. The last few days since their marathon date had been so different. He had worried things would be awkward after that day, the spell broken. But the next day had been just as easy, just as thrilling. If anything, the electricity had sparked stronger. Celia filled his thoughts. He couldn't wait to see her and when he was with her, he couldn't wait to touch her. He loved his aunt, but he found himself counting down the minutes until she'd go to bed or until he and Celia could politely go for a walk so he could kiss her again.

"What are you doing home?" Celia asked when he got closer.

"There's a fire at China Hat. I m-might be gone a few days."

"Where's China Hat?"

"It's a couple hours away."

"You'll be fighting the fire?"

Silas nodded and took the hoe out of her hands and let it fall by their feet. "I wanted to see you b-before I leave."

Celia put her arms around his waist and they pulled each other close. "Is it dangerous?"

"Sometimes, but I'll b-be careful. We'll go to Wild Rose when I get back."

"Please be safe." Celia's voice sounded strained.

Silas put his hands on each side of her neck. "Of course, I will. Don't look so serious." He rubbed his thumb along her jaw and smiled at her. "It's not a b-big deal. I'm trained for this. And I won't be gone long."

Celia smiled but it didn't erase the worried expression. Silas pulled her close again. "I'll miss you." He said it slowly, not wanting to stutter over the words. Then he leaned down and kissed her. It was difficult to pull away, but he knew the sooner they got the fire put out, the sooner he could come home, and coming home was sweeter now than it had ever been.

A crushing weight settled on Celia's heart as she watched Silas walk back to his work pickup. She tried not to picture him out there fighting a fire, flames all around him. She said a silent prayer that he'd return safely. "And please let it be soon," she added aloud.

Of course she hated that he was leaving, but she was also disappointed about the change in plans. Tonight had been the night. They had planned to go to Bend for dinner at a Thai restaurant Silas liked, and Celia had decided this would be the night she would tell him about the baby.

Instinctively, she put her hand on her growing abdomen. There was no denying it was growing and she had wanted to tell Silas before the appointment she had scheduled the following day.

Doctor Vernon had a friend who was an adoption attorney. When Celia explained it was difficult to get to Bend, he had arranged for Mr. Walker to meet with her at the clinic. In Celia's daydreams, she had pictured Silas offering to accompany her to the appointment, but now he would be at China Peak or China Bonnet or wherever it was they were sending him.

She dug the hoe in deeper, taking out her disappointment on the soil. When she accidentally cut off a long, flowering stock of squash plant, she felt ashamed. She had no right to feel angry. Yes, Silas would be gone for a few days and her plans to tell him were delayed, but how could she feel anything but joy right now. Silas had come to see her before he left. It was obvious he was developing strong feelings for her. They had seen each other every day since their drive to Eugene and he was attentive and affectionate.

And it wasn't only that there was attraction. Sure, he was eager to kiss her, but he was also kind and spoke of things they would do in the future. It didn't feel like this was a quick crush that would soon evaporate, and instead of being frustrated that he was leaving, she should feel grateful and excited that he had become part of her life.

She finished the row then turned on the water and watched it flood the channel she had furrowed. When the pickup passed down the lane again, she waved at Silas. Then, unable to stop herself, she blew him a kiss.

"You look nice," Nancy said when Celia came into the kitchen. "You must be working today."

"Yeah. And next week I'll be working every day. Ellis is flying to South Carolina on Sunday."

"He said you sold another big painting."

Celia grinned. "I didn't really do anything. All I did was point out how great the colors were and how it was a perfect example of abstract realism. Don't tell anyone, but I don't even know if that's a real term. It just sounded good." Nancy laughed. "Any word from Silas?" Celia sounded worried.

"No. I don't usually hear from him until he's on his way back. They have a lot going on when they're fighting fires and they don't usually have phone service. I'm sure Jean will call if there's a problem."

Celia nodded. "I guess I'll see you this afternoon."

It was sweet to see Celia worrying about Silas. The poor girl had asked so many questions the night before, Nancy had felt like she was teaching Fighting Forest Fires 101. Maybe they should go to a movie tonight to give them both a distraction.

Nancy hurried to the front door to run the idea by Celia

before she left. Before she could call her name, she realized Celia had turned right and was walking away from the gallery. Come to think of it, it was a little early for her to be going to work. Nancy wondered where she might be going, but then chastised herself. Celia was an adult. If she wanted to stop by the bakery or visit a friend, that was her business.

She would call her at the gallery later and ask her about the movie.

Chapter 30

"Mr. Walker isn't here yet," Lacy said when Celia arrived at the clinic. "Dr. Vernon said to have you meet in his office." Lacy led Celia down the hall and motioned for her to take a seat. "Are you doing okay?"

Celia nodded. "I'm fine. Thank you."

"Let me know if you need anything." Lacy pulled the door almost shut.

On the wall opposite Dr. Vernon's diplomas and certificates hung a painting of a forest. For the thousandth time, Celia thought about Silas out there fighting a forest fire. In her mind, she pictured him with flames shooting high in the air all around him. She hoped reality was safer than her imagination.

"You must be Celia." A tall reed of a man stepped through the door, his hand extended. His appearance was the exact opposite of Dr. Vernon, and Celia thought it might be amusing to see them standing side by side. Celia stood to shake his hand. "Sorry I'm late. I had an appointment in Redmond that took a little longer than I expected."

He settled himself in the chair beside Celia, opened his

briefcase, and put a few folders on the front of Dr. Vernon's desk. Then he turned to Celia, clapped his hands as if he were breaking a huddle and turned his full attention to her.

"I don't know much about your case—doctor patient privilege and all—so I need to ask some basic questions to get us started. Some of these might be sensitive, but we need to establish exactly what we're dealing with here."

Celia was glad Mr. Walker was forgoing small talk. "Of course."

"Dr. Vernon said you've moved from Illinois?" He looked up to see Celia nod. "Good. I've looked over Illinois case law and called a colleague from Champaign to find out the paternity laws there. Should you decide to place your child for adoption, we don't want any father coming along and crying foul."

Celia tried to rein in her panic. She didn't like thinking about Damien at all, but thinking he might have the right to say what should happen to this baby was too much to fathom.

Mr. Walker continued. "Were you married to the father?"

Celia flinched. "No."

Mr. Walker wrote something on his paper and continued speaking without looking up. "Do you know the identity of the father?"

He may not have meant to, but the question made Celia feel sick, like she was on a trashy talk show and the host was trying to establish paternity from among a row of sleazy frat boys.

"I know his first name. And I would recognize him if I saw him in a lineup."

Mr. Walker looked surprised then his expression softened. "Dr. Vernon said there were extenuating circumstances here, but he couldn't give me details. I'm under the same privacy privilege, and I'm here to help you."

"Okay." Celia's hands ached from clasping them so tightly. She forced them apart and rested them loosely on her lap.

"Celia, were you the victim of a rape?"

The words hung in the air for several seconds before Celia trusted her voice to speak, and then it was barely a whisper. "I was."

"Did you report the crime to the authorities?"

"No. I packed my things and moved. I didn't know I was pregnant."

"Under the circumstances, most of these questions are irrelevant." Mr. Walker gently closed the folder he had been writing in and placed it on the desk. "I'm sorry. Questions can sound so harsh and unfeeling. Please know I'm here to help you, whatever you decide to do, and you'll get no judgment from me."

Celia nodded and clasped her hands together again.

"Let me explain a little about how the adoption process works then you can ask me any questions you might have."

Mr. Walker described the steps that would be taken by both the birth mother and the adoptive parents. There was so much information, Celia worried she'd forget it all. He explained the difference between open and closed adoptions and how she would select a birth family. "The earlier you select birth parents, the sooner they can become involved. They often cover your living expenses and medical bills. Sometimes a birth mother becomes good friends with the adoptive parents."

Celia wasn't sure what she thought about that. Did she want a relationship with the parents? Of course, she wanted to be sure the baby was safe and in a good home with security and opportunities. She wasn't sure she wanted to hang out with them. It was all too much to wrap her head around. She needed someone to talk to, someone to help her figure out her mind and what route she wanted to take. This would have been a good time for a mother. But if she had a mother, she probably wouldn't be in this horrible situation in the first place.

The thought made her angry and she suddenly felt protective of the life growing inside her. The most important thing she could do would be to give this baby good parents, a mother and father who would protect it from the terrible people in the world.

"Do you have any questions?" Mr. Walker interrupted her thoughts.

"I don't even know what to ask." Celia could tell her composure was walking a tightrope, and one wrong step would send her emotions tumbling out of control.

Mr. Walker must have sensed how she felt because he reached into his briefcase and pulled out a large folder with a picture of a happy couple—a white woman and an Asian man—holding a laughing, dark-skinned baby. It all looked so neat and tidy and inclusive. "This has most of the information you'll need to help you decide what you want to do. You should read this and maybe go over it with someone you trust. You don't need to make a hasty decision. We have time to do this in a way that is most comfortable for you."

Celia swallowed hard. "Thank you."

"When you decide how you want to handle the process, we'll get you registered so you can sign in and see the files of birth parents who are waiting for a baby. You do have access to a computer, right?"

Nancy had a computer she didn't mind Celia using, so she nodded.

"My card is in there. Feel free to call me with any

questions or to let me know you're ready to move forward."

Celia hugged the folder to her, hiding the smiling family, and left the office.

"Hello?"

"Hey, it's m-me." He tried to put some energy in his voice, but more than two days of back-breaking work had made his weary bones ache, and he knew he wasn't fooling his aunt.

"Silas, are you okay?"

"I'm tired. We're at a little café south of B-Bend. We worked through the night, so now we're getting something to eat and we'll try to get some sleep b-before we head back. I think this afternoon we'll start m-m-mopping up. Unless any hot sp-spots have flared." Silas sighed. He hated how bad his stutter became when he was exhausted.

"So it's mostly contained?" Aunt Nancy asked.

"M-mostly. It wasn't too b-big."

"Good. We've been worried about you."

"Silas?" A waitress holding a plastic basket with a cheeseburger and fries looked from the ticket in one hand to the room. Silas raised his hand and the waitress gave a little nod and delivered his food.

"Is Celia home?"

"No, she left a little while ago. You might be able to reach her at the gallery though."

"I don't think I have the number."

Aunt Nancy gave Silas the phone number. "Do you know when you'll be home?"

"I hope tomorrow, b-but it could be Saturday."

"Well, you take care of yourself. I love you."

"I will. Love you too."

Silas took a bite of his burger and dialed the number his aunt had given him.

"Sisters Gallery. This is Ellis."

"Hi Ellis. This is Silas. Is Ce-lee-ah there?" It was silly, but he didn't want to stutter on her name, so he stretched it out slowly and carefully.

"She won't be in until closer to noon. Do you want me to have her call you?"

Silas rested his head in his hand. "I don't think I'll have service then. Would you tell her I called?"

"We're heading out." Carlos stood at the door of the café and motioned for the crew to join him outside.

The waitress moved quickly through the café handing carryout boxes to the firefighters. Silas dumped his food into the box and threw a few dollars on the table.

"Sorry guys. No sleep yet. Just got word there will be more wind tomorrow, so we need to mop up as much as possible before then."

The men piled into their trucks and drove back toward China Hat.

The long day had gotten longer.

Chapter 31

"I had hoped Silas would be around for our first farmers market," Nancy said as they sorted through the parts of a blue and white striped canopy in the back yard. "I always forget how to put this together until I've done it the first two or three weekends."

Celia measured two poles to each other and put them in a pile with others the same size. This was the first time she had ever put together a tent, and since she would soon be setting up for the farmers market on her own, she listened carefully to Nancy's uncertain instructions.

"What's the longest he's ever been gone on a fire?" Celia tried to keep her voice casual.

"Last year was a bad year and I didn't see him much during the summer. They usually send them out for two or three weeks at a time though and then they get a little break."

Silas had worked four days at China Hat. After he got home, he slept for twenty hours straight. They finally saw him when he joined them for dinner at Nancy's.

"I haven't forgotten Wild Rose," he had said when they

had taken a walk to the creek after dinner. "Let's go Wednesday."

Celia hadn't forgotten either. When Silas had mentioned that Wild Rose had the best Thai food in Bend, she had decided that would be a good time to tell him everything. Mr. Walker had said to talk things over with someone she trusted, and she wanted that someone to be Silas. The only problem was, it was difficult to get his input on adoption when he didn't even know she was pregnant. She needed to tell him, to get that out in the open so he could be her sounding board, her confidante.

"I'll be closing the gallery at seven. Will that work?"

"Oh right. I forgot you're the acting owner this week. Sold any b-big ones?"

"No. I almost sold an eight-hundred dollar sculpture today, but then they decided it was probably too big for the place they planned to put it. I've sold a few smaller things though."

"Can you go from work, or do you need to come home first?"

"You can pick me up at work."

Celia had been surprised when Silas came into the gallery before lunch on Wednesday. She hadn't expected to see him until seven. Then she had noticed he was wearing the dark green pants and yellow shirt of a fire fighter, and before he even said it, she knew he was leaving. Her heart sank, but when she saw his disappointed face, she did her best to hide her frustration. For days she'd been rehearsing how she would tell him about the baby, and now it would be postponed again.

But this wasn't about her and her delayed plans. He was leaving and she needed to be supportive and encouraging. She met his worried expression with a smile.

"You're a little early for our date, and I think you might

be a little overdressed."

Silas stepped to the doorway of an adjoining room that held more artwork and looked around to see if they were alone. "Good. I was hoping no one would b-be here." He leaned across the counter, pulled Celia toward him and kissed her. Celia hadn't been ready for the kiss to end when he pulled away, so she pulled his shirt toward her and stole one more quick kiss.

"So what is this all about?" she asked, pointing up and down at his clothing.

"Another fire."

"I was afraid you were going to say that."

"This one's in Idaho."

"Are you serious?"

Silas nodded. "Last year I fought fires in Washington and California. This is my first fire in Idaho."

"You've hardly had any rest."

"I've had m-more than a lot of the guys. And I was only out four days on the last one. That's p-pretty short."

Celia stepped around the counter to stand by him. "I guess that's a matter of opinion. How long will you be gone this time?"

"It's a two week assignment."

So Wild Rose had been postponed for at least two more weeks. When would she be able to confide in him? Part of her wanted to tell him right now, to get it over with so she could stop worrying about it, but she knew that would be a selfish thing to do. She didn't want him distracted while he worked in dangerous conditions. He didn't need to be stewing over her problems when his life was on the line.

"Don't these fires know I'm craving Thai food?"

Silas laughed. "They're not very thoughtful."

"Do you know where in Idaho you're going?" Celia

wanted to be able to put a name to the place he would be.

"I think the fire's in Nez-Perce."

Celia sighed and touched his yellow shirt. "At least yellow is a good color on you."

"You think so?" Silas pulled her into a tight hug and Celia wondered if he could feel the little bump under her loose blouse.

"Do you like fighting fires?"

"It's hard, b-but I like everything about it. But I don't like m-missing you." He rested his lips on her forehead then dipped his face to hers and kissed her again. It was a long, hungry kiss that would have to last for at least two weeks. His voice was quiet and full of longing when he spoke. "You know I'm crazy about you."

Celia answered him with another kiss.

When the bell above the door rang, announcing a customer, they stepped apart.

"How are you today?" Celia tried to sound professional.

The older gentleman answered. "Not as good as you two. Please, don't let me interrupt."

Celia felt herself blush. Silas took a step toward the door and Celia followed him.

"I'll call when I have service." He had touched her cheek and Celia held his hand there for a moment before he had turned and left.

If Silas had been gone only the two weeks he had expected, he would have returned home yesterday, but last night he had called to tell them his crew had been asked to stay one more week.

Celia had been bitterly disappointed, but Silas had sounded so worn out, she knew she had it easier than he did.

Nancy must have noticed that Celia's thoughts were far away because she stepped over and put her arm around Celia's shoulders. "I'm sure he's okay." Celia nodded, grateful for Nancy's friendship. "Now, I think these poles go through the top and these go on the sides," Nancy said, pointing to each stack of poles.

"Let's give it a try."

A lot could happen in eighteen days. Wind could pick up sparks from a campfire and ignite dry tinder. It could spread and burn over a hundred thousand acres. Crews from four states could work together to try to extinguish it. The aching backs that often plagued firefighters during the first days of fire season could become sturdy and strong, even as the men became leaner from the hard work. Firefighters would become so tired they could sleep on the hard ground while helicopters roared overhead and backhoes dug line a few yards away.

A firefighter cutting a firebreak could die when a gust of wind provoked a meandering, nearly extinguished flame to rise up in anger, a hot, blistering predator chasing down its helpless prey.

Clouds cutting across the sky could give a false sense of hope that rain might help extinguish the hungry flames, but could provide instead nothing but lightning that would start a new fire on the other side of the break the firefighters had spent a week creating. Seven hard day's work gone in one bright, sky-splitting flash.

"Hey, Toller." Silas turned to see Carlos climbing the steep hill where Silas and a few other men were back-burning a slope with fusees. "When was the last time you ate?"

"This morning."

"Bates is cooking burritos. Here, give me that and you go eat something."

Silas handed the long, red torch to Carlos, who took over lighting the dry underbrush. In the distance, smoke plumed into the sky.

"Do you think the line will hold this time?" he asked.

Carlos straightened and looked at the swath of burnt ground they had created. "I hope so. We need the lightning to stay away." Carlos looked at Silas's soot-covered face and grinned. "Don't tell me you want to go home."

"No way. I'm hoping we can all m-move here forever."

"I'm afraid most of the view lots around here are toast." Sarcasm and joking helped ease the strain of the long, often discouraging work. "I got word a while ago that a unit from Washington is relieving us for mop up so we should be home by Thursday." Carlos noticed Silas's grin. "You must have something good to get home to."

"That I do."

"Congratulations. Now go find Bates."

Silas slid down the steep hill to a narrow dirt road that led back to their unit truck. A hundred feet beyond the truck, Bates stood cooking three burritos on a shovel he held over the coals of a burning out stump.

"Nice campfire," Silas said as he approached.

"Too bad we didn't bring the fixins for s'mores." Sometimes local communities brought food to the firefighters. Other times they'd drive into town to eat. The burritos were from a stash of food they kept in one of the trucks along with drinking water.

Bates pulled one of the burritos off the shovel with his gloved hand and gave it to Silas. It was pale and limp and most people would have turned up their noses at it, but for men who were ravenous and didn't know when they'd next see a decent meal, it might as well have been filet mignon.

He couldn't tell how hot it was through his gloves, so he let it cool for a few minutes before he devoured it in a few big bites. He could have eaten three of them, but at least it took the edge off his hunger until they could go eat in Lucile, a tiny town barely big enough to qualify for a zip code.

Silas slapped Bates on the shoulder. "Thanks, chef. That was great."

"Nothing tastes quite like shovel cookin'."

Silas drank a tepid bottle of water before he returned to retrieve his fusee from Carlos and continue back burning the side of the mountain.

Chapter 32

"I'm meeting Inez for a walk and then we're getting a cup of coffee and a muffin at the bakery. You can join us if you want." Nancy finished tying her shoe and looked at Celia for a response.

"That's okay. I've got to finish watering the garden and I need to do a load of laundry."

Nancy slapped her legs and stood. "All righty, then. I'll see you later today."

Once Celia had loaded the washing machine and given Nancy enough time to be well on her way, she pulled out Mr. Walker's card and dialed the number.

"Hello, Celia," he said after his secretary had put the call through.

"Hi. You mentioned I should give you a call to touch base after my next doctor appointment. I saw Dr. Vernon yesterday."

"Thanks for calling. I wanted to see if you've had a chance to look over the information I gave you."

"Yes, I've read it all."

"Great. Do you have any questions?"

"I don't think so. I'll probably go ahead and register soon, but I wanted to talk to my friend before I did, and he's been out of town."

"Of course. It's a good idea to have a support system. We can always put you in touch with a birth mother's support group, but it's nice to have friends and family beyond that. How did your appointment go?"

"It was fine. Dr. Vernon says the baby has a strong heartbeat and is probably about the size of a turnip. I'm not even sure how big a turnip is."

"Sounds like someone needs to make a trip to the produce department. When you can, talk things over with your friend and let us know if and when you're ready to move forward. And please let us know if you want the information about the support group."

"I will. I'll call you after my next appointment, if not sooner."

Celia hung up the phone and rested her head against the wall. She wanted to talk to Silas, but since she had finished reading through the folder, she felt stronger. The more her body changed and grew, the less she thought about how the baby came to be and the more she thought about what she would do to ensure it would have a good life.

She rubbed her belly. "I won't let you down, little one."

Nancy knocked on Inez's front door a second time, and still no one answered. She peered through the window beside the door and saw Inez's calico cat sitting on the back of a recliner, but no other sign of life. She walked around the house and looked through a window into the garage. Inez's car was gone. She must have forgotten their plans.

She reached into her pocket for her cell phone, but it wasn't there. It was probably sitting on the kitchen table where she'd sat to tie her shoes. She didn't mind taking a walk alone, but she knew she would feel more comfortable if she had her phone with her.

As she approached her house, she noticed some trash that had blown into her yard. She stepped around to the side yard and gathered it up. Why would she have McDonald's wrappers when there wasn't even a McDonald's in town? She carried the garbage to the trash can by the back door.

Celia's voice floated through the screen door. Was she talking to Silas? How fortunate she had forgotten her phone. As she reached for the door, Celia's words reached her ears. They didn't make sense.

"Dr. Vernon says the baby has a strong heartbeat and is probably about the size of a turnip. I'm not even sure how big a turnip is."

Nancy stood by the door, frozen in place. If Celia had been speaking Japanese, Nancy wouldn't have been any more confused.

Celia was speaking again. "I will. I'll call you after my next appointment, if not sooner."

She heard Celia hang up the phone and then her voice was quieter, and Nancy strained to hear her. "I won't let you down, little one."

Nancy staggered backward, suddenly afraid Celia might see her. She walked quickly back to the sidewalk and hurried to Inez's house. When she still wasn't home, Nancy collapsed on the front steps. She needed to think. In spite of the cool morning air, Nancy felt flushed. Her knuckles turned white as she gripped the stair rail, trying to hang on to something solid as she battled a myriad of emotions that left her unsteady.

How did you live with someone and not know something this monumental? She had noticed that Celia had purchased loose-fitting, stretchy clothes, but she had thought that was because the poor orphan girl was finally putting some meat on her bones.

And Dr. Vernon. She had known him most of her life, had even gone to a high school football game with him. Didn't he know Celia lived with her? Even as the thoughts crossed her mind, she knew she couldn't blame Sherman. He had that whole doctor patient thing he had to adhere to.

But someone should have told her. Or she should have noticed something. Morning sickness or sleepiness. It didn't matter that Nancy had never been pregnant herself. She was a woman, after all. As she thought of the obvious symptoms, she realized Celia had been a little sick and was often tired. The signs were there, but she hadn't known Celia well enough to know those things might be unusual.

For a moment, she directed her anger at that old busybody, Pearl. Had she known? Had Celia even been pregnant then?

Nancy steadied her breath and thought over the conversation she had heard, hoping she could attach a new meaning to the words. The baby had a strong heartbeat. It was the size of a turnip. She would call again after her next appointment.

There was no other interpretation.

Who had she been talking to? Was it Silas? Could the baby possibly be his? How far along would Celia be for the baby to be the size of a turnip?

It was the kind of conversation a wife might share with her husband after a doctor's appointment. Was Celia married?

Had she left a husband to come to Oregon?

Nothing made sense. If Celia had left behind the father of her baby, why had she taken up with Silas? And if it was Silas's baby, how had she won him over so quickly? They hadn't even seemed to like each other until the first part of June, but if she was carrying his baby, something must have happened between them before that. Had she missed something during those first weeks when Celia had been here? It didn't seem possible. Silas hardly even dated. But that was the very reason the wiles of an experienced woman throwing herself at him might have been problematic. And Nancy had allowed her to live in her home.

As she processed the thoughts, she became more confused. She wanted to know the circumstances behind Celia's baby. Her mind was playing a fierce tennis match, ideas going back and forth. A few thoughts gave Celia the benefit of the doubt. Maybe she felt she'd made a mistake and was trying to make a clean start. Others painted Celia as a promiscuous scam artist, taking in Nancy's vulnerable nephew. Celia hardly seemed like an experienced woman, but they hadn't even known her before she moved in. She had seemed sweet and hard-working and even shy, but maybe that was all an act. Wasn't that exactly how a woman pulling a con would want to come across?

Hurt and indignation battled inside her as she considered the situation. Where was Inez? Nancy needed to use her computer to look up when a baby was the size of a turnip. She certainly didn't want to go home and use her own laptop. She'd never been good at hiding her feelings and Celia would know something was wrong.

There was a computer at The Stitchin' Station. She'd go there. At the very least, it would give her some time to pull herself together before she saw Celia. She couldn't let Celia know she knew. At least not until she had a chance to talk to Silas. Nancy didn't know the details of Celia's pregnancy, but there was one thing she knew for certain. If the baby wasn't Silas's, then Celia had no business being part of his future. He needed to know.

Chapter 33

"Everything okay?" Carlos asked as Silas hung up the phone. When Silas didn't answer immediately, Carlos reached across the truck and put his hand on Silas's arm. "Hey man, what's up?"

Silas pulled his thoughts away from Aunt Nancy's strained tone and directed his attention to Carlos. "Oh, I'm sure everything's fine."

"Good. We're heading home. You're supposed to be celebrating, not looking like your dog died."

Silas couldn't have been happier to be going home, but he was disappointed Celia wouldn't be there. He had called to tell her and Aunt Nancy he was nearly there, but Aunt Nancy had told him Celia was at the farmers market until late evening. So much for the homecoming he'd been imagining. He looked at his grimy hands and reminded himself it would be nice to get showered and take a nap.

A little while later, he stepped out of his bathroom, feeling like a new man. He was hungry, but probably had nothing worth eating in his refrigerator. He pulled on his t-shirt as he headed toward the kitchen, but stopped short when he saw Aunt Nancy sitting on his couch.

"Dang. You freaked m-me out."

"I'm sorry." Aunt Nancy looked even more anxious than she had sounded on the phone. Something was wrong and dread filled his chest.

Silas sat down beside her. "What are you doing here?" Aunt Nancy twisted the handle of her purse in her hands. "You're scaring m-m-me. What's going on?"

"I'm sorry Silas, but I have to ask. Did you and Celia . . . " Her voice faded off as she searched for the right words.

"Did m-me and Celia what?"

Aunt Nancy groaned. "Did you and Celia, you know, hook up when she first got here?" She winched when she said the words "hook up."

Silas laughed at his aunt's choice of words. Did she even know what that meant? "What are you asking m--me?"

"You know, did you . . . during that first . . . Were you secretly seeing each other when she first got here?"

Aunt Nancy wouldn't even make eye contact with him. "What's going on?" Silas asked.

It was a good thing he had sat down because if he hadn't, what she said next would have knocked him off his feet.

"Celia's having a baby."

"What are you talking about?"

"She's pregnant." Silas slowly shook his head and finally Aunt Nancy looked at him, her face earnest and determined. "She is. I overheard her talking on the phone. She said the baby was strong and was the size of a turnip. I don't know who she was talking to, but she said she'd call again after her next appointment. Stop shaking your head, Silas. I'm not making this up." Aunt Nancy's voice caught. She was nearly in tears. Silas held still, but it didn't mean he believed what she was saying. “I looked it up. To be the size of a turnip the baby would have been—” she struggled with the next word—“conceived in March or April, I think. Did you—” She couldn’t bring herself to say it again.

It was impossible. Celia couldn’t have hidden something like this. She would have said something. They had shared so much about their lives and the hard things they had faced. Why would she keep this from him? This was too big a thing to hide. “You’re wrong. There’s no way—”

Aunt Nancy’s voice became steely as she continued. “I’m not wrong. It all makes sense now. She was tired and she threw up. I thought she was sick, but she was pregnant. And after I heard her, I could tell. All the clothes she’s bought are loose so it’s harder to see it, but I asked her to get the cake stand out of the cupboard above the fridge so I could get a better look and when she lifted her arms, I knew. Her stomach is growing. She’s having a baby, and I want to know if it’s yours.” Her voice became soft and she touched Silas’s arm. “I need to know if it’s yours.”

Silas fell back on the couch and looked blankly at the fireplace. He felt hollow inside. “No. It’s not m-mine.”

“So you’ve never . . . ”

“No.”

“Has she told you anything about the baby?”

“No.”

“Has she told you about her ex-boyfriends or if there’s an ex-husband?”

With every question, Silas’s heart sank. “No.”

“I knew she had secrets. I wanted to trust her, but she’s been lying to us ever since she got here.”

“We don’t know that for sure.” Nothing made sense, but he wasn’t ready to turn on the woman he was falling for.

Aunt Nancy squeezed his arm and when she spoke, her

voice was gentle. "After she hung up, she told the baby she wouldn't let it down. I've spent the last two days trying to figure out what she's up to, and all I can think is either she's trying to trick you or maybe she's trying to get back together with the father. She probably should get back with him. The baby has a right to know its father."

Silas groaned. "Either way, it's not good for you." She looked at Silas's tortured face. "I'm sorry. I know you were liking her."

That didn't really cover how he'd been feeling. "Have you asked her about it?"

"No. I wanted to talk to you first. But I'll ask her if you want me to."

Silas shook his head. "I need to think."

"Of course. I'm sure you're disappointed. So am I. She fooled me too, but—"

"No. I don't want to talk about it." He hated that his voice sounded shaky. "I said I need to think."

"I know. I'll go. You can call me when you're ready to talk."

Silas nodded. He didn't get up when Aunt Nancy stood, and after she left he pulled one of the couch cushions off the back of the sofa and tucked it under his head. For the past three weeks, he'd been able to fall asleep on the hard, rocky ground in mere seconds, but right now, on a comfortable sofa, his mind gave his body no rest. He couldn't reconcile the woman he was falling in love with and a woman who would hide something like this while she acted like she was feeling the same way he was. For hours he let his aunt's words settle into his head and then his heart.

It was nearly dark when he heard his aunt's pickup park behind her garage as Celia returned from the market. He didn't go see her. He didn't even turn on the lights. He hoped his aunt wouldn't tell Celia he was home. A tear ran down his temple and into his ear before he fell asleep.

The house looked darker than she had expected it to when Celia got home from the farmers market. She had thought Silas would be here, visiting with his aunt and waiting for her to get home, but the only light in the house was a lamp in the living room and the flashing colored light reflecting off the wall from the television.

"Is Silas not here?" Celia asked from the living room door.

"I'm afraid not." Nancy's voice sounded funny, and she didn't look away from the television.

"I thought he was getting home today."

"I thought so, too. I'm not sure when we'll see him."

Celia was confused. "Have you talked to him?"

"Earlier today. I'm sure he'll be in touch. How did the market go?"

Celia sat down in the corner of the couch. "It was good. I sold out of almost everything. The money's in the kitchen. Do you want me to get it and we can divide it up?"

"You can take care of that. I trust you." There was a strange edge to Nancy's voice.

"Is something wrong?"

"Everything's fine." Nancy glanced at her and even though she smiled, something still felt off.

"I'm pretty tired. I think I'll go to bed."

"Goodnight, Celia."

At the door, Celia paused and looked back at Nancy. She wanted to ask more questions, to get to the bottom of the older woman's strange mood, but she wasn't even sure what to ask.

"Will you wake me up if Silas calls?"

"Of course."

Silas didn't call. She still hadn't heard from him three days later. She tried his cell phone, even left an awkward message when he didn't answer, but he didn't call her back. Celia was worried about him, and she didn't understand why Nancy wasn't.

"Shouldn't he be home by now?" she asked.

"I thought he would be, but these things are unpredictable."

"I thought they didn't keep them longer than three weeks."

"I'm sure he's fine. We'll see him when we see him."

On Sunday, Celia walked to church. She had felt so uneasy the past few days, she yearned for the peace of the quiet chapel and the comfort of the minister's calm voice. She went a little early and sat on the back pew, praying Silas would return soon so she could talk to him. Every day the baby grew, and she knew it wouldn't be long before everyone would be able to tell she was pregnant. She had been so ready to tell him before he left, but now, even though the urgency was still there, she felt less confident of what his reaction would be. The longer he was gone without hearing from him, the more she wondered if the connection she had felt was real.

Celia slipped out a little early. She was tired and didn't want to risk an invitation to stay and eat or socialize. Nancy would be working at The Stitchin' Station, and Celia would have the house to herself. She would make a cheese sandwich and take a long nap.

She was almost home when she saw the Jeep driving up

the lane. Silas was back. Her prayers were being answered faster than she had imagined they would be. She picked up her pace to a brisk walk then, eager to see him, she started running. He stopped at the road then turned left, away from her.

"Silas," she called and waved, but he hadn't seen her and kept driving. But he was home.

Celia was out of breath from running when she let herself in the back door. She paused for a moment to catch her breath then dialed Silas's cell phone from the wall landline in the kitchen. It rang five times then went to voicemail. She hung up and dialed it again with the same result. This time she waited for the tone.

"Hi Silas, it's me. I got home from church and saw you leaving. I'm here now, so if you want to come by, that would be great. I can fix us some lunch or something. I'm so glad you're home safe. I've been worried about you. Anyway, I guess I'll see you soon."

She hung up the phone and waited. She went to the bathroom and checked her reflection to see if she looked okay. She turned and looked at herself sideways to be sure her loose-fitting skirt and blouse didn't give away her secret before she had the chance to tell him. She brushed through her hair and decided she looked fine. She sat on the porch swing and watched the road he had driven down. When a half an hour had passed, and she hadn't seen or heard from him, she considered walking to The Stitchin' Station to see if he had gone to see his aunt. But what if he came home while she was gone.

She went inside and called Nancy.

"He's home. Silas is home. I saw him leaving in his Jeep when I was getting home from church, but he didn't see me. Is he there?"

"He's not."

"Do you know where he is?"

Celia heard Nancy let out a long breath before she spoke. "Celia, he and his crew left a little while ago for a fire in Washington."

Celia leaned against the wall and slid to the floor. "But he needs some rest. I thought they were supposed to get a break between jobs."

"I guess it's a pretty big fire, and they're calling up as many crews as they can."

"But I didn't even get to see him."

"I'm sorry, Celia." For the first time in several days, Nancy's voice sounded gentle and kind. "He had to go."

Celia sat on the floor after Nancy had hung up, the phone hanging from its coiled cord beside her. She didn't understand why Silas had left again so soon and why he hadn't answered her phone calls. Did he not want to see her before he left? Even for a few minutes? She thought about the day he had come into the gallery to say goodbye. There hadn't been much time then either, but he had wanted to see her.

When the phone started an unpleasant beeping, Celia dragged herself to her feet and hung it up. The thought of a cheese sandwich made her stomach roil, so she curled up on her bed and cried herself to sleep.

Chapter 34

"What are you doing, man? You got a death wish?"

Silas shot a questioning look at Jed, the leader of a thrown-together crew Silas had volunteered for. While Carlos and the remainder of his crew were taking the rest of the week off to recover, Silas had volunteered to go out on the next available assignment. That put him with Jed and a unit from Ashland. Jed had been thrilled to have an extra guy until he realized Silas's thoughts were preoccupied with something going on at home.

"I don't know where your head's been, but you gotta get it here. Right now. I can't have you being a liability out there with the other guys."

Silas knew he deserved the chastening. "I'm sorry. I'm here now."

"Good. Jean said you're one of the best, so prove it."

"I will."

"It's hot in there. I said get completely geared up. Now get your gloves on and pull down your shroud." Silas removed his helmet and pulled down the Nomex shroud that hung from the helmet over his shirt to protect his neck and face. Then he pulled on his gloves. He may have been distracted by the mess he had left at home, but he certainly didn't want to die because of it. Hard work would take his mind off Celia, and now that he'd made Jed skeptical of his value, Silas would have to work extra hard to convince Jed he was an asset.

The Okanogan fire had already burned almost two-hundred-thousand acres along with more than sixty cabins. Now the flames were threatening the little town of Skykomish, and Jed's crew was joining four others at the line. The residents had been evacuated, but the firefighters were determined those people would have homes to return to.

The dirt road they bumped along got narrower and soon it was hard to call it a road. It was more like a wide hiking trail. Smoke and ash darkened the sky and up ahead they could see orange flames rising thirty feet into the tree canopy. The men closed their shrouds and lowered the safety glasses. Adrenalin coursed through Silas's veins as he and the other firefighters jumped out of the truck.

"Pay attention in there," shouted Jed to the men, but his eyes were on Silas. "Follow protocol and watch each other's backs. Don't let anything happen to any of you."

Silas nodded, irritated that he was being singled out, even though he knew it was his own fault. Waves of heat slammed into the men as they started up the hill. Silas pushed aside every thought except one. There was a job to do, and Silas couldn't afford to think about Celia or his crushed hopes.

Days passed and Celia didn't hear from Silas. At first she had convinced herself it had only been bad timing, and she had blamed it on the wildfires, but as the days passed, she knew things were different. Silas must not have liked her as much as she had thought he did. She had misread things before. There had been many times she had believed her mother would turn things around so Celia could count on her. She had been wrong. She had thought the Hundleys loved her enough to keep her, but they hadn't. Silas would be one more in a long line of people to let her down, but as she had every other time it had happened, she would pick herself up and forge ahead.

She had no choice.

Silas had been gone to Washington for almost two weeks when Celia jolted awake in the night. At first she thought she must have heard something. She threw back the covers from her damp skin, but as soon as she did, the cool night air chilled her. She listened intently for something that might have interrupted her sleep, but there were no sounds at all. Not even a fan running or a cricket chirping.

And then her abdomen seized as if an arm wrestler had gripped it tightly and slammed it into her spine, and she recognized that this is what had awakened her. She rolled onto her side and pulled her knees up, trying to find a position that relieved the burning cramp. Celia did her best to relax and after a few minutes the pain subsided and she fell back into a restless sleep.

Nancy glanced up from the crossword puzzle she was working on at the table when Celia walked into the kitchen for breakfast. "Celia, are you okay?" Nancy nearly knocked the chair to the floor as she stood from the table and hurried to Celia.

"I didn't sleep very well."

"Do you have a fever? You look so pale." Nancy put the back of her hand on Celia's forehead. "You don't feel hot."

"I'll be fine. I probably need to eat."

"Sit down and I'll make you something. Do you want eggs? Or oatmeal?"

Nancy guided Celia to the chair across from the one she had been sitting in.

"Thank you. Oatmeal sounds good." Celia sat at the table while Nancy microwaved a bowl of instant oatmeal and added brown sugar and milk.

Celia had eaten half the bowl when her stomach began to clench painfully. She dropped her spoon in the bowl and leaned over, hugging her abdomen.

"Celia, what is it?" Nancy sounded afraid.

Celia spoke through clenched teeth. "I'm not sure."

"I'm taking you to the doctor."

All Celia could think about was that she couldn't let Nancy know about the baby. If Nancy took her to Dr. Vernon, he might let it slip that Celia had been in before. What if Nancy wanted to go with her to the examination room? What if Lacy made it clear she and Celia knew each other?

"I can go myself."

"Nonsense. I'm going with you. Do you need me to get you anything before we go?" Nancy was already gathering her things. She retrieved her purse off the coffee table and slipped her feet into the sandals she kept by the back door. "Is your bag in your room?"

"It's hanging on the door."

Nancy returned with Celia's bag. She held the door for Celia and within a few minutes, they were in front of Dr. Vernon's office. Nancy pulled as close to the door as she could. "Can you make it in while I park the car?"

"Yes." Celia tried to hide her relief as she exited the car

and walked into Dr. Vernon's office.

"Hi, Celia. I don't remember seeing you on the schedule today."

Celia walked to the counter and spoke softly. "I don't have an appointment. I'm having terrible cramps and Nancy brought me in. She's parking the car." Celia glanced toward the door. "She doesn't know. I don't want her to find out like this."

Lacy nodded as Nancy entered the waiting room. "All right Miss Edwards. Dr. Vernon is with a patient, but I'll see if I can work you in."

"Thank you."

"You don't have to wait with me," Celia said after they chose two seats with a view of the small television in the corner.

"I don't mind. I don't have anywhere else to be today."

The television screen scrolled through health tips and statistics. Celia had learned that more than seventy-three thousand people are diagnosed with skin cancer each year and that antibiotics are not always the answer to childhood ear infections by the time Karen, Dr. Vernon's nurse, came to the door.

"Celia Edwards?"

"I'll wait out here for you," Nancy said.

"Thank you."

"I'm feeling a hankering for Harrison Ford lately. Want to watch *The Fugitive* with me tonight? You can take my recliner or the couch. Whichever would be more comfortable."

"The couch is fine," Celia said. "You take your chair."

Nancy had been waiting all day for Celia to open up about her doctor's appointment. She had hoped this would be the opening Celia needed to tell her about the baby, but Celia's explanation had been cryptic. "Dr. Vernon says I'm worn down and need to rest. He said it could be stress."

"Have you been pushing yourself too hard? If the garden and the farmer's market and working for Ellis is too much, maybe you should think about cutting back."

"It's not that."

"What could be causing stress then if it isn't all the work you're doing?" This was her chance to talk about the baby. Nancy knew she had given Celia the perfect opening and she waited eagerly for her to confess. And she did, but not to what Nancy had been expecting.

"Maybe it's because of Silas."

"He's been trained, you know. It's dangerous work, but it's rare that something bad happens to one of these guys."

"It's not that." Celia was always so skittish that Nancy was afraid to prod her too much, so she waited for Celia to continue on her own. "I thought . . . I don't know. I thought we were friends, but he didn't even try to see me when he came home."

In spite of Nancy's irritation with Celia's secret, she felt a pang of guilt. She knew why Silas had left, even knew Silas had offered to go out with another unit when the rest of his crew was still taking the days off they had earned. As much as she wanted to blurt out that Silas had left because Celia had kept a secret from him and had led him on, she knew this wasn't the time for that. No matter how frustrated she was with Celia, she wouldn't endanger her baby.

"The men are exhausted when they're fighting fires. I

wouldn't take it personally."

Celia nodded and turned toward the television. Even though she kept her eyes trained on the movie, Nancy could tell Celia's thoughts were nowhere near Sisters, and while Nancy thought Harrison Ford was handsome enough to stir a woman's emotions, she was certain that when Celia wiped a tear from her cheek, it had nothing at all to do with the wrongful conviction of Dr. Richard Kimble.

Chapter 35

Nancy folded the empty bank bag and tucked it into her purse.

"Are you still growing that Black Beauty eggplant?" asked Millie Watson, the teller at Oregon National Bank, as she handed Nancy the receipt for the day's deposit.

"I'm not doing it myself this year. Got a girl working for me, but yeah. We've got some."

"I need to come by and pick up a few. Those make the best sandwiches."

"Come by and get some," Nancy said. "And take a couple to your mom, too."

"I'll do that. You have a nice day."

Nancy was almost across the marble floor of the lobby when Dr. Vernon stepped through the door.

"Nancy Toller."

"Hi, Sherm. How've you been?"

"Can't stop smiling. How about you?"

Nancy grinned. Sherman Vernon had been using that line for more than thirty years. "I'm fine. Enjoying this nice, sunny day, although I wouldn't mind a little rain."

"Probably wishing for a downpour, aren't you? I'm always at odds with the farmers and gardeners who want to trade in this perfect weather for rain."

"I always want the water for the garden, but right now I'd like a good cloudburst to help put out all these fires. As long as it doesn't bring a bunch of lightning with it."

Sherman looked rueful. "Now you've shamed me into hoping for some rain. Of course we need whatever we can get. It seems the whole western United States is ablaze. Is your nephew out there?"

Nancy nodded. "He's in Washington right now. He's been there more than two weeks. He's fighting the Okanogan fire."

"I hope he gets back soon and safe."

"Thanks, Sherm. Tell Susan hello."

Nancy was about to leave when Sherman touched her arm lightly to stop her. "How's your . . . I'm not sure what to call her. Is she your boarder?"

"Celia? Yes, she's my boarder. She's helping me out with the garden this year in exchange for a place to live."

"Yes." The way he said it told Nancy he was already aware of their living arrangement. Why was Sherman asking her questions? Celia had confided more to him than she had to Nancy. It occurred to her that maybe she could catch Sherman off guard and get him to slip with some new information. Maybe she could pretend Celia had already told her about the baby.

"Celia seems to be doing better. You know I brought her in last week. Stress, and exhaustion, and . . . you know."

Nancy thought she caught a wary expression, but then it was gone. "Tell her to drink plenty of water. Dehydration's always a problem in this hot weather."

"I'll tell her."

Sherman paused before he continued. "That's one brave girl you've got there." He glanced at his watch. "I'd better get going. Susan's invited her sister's family for dinner, so if I know what's good for me, I won't be late."

Nancy stood there, surprised at his complimentary remark about Celia, before she recovered and responded. "You'd better get out of here. Have a nice time."

All evening, Sherman Vernon's words niggled the edge of her mind. When she had first met Celia, Nancy had had the same reaction. Celia was here alone, far from home, starting a new life in a town full of strangers. But lately those thoughts had been replaced with other, less glowing judgments. Here was a pregnant girl, sneaking away from her life and her commitments, a woman with secrets and ulterior motives. There was nothing courageous about sneaking around and dating people who don't know about your past.

Which opinions were right? Were Nancy's conclusions correct or did Sherman know something she didn't? He had lived up to his responsibility to keep Celia's secret confidential, and maybe what he had said meant nothing at all, but the thought wouldn't leave Nancy alone. It poked at her as she watched Celia carry a grocery bag full of Swiss chard in from the garden for dinner. It nagged at her while they loaded the dishwasher. It distracted her as they watched Home and Garden Television.

All her life, Nancy had prided herself on her fairness. She always cheered for the underdog, and even though she wasn't a particularly religious woman, she had always felt a connection with the story of David and Goliath. She believed everyone deserved the benefit of the doubt, so why had she decided to think the worst about Celia? What was it about Celia's story that impressed Dr. Vernon enough to make him comment on her bravery?

Nancy looked at Celia. Sometime in the last few minutes, she had fallen asleep, her head on the soft arm of the sofa and her knees tucked up beside her. Even in sleep, her face looked tense and full of worry. She knew of some of the difficulties Celia had endured, but what didn't she know? An exquisite sadness pierced Nancy's heart. She didn't approve of Celia leading on her nephew, and she wanted to protect Silas from carrying around Celia's baggage the rest of his life, but that didn't mean she had no heart. How could she be loyal to Silas and keep him from being hurt while still being kind and generous to this lonely girl?

Nancy couldn't remember a time when she'd felt so conflicted.

She turned off the television and gently shook Celia's arm to awaken her.

Celia flinched and pulled away, a panicked look on her face. "No. Please don't."

"Celia, it's me. Come on, dear. You'll end up with a terrible kink in your neck if you stay out here." She reached for Celia's hand and gently pulled her to a sitting position. "Come on. Let's get you to bed."

Celia met Nancy's gaze, and when she saw it was Nancy, the panic drained away. "I'm sorry. I'm not very good company, am I?"

"You're fine company. How are you feeling?" She linked her arm through Celia's and walked her to the bedroom door.

"I'm so tired." Nancy squeezed Celia's arm then pushed open the door. Celia turned toward her before she went inside. "Thanks for everything."

Nancy's throat was too tight to speak so she nodded and turned away. She had never been much of a crier, but by the time she reached her bedroom door, the tears couldn't be stopped.

July had been one of the hottest on record and the entire northwest was parched. Three mornings per week, the thirsty ground sucked up the water Celia and Nancy guided into the irrigation ditches that lined the rows of plants. Some mornings Celia watered while the sun crept up over the horizon, so the heat of the day wouldn't evaporate the water before it could soak the ground surrounding the roots.

Celia carried a box from the shed to the middle of the long, thin Chinese eggplants. When the box was half full, she carried it to the back of Nancy's pickup, retrieved another box from the shed, and headed to the row of Black Beauties. It wasn't efficient to fill the boxes halfway, but Dr. Vernon had given her specific instructions that she was to lift less and pace herself. She was doing her best to follow his advice.

In a few hours, she would take the morning's harvest to the Redmond farmers market, where she would spend the afternoon selling the vegetables she had worked so hard to cultivate.

Nancy stepped out onto the porch when Celia brought the box of dark purple eggplants to the pickup. Celia saw her look at the half-filled boxes, but if she wondered why Celia was wasting so much space, she didn't mention it. "I'm scrambling some eggs. Would you like any?"

"No thanks. I already ate a bowl of oatmeal."

Celia carried two small baskets to the tomato section of the garden and knelt down beside the vines, pushing aside the leafy stems to find the ripest ones. She twisted them off the vines the way Nancy had shown her, and carefully placed them in the basket so they wouldn't bruise. She held one to her nose and took a deep breath. She loved the sweet, acidic smell. She looked across the expanse of green, healthy plants. She had never done something that required so much work and patience and attention, and with each squash and eggplant and tomato she picked, she felt a sense of pride. Almost every evening this week, they had eaten something she had grown. She had never felt so self-sufficient, so accomplished, so productive.

Celia pulled the second basket closer and placed a red and green variegated tomato in the bottom. As she leaned toward the next plant, hummingbird wings flapped inside her belly. The feeling was fleeting, and Celia wondered if she'd imagined it. And then it came again, a barely-there flutter from inside her.

She sat down in the dirt and put a gentle hand over the place she'd felt the movement. A dog barked down the street and a potato bug crawled across the ground in front of her, but she held perfectly still and focused on her stomach, hoping she'd feel it again. "Come on little one, I know you're there. You can do it," she whispered.

"Celia, what's wrong?" Nancy's frightened voice jarred Celia out of her communion with the baby inside her. She turned and watched as Nancy hurried the last few feet to her. "Are you okay?"

Celia nodded.

Nancy leaned over, resting her hands on her thighs, trying to catch her breath. "I thought you fell."

Celia reached up her hand and Nancy took it. When she spoke, her voice was shaky and uncertain. "Nancy, I really need a friend."

Nancy knelt down beside her and held Celia's hand between both of hers. "Oh sweet girl, I know you do. Do you mind if your friend is an old woman?"

Chapter 36

Celia sat cross-legged in the corner of the couch and hugged a pillow in front of her to occupy her hands. Now that she had felt the baby move, it was difficult to concentrate on anything other than when she would feel that gentle flutter again, but for the moment, she needed to focus. It was time to tell Nancy what had happened to her and about the resulting little life growing inside her.

Nancy sat on the other end of the couch, facing Celia. "I know you've had something on your mind."

It was the opening Celia needed. A surprising calm settled over her. Nancy hadn't been her planned confidante, but now that they were sitting here together, she knew there were advantages to telling Nancy. If she had told Silas, she would have worried about his reaction. Would he still like her? Would he be upset or embarrassed by her past? Would the truth change his feelings?

She didn't have to worry about those things with Nancy. There was nothing more than friendship between them, and if Nancy thought less of Celia, the disappointment would be no worse than what she had dealt with most of her life. There had been more at stake with Silas, and while Celia felt sad that she had misread his intentions, she also felt grateful that his feelings had cooled before she had served up her soul to him.

"I'm pregnant." Celia watched for Nancy's face to express horror or disgust, but it remained impassive. She didn't even look surprised. "I'm eighteen weeks along."

Nancy didn't say anything, just gave the slightest bob of her head, so Celia continued, tearing down the wall she had been hiding behind brick by brick, sentence by sentence. "My last foster family were the Javorseks. I turned eighteen while I lived there, and technically they could have kicked me out, but they let me stay as long as I paid them rent and helped with the housework. I lived there for almost a year after I graduated from high school. About a year ago, I met a girl at work—we both waited tables at Applebee's—and she wanted to get an apartment. Once I did the math, I realized I could share a little apartment for less than I was paying the Javorseks, so we moved in together.

"It turned out to be a mistake. I didn't know she used drugs and that she had friends that would come over to party all the time. Sometimes they stayed for days, but they never helped pay the bills. I asked the Javorseks if I could move back in, but they had already signed up for another foster child and if I was living there, they wouldn't qualify. Something about too many people in the house or an unrelated adult living there. Cassidy—that was my roommate—tried to get me to come have fun with them, but it reminded me of the mess my mom had made with her life, so I spent most of my time in my bedroom. Cassidy and her friends didn't trust me because I didn't party with them. At first they made fun of me, but then they ignored me."

Celia twisted the fringe on the pillow. She hadn't ever told the details of that night and she wasn't sure she wanted to now.

Seconds passed as she tried to choose her words, but she couldn't find a way to describe the ugliness she had endured. Finally Nancy softly spoke. "So the father is from Chicago?"

"Yes."

"Does he know you're pregnant?"

"No. And he never will. I don't think he even knows my name. I was just Cassidy's boring roommate. I'm not even sure he'd remember what he did to me. He was tripping pretty hard."

Nancy slid closer to Celia, and although she didn't touch her, the gesture felt like a gift of compassion and clemency. "Do you know his name?"

"His name is Damien. I don't know his last name."

Nancy sighed. "Is that when you left?"

"I was scared. He was a big guy and I was afraid he'd do it again. So when he left, I packed my things and never went back."

"And you took a bus to Sisters all by yourself."

"That wasn't nearly as scary as staying and seeing him again."

Nancy covered her face hands with her hands. "Oh, Celia. I'm so sorry."

Celia forced a half-hearted laugh. "You're not the one who should be sorry. You've been so kind to me. I'm sorry I didn't tell you sooner. I was going to tell Silas before . . . you know. But then this morning, while I was working in the garden, I felt the baby move, and I couldn't keep it to myself."

Nancy reached for Celia and pulled her into a hug. Celia felt Nancy's damp cheek against her temple and knew Nancy was crying.

The bell on the front door of the gallery rang as Celia switched off the lights in the back room.

"We're about to close, so if— Oh . . . hi." Silas stood inside the door. He looked different. He looked leaner and had at least a month's growth of beard.

Celia took a deep breath and clenched her hands into fists to ground her. He looked good, and it was hard not to feel excitement that he was here. But it was too late for that. Silas had left without a word and the confusion and disappointment had left her shaken and exhausted. She couldn't deal with that right now. This wasn't the time for romance and dating. She needed to put the baby first.

"Did you get home today?" She did her best to keep her voice casual.

"This m-morning." He stayed by the door, and Celia was struck by the reversal in his confidence. A few weeks ago he had been sure of himself around her. Now he seemed tentative. The change made Celia sad.

"I'll bet Nancy was relieved to have you back in one piece."

"Yeah. She said if I sign up again b-before next summer, she'll disown m-me."

"She's been worried about you."

Celia dragged her gaze away from Silas and busied herself straightening up the counter.

"Can I walk you home?"

"That's okay. I've got to straighten up a bit and I want to vacuum so it's clean for Ellis in the morning." She didn't tell

Silas she had done all of this less than an hour ago.

"I can wait. I'll vacuum for you." Silas headed to the closet by the office where the cleaning supplies were kept.

"You don't have to do that."

"I don't m-mind."

The floor didn't need vacuumed, but if she admitted that, she'd have to admit she wanted to avoid him, so while Silas vacuumed, Celia pulled out a painting and hung it in the empty space where she had sold a small landscape earlier in the day. It was hard not to watch Silas. He looked good, and her mind wandered to the last time she had seen him in the gallery, and the easy affection they had shared.

She didn't let her mind remain there long. It was too disappointing. Instead, she dredged up the memory of her walking home from church and breaking into a run when she saw Silas in his Jeep. She reminded herself that he had turned away from her and had never tried to reach her during the past nineteen days. That was the memory she needed to keep front and center so she wouldn't make the mistake of falling into his pale blue eyes and helpful ways. She was going to have a baby and that needed to be her focus. She didn't have the time or the emotional stability for a roller coaster relationship.

Silas put the vacuum cleaner away and stood by the counter, his hands in his pockets. "Is there anything else you need to do?"

"No. I guess I'm ready to go."

Celia turned off all but one light and locked the door behind them. They walked more than a block before Celia finally spoke. "Did you get the fire put out?"

"Yes. It was a b-big one. Almost took out a little town called Skykomish."

"I'll bet they appreciated your help." She meant it, but realized it might have sounded sarcastic. "I mean, all of you that were there."

"C-C-Celia, I should have come to see you b-before I left."

Silas's stuttering filled Celia with sorrow, and she would have tried to put him at ease, but she wasn't sure how to do that while keeping a safe distance.

"I'm sure it was pretty hectic, getting home and leaving so soon."

The conversation lagged again.

"They needed volunteers, b-but I still should have said goodbye."

Celia shrugged. "Or hello."

Silas nodded. "I'm sorry."

"It's okay." Celia gave him a regretful smile. "You know, I've got a lot going on right now, and I'm not in a very good place to be dating anyway."

Silas looked stunned for a moment, but recovered quickly. "Oh. I thought—"

"I'm going to have a baby." Silas stopped walking and Celia turned to face him.

"I know. Nancy told me."

Celia couldn't read his expression so she continued. "I wanted to tell you, but at first I was afraid. And then you left. And then you left again and I didn't have a chance."

"I shouldn't have l-l-left l-l-like that. I'm s-s-sorry." Now he was stuttering on sounds she'd never heard him trip on. She looked at his feet, afraid if she looked in his eyes, she'd lose her resolve.

"My whole life has been full of people leaving me."

"I'm not that kind of m-man."

"Then what happened?"

"I knew there were things you weren't telling m-me and I guess I freaked out."

Celia and Silas started walking again, slowly. They were nearly home when Celia said, "I should have told you sooner."

"M-maybe we can, you know . . . "

Celia looked up at Silas. She hadn't noticed his tired eyes. She put her hand on Silas's arm to soften her words. "Silas, you should go home and get some rest. Let's talk later."

If he would have taken her in his arms, she'd have burrowed in and stayed there forever, but he nodded and spoke slowly and carefully. "I'll see you tomorrow."

Chapter 37

Silas climbed the ladder to the second-story windows of the Sisters Brewhouse, and reached down for the quilt Nancy was handing him. For the last couple of years Silas had pitched in to help his aunt and about a hundred other volunteers set up for the annual quilt show.

"I love this one." Nancy held up the beautiful art quilt that had been sent from New Zealand. Every year she looked forward to the variety of quilts from around the world, especially the ones that paid tribute to the beauty she sometimes took for granted. The quilt painstakingly depicted Smith Rock set against a colorful sunset. "I wish this one was for sale."

When the quilt was secure, Silas climbed down. He had barely spoken during the three hours he and Nancy had been hanging quilts, and he hadn't smiled once.

"Silas, you've got to snap out of this."

"She hardly talks to me."

"That's because you're not listening to her. She doesn't want a boyfriend right now and you keep asking her out on dates."

"Nothing b-big. Just movies or out to eat." Silas had been home from Washington almost a month, and although Nancy was impressed with his determination, she worried he was driving Celia away.

Nancy looked at him like he was a silly child. "Those are dates."

"I wish you'd never told me."

Nancy sighed. How different would Silas and Celia's relationship be if Nancy had minded her own business? She tried to reassure herself that she had acted out of love and concern for her nephew, but she couldn't completely convince herself that there hadn't been a little bit of meddling old woman involved. "So do I. I didn't know she was planning to tell you, and I didn't want her to try to trick you. I was wrong and I'm sorry. But maybe it was for the best."

Silas looked disgusted. "It wasn't for the b-best." He turned away. "I like her. A lot. I don't care if she's p-pregnant. She's still Celia." His voice got softer. "And I want her back."

"I know you do. And she might like you back, but she's got a lot to work out, and she needs us to let her do that." When Silas began to walk away, Nancy caught his arm. "Be her friend. That's what she needs."

"Yeah, but I wanted to be m-more than friends."

"Right now it isn't about you. It's not even about Celia. It's about that baby, and we need to be her friends and support her. So stop being moody and stop asking her on dates. Maybe after she has the baby, she'll be ready to date again, and if you haven't scared her off, maybe she'll even go out with you."

Nancy smiled and gave Silas a maternal side hug.

"How can I be her friend if she's avoiding m-me?"

"Oh, Silas. You're a smart boy. I'm sure you can figure that out how to be her friend."

Most of Main Street and the two streets that ran parallel to it were closed off, and thousands of people milled about admiring quilts, eating good food, and socializing. Under tents at the park and in The Stitchin' Station's parking lot, teachers taught interested visitors about quilting, fabric selection, and the latest tools of the trade.

Celia paused to admire a cluster of quilts hanging from branches. The display, "A Handmade Forest," featured long, thin quilts that interpreted trees. One had pink, three-dimensional flowers and reminded Celia of dogwood trees she'd seen as a child.

"Hey, Celia." Lacy practically bumped into Celia before she realized who it was.

"Hi. Out enjoying the show?"

"I come every year. Looking at all this gorgeous handiwork is the closest I'll ever get to being crafty."

"You live here and you don't quilt?"

Lacy waved her off. "I know. There's probably a law against it. Have you taken up our community pastime?"

"I don't know how good I am, but I've made three quilt blocks." Celia was being modest. Nancy had said Celia's stitching looked better than some of the women who had been coming to The Stitchin' Station classes for years.

"You're already ahead of me. Didn't you have an ultrasound while I was on vacation?"

"I did."

"And?" Lacy stretched out the word and rubbed her hands together excitedly.

"Didn't Dr. Vernon tell you?"

"No." Lacy put on her best innocent voice.

Celia stepped around a quilt to get a look at the back. "It's a boy."

"Oh." Lacy made the word three sing-song syllables. "How exciting." They moved together down the row of quilts, stopping to admire them as they talked.

"Dr. Vernon called him 'the little thinker.' Said it looks like he'll be an Einstein or something."

"That'll be a perk when it's time to do his homework." Lacy stopped, and her voice became serious. "Oh. Sorry. Have you decided what you're going to do?"

Celia lifted a bright orange and green quilt and examined the intricate stitching. "I'm going to find a family for him."

Lacy gently rested her hand on Celia's arm. "I'm sure it's such a hard thing." Celia nodded. "If I can do anything for you, let me know. I mean, I'm great at listening, so if you need to talk . . . " Her uncomfortable laugh made Celia smile a little. It was hard to believe this was the same woman who had been unfriendly and difficult at her first doctor's appointment.

"Thank you. I want him to have a happy life and a good dad. I can't give him that."

"It's such an unselfish thing to do."

Celia didn't want to talk about unselfishness or hard things or the shortcomings of her own life. "It's all so overwhelming. Sometimes the only way I can get through it is to not think about it, but thank you." Eager to change the subject, she moved to the next quilt. "I can't even believe the work in some of these."

Celia was thankful when Lacy welcomed the new subject. "I know. Who would even think about making an entire quilt of dogs?"

Nancy still slept when Celia quietly slipped out to walk to church. Saturday had been a busy day for Nancy and she would be putting in many more hours as the quilt show wrapped up tonight, so she deserved to sleep in.

Celia was surprised how many people were already out, probably to beat the elevated temperatures that had been forecast. Despite the early hour, the cool night air had already surrendered to a stifling heat, and she welcomed the air-conditioned chapel. Some of the out-of-town guests must have decided to attend church, because the pews were nearly full, and it was still five minutes until the services were to begin.

Celia smiled at a few of the people she had met in the last few months as she chose a seat. She was grateful for the friendly faces. She had wondered how people would react to her when she began to show. Would they judge her and look at her with disgust? She needn't have worried. Whether it was the minister's mindfulness or God's kindness, she wasn't sure, but the last time she had attended services, the sermon had been on not judging others.

"Some of our sins and weaknesses are obvious to those around us, and it's easy to point fingers," the minister had said. "But for many of us, we carry our sins and burdens privately, secretly. There's only one thing that makes the visible sin worse than the secret sin, and that is that it sometimes causes others to give in to the temptation to point and scrutinize and judge. Let's each worry about ourselves. And when it comes to the misdeeds of others, let us simply do as the scriptures tell us. Love our neighbor. Serve each other. Forgive. Let's leave the judgments to God."

Celia had been grateful for the message.

Now, more than ever, she needed the peace she felt when she walked through the doors of the church. Ever since her ultrasound, she had felt like a woman on a medieval torture rack, painfully pulled and stretched in different directions. From the time she had discovered she was pregnant, she had known she would give the baby to a family who could provide a better life. The inconvenience and discomfort of her condition were difficult, but they would end, and she would get back to being the person she had been before this had happened to her.

Then she had felt the first flutter of life inside her, and days later, she had seen the tiny boy on the screen, his heart beating, his hand on his chin, as if he were thinking, pondering what the future would hold for him.

And she loved him. For the first time, she realized that even after he was gone from her life, she would never be the same. There would always be a piece of her heart that belonged to him. Celia thought of herself as a fighter. She had survived the uppercut of her father's abandonment and the left hook of her mother's neglect. She'd been knocked down time after time, but this might be too much. Would giving up this baby be the sucker punch that put her down for the count? Would she ever truly recover?

The stained glass depiction of Jesus in the Garden of Gethsemane blurred, and Celia blinked hard, clearing her vision. The organist stretched out the last note of the prelude, and as the minister stood to welcome the congregation, Silas slipped in and sat beside Celia. He gave her a quick smile then focused his attention to the front of the chapel.

Silas hadn't joined her at church since before he'd gone

firefighting, and Celia wondered about his motives. He had been asking her out ever since he had returned from Washington, and while it had been flattering at first, she was determined to keep him at arm's length. Circumstances outside her control had inflicted too much pain on her heart already. She didn't need to willingly subject it to more.

Celia recited in her mind the way she would refuse an invitation to get lunch or go for a drive, something polite but firm. Halfway through the service, she realized she was thinking more about how to handle her rejection of Silas than she was of the spiritual message being shared. She focused on the man standing in front instead of the man sitting beside her.

When the meeting ended, Celia braced herself as Silas turned to her.

"I'm going to B-Bend, but if you need a ride home, I can drop you off before I go."

No invitation, just an offer of a ride. No need to have worried.

"Oh. Thanks." Celia thought about declining, but it was so hot today. "If you've got time, that would be great."

He didn't say much as he drove her home, just a casual comment about the quilt show and how Aunt Nancy needed to slow down a bit.

After he dropped her off, Celia watched from the porch as the Jeep stopped at the corner before it turned toward Bend. Instead of feeling the calm she usually felt after church, she felt restless and agitated.

Chapter 38

"Have you registered on the website yet?" Mr. Walker asked.

Celia sat in the plush offices of Walker and Labrum Law. "Your secretary helped me set that up last week."

"Good. Have you had a chance to check out some of the families?"

"I've looked through some of them." Celia didn't tell him she had spent hours looking at pictures and reading biographies and letters of recommendation. There were hundreds of hopeful couples who wanted to adopt. Some were childless, some had one child and didn't want their little boy or girl to be raised without siblings. It was daunting. She had the power to make these people's dreams come true, but more important than that, she wanted to be sure she found the best situation for her baby boy. A good life was the last thing she could give him, and she was terrified she would fail.

Mr. Walker saw Celia's expression, and his tone became appeasing. "I know it feels like a lot to take in."

"What if I can't choose?" It was a question Celia had been

asking ever since she opened the file of the first couple. They had been an attractive couple from Roseburg, but the first thing Celia had noticed was that the mother's eyes were too close together. She knew that didn't matter. She sounded like a lovely woman—she baked and played piano and volunteered at a homeless shelter—but all Celia could see when she looked at their pictures were the woman's eyes.

"Be patient. Most birth mothers say when they find the right couple, they know right away. So don't be rushed. Keep looking until it feels right."

When Celia left his office, Mr. Walker handed her a pamphlet. "I know it's a long drive, but there's a birth mothers support group that meets in Eugene two afternoons a month. You might find it helpful to hear from other mothers who have gone through this or are going through it."

Celia was disappointed. "Eugene is so far."

"I know. We tried to have one here, but there were times we'd only have one or two women show up. It might be worth it to go once or twice."

"Are you kidding me?" A red-haired woman in running clothes with an even redder-haired child that looked too old for the stroller he was strapped into stood by the boxes that had held the day's tomatoes. "One stinking tomato left?"

The child cried and pulled on the straps that held him in, trying to escape the confines of the seat.

"Shhh," the mother scolded.

"Cookie. I want a cookie."

"I told you no cookies. Too much sugar."

"Dad gives me cookies."

"Which is probably why you're acting like this."

Celia reached under the table to see if there were any tomatoes left. She pulled out the empty basket and held it up. "I'm afraid that's our last tomato."

"Get me a cookie!" the child screamed.

The woman ignored her child and raised her voice to be heard over his fit. "You need to bring more tomatoes. This is the second time in the last month that you've been sold out before I could get here."

It had been a busy day at the market with customers coming in a steady procession. Celia's feet hurt and her head ached. She was hungry and tired and still had to load up the truck, tear down the tables and tent, and drive thirty minutes before she would get to eat. She took a deep breath and let it out slowly before she responded to the woman.

"I brought every single ripe tomato this morning. I didn't even leave any home for my own dinner. I wish you had come even a few minutes earlier."

"Yeah, well, when you have to wait around for your ex to bring your kid back, there's not a lot you can do."

"Give. Me. A. Cookie!" The child's shriek hit a nerve in Celia's ear that actually hurt, and it was difficult not to cover her ears with her hands. Celia held back a smile when she thought how angry that gesture would make the woman.

"I came all the way down here for your tomatoes."

"Someone else might have some left."

"COOKIE!"

The woman turned the stroller and started away, her long shadow stretching out twenty feet behind her in the evening sun. A few feet from the stand, she turned and spoke to Celia over her shoulder. "I'd suggest next year you plant more tomatoes."

Celia sighed and looked at her watch, glad it was almost time to go.

"I wonder why her husband is an ex?" Celia muttered and was startled when someone behind her laughed. She turned to see Silas standing outside the tent. What was he doing here?

"You heard that?" Celia asked.

"Some p-people are so rude."

"Everyone else today has been really nice." She stretched her back. "What are you doing here, anyway?"

"The Jeep needed an oil change so I thought I'd swing b-by and help you load up."

Overcome with gratitude, Celia turned away and busied herself in the back of the booth, stacking boxes. She knew he could have taken his Jeep to Carter's Garage in Sisters.

She stopped working when Silas put his hand on her arm. "You look tired."

"I am tired."

"You sit down. I'll do this."

"I can help you."

Silas put his arm around her shoulder and guided her to the camp chair she had almost forgotten she had. "Sit down."

Celia sat and watched while Silas loaded the mostly empty boxes into the back of Nancy's old, rickety pickup.

"Is this getting to be too much?" he asked while he put the legs down on one of the folding tables.

"There are only three more weeks before the market closes down. I'll be fine."

It was hard for Celia to believe that September was half over. She had lived in Sisters longer than she had lived in two of her foster homes. It didn't seem possible she had been here this long, but when she looked at how much her midsection had grown, she knew it was true.

When all that was left to pack up was the tent and the camp chair, Celia stood to help. "The tent is easier with two people."

"You do it yourself every time though, right?"

Celia shrugged. "Usually, but it's easier with two." She and Silas each took a corner and untied the canopy. Together they folded the tent and took apart the poles.

"There you go," Silas said when the last of the booth had been stowed in the truck.

Celia hesitated. She wanted to show her appreciation but wasn't sure how to do that without misleading him. Guilt won out. "If you haven't eaten, you should come over. Nancy said she'd have dinner ready when I got home and I'm sure there's enough for you too."

"M-maybe another time. I'm not going b-back to Sisters yet."

"Okay. Another time then."

Celia sat in the front of the pickup and watched Silas walk across the park to his Jeep. He was the best kind of man, and a longing for him wound its way around her heart.

Celia folded and unfolded the pamphlet in her hand. For the past couple of weeks she had felt a growing urgency to go to the birth mothers support group. She'd put aside the idea because of the two-and-a-half-hour drive to Eugene, but after she had nearly thrown the laptop across the room in frustration earlier in the day, she knew she needed to talk to other women who understood what she was going through.

Now she had to figure out how to get there.

"Silas, would you turn that up a little?" Nancy asked.

Hindsight, a television news program, had filmed a spot on the Sisters Outdoor Quilt Show and they were airing it tonight.

Silas turned up the volume and together they watched as the reporter interviewed the mayor and Val.

"I look terrible. Why didn't anyone tell me that shirt makes me look fat?" Nancy could be seen in the background cutting fabric while Val was interviewed.

"You look great," Celia said.

"The camera adds ten p-pounds," Silas added.

"Looks more like fifty," Nancy muttered under her breath.

The piece ended with a banjo playing a lively tune while they showed a montage of the most impressive quilts.

"That wasn't too bad," Nancy said when the piece was over.

Silas turned off the television. "It was great."

Nancy turned to Celia. "What have you got there? You're going to wear that paper right out?"

Celia smoothed out the pamphlet. "It's about a support group Mr. Walker told me about. For birth mothers."

"What a good idea? Are you going?"

Celia lifted one shoulder. "I really want to. But it's in Eugene."

"That's a ways away." Nancy saw Celia's face and added. "But you could take my car. When is it?"

"Tomorrow afternoon."

"Shoot. I have a doctor's appointment tomorrow."

Celia bit the side of her lip and asked, "Do you think I could take the pickup?"

"Oh dear, I don't know if that's a good idea. That old

thing might not even make it to Eugene."

"You can take the Jeep." Surprised, Celia and Nancy looked at Silas. "It'll just be p-parked at work anyway."

"Maybe you could take the afternoon off and drive her there," Nancy said. "I worry about her driving that far alone." Before she had even finished the sentence, Silas was shaking his head.

"I can't. B-but she can take it."

Celia refused to admit she was a little disappointed he'd rejected Nancy's idea so quickly.

"Can you drive m-me to work in the morning?" Silas asked.

"Of course."

Nancy still looked concerned, but Celia pretended not to notice. She didn't want anything to change Silas's mind.

Chapter 39

Celia turned onto Sycamore Street and craned her neck, looking for the building number. With a baby growing inside her, how was there even room for the monster-sized pit she felt in her stomach? The only thing that kept her moving toward the support group meeting was the knowledge that Silas and Nancy would be asking about it and she didn't want to admit she had chickened out, or worse, lie to them about it. Especially since Silas had trusted her with his Jeep.

The building was dark gray stone and looked gothic and forbidding, the kind of place you might imagine women going to sacrifice their babies to the screaming gargoyles. Celia chastised herself for letting her imagination get carried away.

Eleven women looked toward the door as Celia entered. One stood and took a few steps forward to greet her, while a few others expanded the circle and pulled in another chair.

"We're just getting started, so you haven't missed a thing." The woman who appeared to be in charge, shook Celia's hand then motioned toward the spare chair. "We were going to introduce ourselves. You can share as much or as little as you want. My name is Yvonne and I'm a social worker.

I love working with you birth mothers because I was a birth mother myself, so I understand. I was sixteen when I placed my baby. He's twenty-seven now and has a baby of his own. Why don't you go next, Jackie?" She touched the leg of the woman sitting to her left.

Jackie had a short, dark afro and was thin as a twig, except for a belly that looked like she might deliver today, right here in this room. "I'm Jackie and I'm thirty-nine weeks along. I been coming here for almost six months now. I'm giving this here girl to a couple that lives in Phoenix. I hope she likes the desert so she won't hate me."

"I've been to Phoenix. Your little girl is going to love it," said a blond woman sitting beside Celia.

"Fiona?" the social worker said to a tiny girl with short, brown hair.

"I'm Fiona. I'm seventeen. I'm twenty-two weeks along, and last week I found out I'm having a little boy. I haven't picked a family yet."

The next woman didn't wait for a prompt. Except for the social worker, she looked like the oldest woman in the room. "I'm Andee and I'm due on Christmas day. Merry Christmas to me." Celia was shocked at her bitter tone. "My soon-to-be ex-husband thought he could coerce me into staying married by getting me pregnant, but he was wrong. I can't stand him, and there's no way I'm keeping his child. I'd have had an abortion, but I could practically hear my mother threatening me from the grave if I did. So here I am. Waiting to send this baby to its new home in Colorado so I can get back to my life."

The woman folded her arms across her chest and glared at the next woman.

Celia listened with interest to each of the women's stories. They were all so different—different ages, backgrounds and feelings. When it was her turn, she took a deep breath and reminded herself of the promise she had made as she drove to Eugene. No matter what, she would be completely honest.

"My name is Celia. I'll be twenty-one next month."

"Happy birthday, girl," Jackie said.

Celia smiled at her. "Thank you. My baby is due the eleventh of December. I'm pregnant because I was raped."

A couple of women gasped and Yvonne put up her hand to quiet them.

"I haven't chosen a family yet. It's like I'm so afraid I'm going to make a mistake, it paralyzes me." A few women nodded their understanding. "But I want him to have the very best."

After the introductions, the women talked for almost two hours. They passed around the tissue boxes several times, and by the time the meeting ended, Celia felt a kinship with most of the women.

"I'm glad you came," Yvonne said at the drinking fountain after the meeting.

"Me too. I didn't know if it would be worth the drive, but it totally was. I feel better, like I'm not so different from the others."

"Sometimes it feels like no one can understand, like we're the only one on earth who feels like we do, but we're not. All of us feel scared and lonely and we wonder if we're doing the right thing. Even Andee. It's good to talk to each other, so we know that."

Celia smiled and nodded. "I needed to hear that others have had a hard time choosing families. I've felt so stuck. Every time I look at potential parents, I think I might throw up. I don't want to make a mistake."

"And you won't." When a man stepped up to the drinking fountain, Yvonne took Celia's arm and led her a few feet away. "Even though you're giving your baby up, you still have a mother's intuition. You'll study the options, and when all is said and done, you'll pick the right family for your baby."

It was dark when Celia drove the Jeep down the lane to Silas's house. The porch light created a wide, yellow circle that almost reached the driveway, and she could see a light from somewhere inside.

"Thank you," she said when Silas opened the door. "That was exactly what I needed."

"Worth the drive?" he asked.

"So worth it. I can't tell you how grateful I am you let me take your car."

"You're welcome. Did you stop for ice cream?"

"Stop where?" Celia asked innocently.

Silas smiled and shook his head. "You think I can't say it?" The next words were slow, and although his lips pursed tightly, he managed to say them without stuttering. "Prince Puckler's. I'm glad you didn't stop. You don't deserve any ice cream."

Celia grinned. "But you do. If it wouldn't have melted, I'd have stopped and picked up some strawberry ice cream for you."

"Oh well. It's the thought that—"

"Whoa," Celia interrupted him and put her hand on the side of her stomach. "Sorry. I think he just scored a goal."

"That's crazy. You can really feel that?"

"Yeah. Here." Without overthinking it, Celia placed

Silas's hand where hers had been. They waited, his hand warm, her hand over his. She ignored her own surprise that she had been so forward.

"I guess the game's over," he said quietly.

"He's messing with us," Celia said. She was about to let his hand go, when the baby kicked again. "There. Did you feel that?"

"That's the b-baby?"

Celia laughed. "I'm not kicking myself."

"Wow. That's amazing."

When the baby didn't kick again, Silas pulled away his hand, and Celia took an awkward step back.

"Thanks again. I really appreciate it."

"I can walk you home."

Celia stepped off the porch and out of the circle of light. "It's not far. I'm fine."

Silas followed her to the lane. "I'll stand here and watch. M-make sure there are no b-bad guys."

When she reached Nancy's house, she looked back down the lane. Silas's white t-shirt glowed in the moonlight. He waved and she lifted her hand in answer before she went inside.

Chapter 40

"What's for lunch?" Silas asked as he came through Nancy's back door.

"Since you've only got an hour, I thought I'd make ham and cheese sandwiches."

"Sounds good." Silas opened the refrigerator and poured himself a glass of orange juice.

"Sit down while I fix these," Nancy said. "And start talking. You've had me worried ever since you called last night."

"I told you not to worry. I just wanted to talk to m-my dear old aunt." Silas squeezed her shoulder, and she swatted off his hand.

"Old? And you want me to fix lunch for you?"

"I'm hungry, b-but this isn't about the food."

Nancy leaned against the counter and studied her nephew's face. "What is it about?"

"The garden."

Nancy looked skeptical. "The garden?"

"Isn't it about time to tear it out? Rototill?"

"Yes."

"I'm sure Celia will be stubborn about doing it. You know. For the rent. B-but I don't think she should."

"I don't either. That's why I haven't said anything to her about it being time. I was thinking I might hire Frank and his son to do it after they finish their garden."

"I'll do it."

"It's not a big deal to hire them. You already work more than forty hours a week."

"I want to."

Nancy shot him a teasing smile. "Trying to impress her?"

Silas grinned. "Think it will work?"

"Maybe. But I wouldn't count on it. She hasn't given you much encouragement even though you've been wooing her pretty hard."

"I haven't b-been wooing. I'm being her friend. Like you told m-me to. And a friend wouldn't want his pregnant friend to hurt herself tearing up the garden."

"No, I guess a friend wouldn't." Nancy put the sandwiches and a bag of chips on the table and sat down across from him.

"Thanks." Silas took a bite.

Nancy's teasing changed, and her voice became serious. "What if you do all this and then she leaves?"

Silas swallowed. "What if I don't do all this and she stays?"

Nancy chuckled. "I don't want you to get hurt."

"It's too late for that."

A couple of minutes passed before Nancy said, "Has she told you about the baby's father?"

A pained expression passed over Silas's face. "No. Has she told you?"

"I know a few things."

Silas leaned forward. "What? If there's something I need to know, tell me."

Nancy shook her head and her face looked sad. "Silas, there are some things that aren't mine to share. This is Celia's to tell. Maybe you should ask her." She took a sip of water. "Or maybe you should wait for her to bring it up." Nancy slapped the table with her hand. "I don't know what you should do, and if there's one thing I learned when I told you she was pregnant, it was that I need to keep my meddling old nose out of things."

"Old?"

Nancy smiled. "I love you, Silas."

"I love you too."

Celia was still in bed when she heard the shed door slam shut. Nancy had gone for a walk with Inez, so who was out there?

She couldn't see anything through the bedroom window, so she quickly dressed and headed to the back yard. Silas was bent over pulling up plants and throwing them in the wheelbarrow.

"What are you doing?" she called as she walked toward him.

He straightened and watched her approach. When she was close enough that he could respond without shouting, he answered. "I'm taking out the garden."

"Is it time for that? Nancy hasn't said anything."

"It's time." He leaned over and pulled out another

cucumber plant.

"I should be doing this."

"No, you shouldn't."

He smiled when Celia put her hands on her hips. "It's my job. And what are you smiling about?"

"You look cute."

Celia looked down at her large belly. "Don't be ridiculous. I don't look cute. I look huge. And don't change the subject. I'm supposed to take care of the garden."

"Not today, you aren't." He moved the wheelbarrow down the row a few feet. "And yes, you look cute."

"Stop it, Silas." Silas stopped and looked at her. "I need to do my job."

"Look at you." He pointed at the baby.

"So?"

"I'm doing this. Don't fight me."

"Let me at least help." Celia leaned over and pulled on a tomato plant. It didn't come up so she put her hands closer to the ground and pulled again, grunting with the exertion. Silas watched for a few seconds then put his hand out to stop her.

"You really want to help?"

"Yes."

"I'm hungry and I've been wanting a salmon hash omelet from M-McKay's for weeks. Take the Jeep and go get us some food. When you get back, we'll eat and then you can help me."

"You promise you'll save some work for me?"

"There's no way I'll be finished when you get back." Silas fished in his pockets and handed her the keys to the Jeep and two twenty-dollar bills.

"I should be paying for this," Celia said, halfheartedly.

"You can p-pay next time."

Silas watched her walk back into the house before he returned to pulling up plants.

"Look at the snow up there." Silas pointed out the windshield at the Three Sisters Peaks. The top fourth of the mountains glowed white with snow that had fallen overnight.

"I was wondering what snowfall the minister was talking about," Celia said. "It's beautiful."

"I told Adam I'd drive out to B-Broken Top and make sure the trailhead is closed."

"Is that very far?" A drive sounded nice, but Celia didn't want to invite herself along.

"Not too far."

"Will there be snow there?"

"P-probably. We need it closed b-before anyone gets trapped out there in the bad weather."

"I'll bet it's pretty." Why didn't he invite her?

"Yeah. The forest looks great after a snowfall. Like Christmas." Silas pulled the truck into Nancy's driveway. "I'll see you later."

Celia smiled to hide her disappointment. It was better not to waste the day in the mountains anyway. She needed to find a home for her baby and this afternoon would be a good time to sort through files.

A few hours later, Celia was looking at pictures of a couple from San Diego when she heard the Jeep. She pretended she didn't notice when it stopped in Nancy's driveway instead of continuing down the lane. She heard the back door open and voices as Nancy and Silas visited in the kitchen.

A short time later, Silas leaned his head into the room. "Dinner's ready."

Celia closed the laptop. "Are you eating with us?"

"She made b-beef stew, so I'm not going anywhere."

"What did you two do all afternoon?" Silas asked as he buttered a biscuit.

"I worked until two," Nancy said.

"I've been wasting my time looking at adoptive parents."

"Still can't find any you like?" Nancy asked.

"I like a few of them. But I don't know who would be the best parents for him." Instinctively, she laid a protective hand on her stomach. "It's so confusing."

"Do you want some help?" Silas sounded tentative.

"This is probably something she wants to do alone," Nancy said and patted Celia's arm.

"Actually, I think it would be nice to get another opinion or two."

"Really?" Nancy sounded excited. "I would have offered a long time ago, but I thought I'd be intruding.

"We could come up with a system to help narrow it down," Silas said.

"Of course, you'd have the final say," Nancy added.

After dinner, they cleared the table and pulled three chairs up to one side. Nancy and Silas sat on either side of her while Celia pulled up the website.

"So three yesses means we put them in the saved file," Celia said.

"Let's look until we have ten keepers." Nancy shook her hands out.

A picture of a couple standing in front of a lake came up on the screen. "Jan and Paul," Celia read.

Nancy read as she scanned the page. "From Corpus Christi, Texas. He flies helicopters to the oil rigs and she's a librarian at a middle school."

"Flying helicopters sounds dangerous," Celia said. "I don't think I like that."

"So is that a no?" Silas asked.

"That's a no."

Celia pulled up the next couple, and they began to scan the page. "Dave and Kathy, from Seattle. Is Seattle a nice place?" Celia asked. After Silas and Nancy assured her Seattle was a great city, they continued reading. "She designs jewelry and he's a school teacher. I like that."

Nancy tipped her head so she could read better through her glasses. "They enjoy backpacking, reading and fishing. Uh oh. They don't believe in God."

"They don't?" Celia asked, and Nancy pointed at the line that asked about their religion and spirituality.

"That's too b-bad," Silas said. "I was liking them."

"Is that a deal breaker?" Nancy looked at Celia who nodded and moved on to the next couple.

"Jim and Denise, from Twin Falls, Idaho. Oh look, they have a four-year-old girl."

"She's a cutie," Nancy said.

Silas ran his finger down the side of the computer as he read the bio. "He's a manager at a department store and she's a p-part-time nurse and full-time m-mom."

"They like to cook together. I like that." They finished reading then scrolled through several pictures. Celia leaned back in her chair.

"I like them," Nancy said and Silas agreed. They both looked at Celia.

"They're okay, I guess."

"Great. One in the save file."

They continued searching the files, but after an hour, they hadn't agreed on any more.

"Ron and Vicki," Celia read.

"From Naperville, Illinois," Nancy continued.

"They're a no." Celia exited out of the file without reading any further.

"Why?" Silas asked.

"That's too close to Chicago."

No one spoke until Celia had pulled up the next couple. "Randy and Diane. They're from Henderson, Nevada." Celia closed the laptop and slid back her chair. "Do you mind if we stop? I'm really tired, and at this rate we won't have ten until sometime tomorrow."

"I can see why this is exhausting." Nancy removed her glasses and rubbed the bridge of her nose.

"So Jim and Denise are the only couple to move p-past the first round of eliminations."

Celia smiled. "At least we sorta liked one couple. I didn't find any I wanted to move on when I was looking alone."

"We can help again. If you want," Silas said.

Celia's voice was weary. "That'd be great."

Chapter 41

"Happy Halloween, your majesty," Val said as she bowed low and rolled one arm with a flourish. Unfortunately, the low bow caused her witch's hat to fall to the floor.

"Taking advantage of my gray hair." Nancy straightened the wide-brimmed, pale blue hat that perched jauntily on her head. It perfectly matched the matronly skirt and jacket she wore along with droopy pantyhose and low-heeled pumps.

"Ladies, I present the Queen of England," Val said when she and Nancy walked into classroom behind The Stitchin' Station.

"Don't worry," Nancy said. "We're good enough friends that I'm not going to call you my loyal subjects."

"Nice costume," said Sandra, who sat at a table wearing a period renaissance gown.

"You too. Did you make that?"

"It only took most of the last year." Sandra said.

Soon the nine women present were assembling quilt blocks in harvest golds and oranges. "I'll bet we'd have better attendance if we did this a day or two before Halloween. A lot of moms had to stay home and take their kids trick-or-treating. Luckily I won't have to worry about that for a few years yet." Ellie patted her pregnant belly.

"I told Alan he'd have to take care of the trick-or-treaters this year," said Val.

"Celia offered to hand out treats at my house, so I don't even have to feel guilty." Nancy walked around the group, offering Halloween treats. She caught a few of the women sharing meaningful glances and stopped. "Did I miss something?"

A couple of the women shrugged, but Sandra, who was known for her bluntness, cleared her throat. "So what's that girl's story, anyway, Nancy? Is she still dating your nephew?"

"Not at the moment."

"I could be wrong, but I don't think they were dating when she would have had to get pregnant. So it's not Silas's, is it?"

Nancy felt her normally pleasant demeanor slipping. "No, the baby's not Silas's."

"Whew." Ellie made a brow-wiping gesture. "I guess he dodged the bullet then. Why would she come here and take up with Silas anyway? She obviously had a little sumpin' sumpin' going on with someone before she got here."

Nancy felt a combination of anger at the accusations being made and shame that she had made the same assumptions. When a few of the women started discussing Celia among themselves, she put up her white-gloved hand to get their attention.

When the ladies immediately turned toward her, she gave them a playful smile. "Hmm, this queen stuff isn't so bad."

They all laughed.

"It isn't my place to share Celia's life story, but I will tell you this. If anyone in this room had been through what that girl has been through, you'd have room to judge her, but none of us have. Someday, if you're lucky enough to become her friend, she might share her story with you, but until then, you'll have to take my word for it. She's a good girl who's been dealt a pretty crappy hand, and she's come through it better than most of us would have. And if she and Silas get back together, I'd be behind them a hundred percent."

The room was quiet for a minute as the women took in Nancy's words. Finally, when it began to get awkward, Val raised her hands in the air and said, "Here, here. All hail the queen."

Celia had offered to hand out Halloween candy so Nancy could help with a Spook & Spool Quilt Club at The Stitchin' Station. In spite of the cold fall temperatures, children began ringing the doorbell a little before dark. When Celia opened the door the third time, Silas stood there holding a bowl of miniature candy bars, Winston wagging his tail beside him.

"No one lets their kids come down the lane. Do you m-mind if I give out candy here?"

Celia held the door open wide. "Is it the lane the parents are worried about? Or is it you?"

"I hope it's the lane."

Winston padded to the back porch to snuggle with Nubia while Celia rifled through his bowl. "You've got better candy bars than we do." She picked out a Butterfinger and opened it. "Did you see Nancy tonight?"

"What was she this year?"

"Queen Elizabeth. It was scary how much she looked like her."

"She dresses up as real people every Halloween. She's been Oprah, M-Madonna, some figure skater. M-make her show you pictures. Last year she was LeBron James."

Celia laughed. "Nancy was LeBron James?"

"I swear. She even had fake tattoos on her calves that said 'King James.'"

The doorbell rang and Silas handed treats to a ghost and a princess.

"Why aren't you in a costume?" Celia asked after he closed the door.

"I always dressed up as a fireman when I was a kid, and now I am one, so it's b-boring. What was your favorite costume?"

"I never really did Halloween."

Silas looked surprised. "Never?"

"I always wanted to be a princess with a beautiful sparkly dress and crown, but Mom never had money for silly things like that. One year, she made a crown out of tin foil, but it wasn't very good and I was too embarrassed to go out in it. Then when I was in foster care, I pretended like I was too old to dress up."

The doorbell rang, so Silas was spared responding to the sad story as Celia handed animal crackers to a mushroom, a little pig, and a baseball player.

By eight, the trick or treating had nearly stopped. Silas and Celia ate a few treats and worked on the puzzle of Saint Basil's Cathedral Nancy had started a few days earlier. Celia thought back to the first time they had worked on a puzzle at this table, days after she had arrived in Sisters. She hadn't even known she was pregnant then. Silas had been distant and shy. Even though she was disappointed with how he had treated her in the summer, she was grateful for the kind friend he had become.

The last few weeks of farmers markets he had shown up every evening to help her pack up. He sat by her nearly every week at church. And then there was the garden. She would have been out there forever trying to pull all those plants out.

"What are you thinking about?" Silas asked.

She didn't want to admit she had been thinking about him. "How nice everyone in Sisters has been. You're lucky to have grown up here."

A shadow passed over his face. "It isn't all p-perfect."

She knew Silas had had plenty of disappointments here. Celia softly touched his arm. "I know. No place is perfect."

Silas looked at her hand and she pulled it back. "Celia?" She loved how he always said her name so carefully, like it was a word too important to mess up. "Are you going b-back?"

"To Chicago?"

"To him."

Celia looked confused. "To who?"

Silas inclined his head toward the baby. "His dad."

Stunned, Celia slid her chair away from the table. "What are you talking about?"

Silas looked bewildered, like suddenly the conversation was being spoken in a foreign language and he didn't understand what was being said. "I . . . I . . . I thought m-maybe since you didn't want to go out with m-m-me again, that you might b-be going back to him."

Celia let his words settle into her mind for several seconds. Could he really not know?

"I thought Nancy told you."

"Told m-me what?"

"Silas, I was raped."

Silas looked like someone had hit him with a baseball bat.

"I'm sorry. I didn't know," he finally said. "Aunt Nancy said you would tell m-me what you wanted me to know."

The doorbell rang and Silas sprang up to answer it. After he had given candy to four teenagers dressed as ninja turtles, he closed the door and leaned against it, the bowl of candy hugged against him, his gaze on Celia. "I took the job in Washington b-because I thought you were p-pregnant with an ex's b-baby. I thought you were keeping secrets from me and it about killed m-me. I knew if I saw you, I'd want to stay even if there was an ex. When I got b-back and found out you were going to tell m-me, I wanted to fight for you." Silas laughed bitterly. "I thought I was fighting someone you had loved. I didn't know. I'm s-s-sorry." His stuttering told her how flustered he was.

Celia stood and took the bowl of candy from his arms and put it on the entry table. "I saw you leave. I was walking home from church and I saw the Jeep coming down the lane. I was so excited you were home. I started running to meet you and you turned the other way and left. Nancy told me later that day that you had left for Washington. I hadn't seen you for three weeks, and you didn't even come to say goodbye."

Silas took Celia's hands in his. "I didn't see you."

Celia linked her fingers with his. "I decided while you were gone that I couldn't let you break my heart. I've been disappointed so many times and I have to gear myself up for probably the worst heartbreak of my life when I give up this baby. If I let you break my heart, too, I might never recover."

Silas slowly lowered his head toward Celia. When she didn't turn away, he kissed her gently. His hand came up and touched her cheek. "I'm not going to break your heart."

"Please don't say that unless you're sure."

Silas kissed her again, as if he were trying to make up for the last four kiss-less months. "I'm sure," he said against her neck.

Celia tried to pull him closer but when the baby bumped up against Silas's stomach, they both started laughing. "I guess we have a chaperone."

"He can't stop me from this," Silas said and kissed her again.

Chapter 42

Wind whistled through the attic and rattled the back screen door.

"Sounds like winter's here," Nancy said as she handed Celia the last of the dinner dishes.

Celia finished loading the dishwasher and started it before coming to the table.

The front door blew closed with a bang and Silas came into the kitchen. "The swing is now in the shed."

Nancy placed the laptop on the table. "No more banging against the rail. Thank you, Silas."

"Shall we get started?" Silas asked.

Celia reluctantly sat down, and Silas and Nancy followed.

"Is there still only one saved in the potentials file?" Nancy asked.

Celia clicked open the folder and Jim and Denise from Twin Falls smiled back at them. "Yep. They're still the frontrunners."

Silas put his arm on the back of Celia's chair and let his fingers graze her neck. "Let's see if we can add one or two m-more tonight."

They worked through three couples from California, two from Arizona, and potential parents from Arkansas, Iowa, and Montana. Celia found a problem with each of them.

"They look nice," Nancy said when she opened the file for Damien and Amanda, from Knoxville, Tennessee.

"I don't think so," Celia said too quickly, and exited out of their file.

"Why not?" Nancy's voice held a hint of impatience. "We hardly saw them."

"I don't like their names."

"You're fast. I didn't even have time to see their names. What were they?"

Celia shook her head. "He had the same name as . . . " Her voice trailed off.

"Oh. Of course. Let's move on," Nancy said, and Silas leaned over and gently kissed her temple.

Celia opened the next folder and they studied it quietly for a few seconds.

"She looks a little like you," Silas said, looking at a picture of Kate and Matthew.

"She does. She has your eyes," Nancy agreed. "And her hair is the same color as yours."

It was true. Even Celia could see the similarities. She began reading their information. "Hershey, Pennsylvania. I like chocolate." She smiled, eager to put the awkwardness caused by the last couple behind them. "Oh look, he even works for the Hershey Company. She owns a daycare center. I don't know. Would he be competing for her time?"

"Keep going." Silas's voice was gentle. "Don't count her out b-because she's good with kids."

Celia continued. "They have a church they go to. He would have seven cousins. She plays the guitar. They sound like nice people."

They looked like they enjoyed themselves. There were pictures of them traveling and celebrating the Fourth of July. It wasn't until she saw a picture of them toasting in the New Year that she noticed a troubling trend. Maybe it was Kate's slightly glazed-over eyes that Celia had seen so many times on her own mother that caught Celia's attention. She scrolled back to the beginning of the pictures and saw them sitting at a table on a cruise, on a boat at Lake Harmony, and around a campfire. In most of the pictures, they were drinking. When Celia reached the New Year's Eve picture, she couldn't take her eyes off Kate's eyes.

Celia scooted her chair away from the table. "I need to go for a walk."

Silas and Nancy exchanged a worried glance as Celia pulled her jacket from a hook by the back door.

"I won't be gone long."

She welcomed the cold air and the stinging bite of the wind. Maybe it would help clear her head. After a block, she saw the park in the distance and started for the pavilion. Perhaps the large brick fireplace would offer a reprieve from the bitter gusts.

She was almost there when she heard Silas calling her name. She turned to see him walking quickly toward her, his arms full.

In spite of her somber mood, she laughed when he reached her. "What did you do? Strip Nancy's bed?" In his arms, he held a large, down comforter and a stocking hat.

"No. The closet. I didn't want you to freeze out here."

Celia pulled the hat low over her ears and Silas wrapped her in the blanket, then put his arm around her and guided her to one of the picnic tables in the pavilion.

Celia was grateful for the warmth. She removed one side of the blanket and put it around him, so they were cocooned inside, holding it closed with one hand and holding his hand with the other.

"What happened back there?"

Celia shook her head against his shoulder. "They looked great. I thought they might be a good option, but then I saw something in her eyes that reminded me of my mom. When they were toasting in the New Year, she looked drunk."

"Lots of p-people drink on New Year's Eve."

"They were drinking all the time. This is what scares me. In pictures and on paper, they might look great. But I don't know how often they drink or if they do drugs. They're not going to say that in an adoption package that's meant to make me choose them. How often do they fight? Does one of them have a gambling problem? Are they trying to save their marriage by adopting a baby? Will they yell at him if he has trouble with math? Will they take him places or will he always be with a babysitter?"

Hot tears burned Celia's cold cheeks.

"I'm afraid I'm going to miss something and make a mistake."

Silas shifted and straddled the bench, pulling her into his arms, the blanket still around them. "I don't know what to do to help."

Celia shrugged. "I don't want to let him down."

Silas ran his hand up and down her back until she stopped crying. "Would you like to go b-back to the support group?"

"I wish it wasn't so far away."

"When is the next meeting?"

"Next Thursday." Celia wiped her eyes on her sleeve.

"How about I take the day off and I'll drive you there. Then we can get some dinner."

"I don't want to make you miss work."

"Stop it. I'd rather b-be with you."

Silas's lips felt hot when they met hers and she felt a cozy warmth spread through her. She couldn't remember a time someone had put her first. Drugs had been her mother's top priority. Who knows about her dad? Celia had been a means to a check for most of her foster families. Even the Hundleys, who had shown her the most love, had chosen a job over her.

But Silas recognized that she needed support he couldn't give her, and he was willing to sacrifice to be sure she got it.

She held tightly to his jacket and kissed him back, praying he wouldn't let her down.

A light snow fell as they drove out of Sisters toward Eugene, and Silas was glad he was driving Celia to her meeting.

"Is it supposed to snow very much? Should we be staying home?"

"This is a Jeep. We'll be fine."

"I don't want us to get stranded."

"We won't. You need this m-meeting."

Silas knew Celia needed to make some decisions. The baby was due in five weeks and it seemed the closer that day got, the harder the choices became.

"Besides, I want to eat at Fisherman's."

"Should I come with you?" Silas asked when he pulled up to the curb in front of the gray stone building.

"It's just the birth mothers. There weren't any other people there last time. Sorry you have to kill two hours."

"Don't worry. I have things I can do."

Silas watched Celia walk from the car to the doors. He wished he could make things easy for her. He wanted to lighten the burdens she carried, to ease the worry lines that creased her forehead when she thought no one was looking.

He didn't have anywhere to go, so he drove around the college campus. The trees had shed their leaves and the bare branches looked bleak against the white sky. Despite the cold weather, students stood outside some of the buildings, laughing and talking. It surprised him to realize Celia was the same age as these women. She could have been at a college, socializing and flirting, if she'd been given the chance. If her mother's poor choices hadn't robbed her of opportunities and if some drunken loser hadn't hurt her. Anger welled up in him. Why had no one protected her?

He drove away from the campus and toward a shopping area. He nearly drove into a department store parking lot, when he noticed a bookstore. That would be an easy place to kill an hour and a half.

He walked up and down the aisles looking for something that interested him. He stopped when he reached the parenting shelves. He read the back of a few of them then took two to an overstuffed chair near the coffee shop in the corner. For the next two hours he read about pregnancy and childbirth and a guide for new fathers.

Celia stood by the window, watching for Silas's Jeep. He was almost thirty minutes late.

"Do you need a ride somewhere?" Yvonne stepped up beside her, pulling on her gloves.

"My friend is picking me up. He should be here any minute."

The two women stood together, looking out at the black and white afternoon. "I didn't know if we'd see you again before you have your baby."

Cold air blew into the lobby as someone entered the building. "I needed to come," Celia said, rubbing her arms. "I've been so confused lately."

"There are no easy choices when you find yourself in this situation."

"I didn't know I'd care so much about what happens to him."

"Good mothers always care. Even when their child is grown and they haven't seen them for decades, they still care." Celia knew Yvonne was thinking about the boy she'd given up for adoption many years ago. "Is that your ride?" Yvonne pointed toward the street.

Silas was parked at the curb, standing by the door of the Jeep.

"Yes."

"Good luck, Celia."

Silas held the door open when she reached the Jeep. "I'm sorry I'm late. I lost track of time."

"It's really okay."

"Hungry?"

"Starving."

Chapter 43

Even though it was the day before Thanksgiving, the offices of Walker and Labrum were already decorated for Christmas. A lighted tree covered with angels sat in the corner and a garland with red and gold balls festooned the reception desk. Johnny Mathis sang "Chestnuts Roasting" softly in the background.

Silas could tell Celia was anxious. She shifted uncomfortably in her seat, her foot tapped nervously, and she gripped his hand like it was the only thing keeping her from plunging to her death.

The receptionist, a pretty blond with huge eyes and porcelain skin picked up her phone after it buzzed then smiled at Celia.

"Mr. Walker's ready to see you," she said.

"You should come with me." Celia's voice was trembling, and he didn't want her to have to face this alone.

"Is that okay?" he asked, speaking to both Celia and the receptionist.

"It's up to Celia," the woman said.

"I want you to."

Silas walked with Celia down a short hall and into Mr. Walker's office.

"Celia, I was beginning to wonder if we were ever going to see you again. Come in." When he turned to look at Silas, Celia introduced them.

"This is Silas. I asked him to come with me."

Mr. Walker extended his hand. "Nice to meet you, Silas." He motioned to the black leather chairs across from his chrome and wood desk and they sat down.

The first couple of minutes, they dispensed with small talk about Thanksgiving and the always busy holidays. Then Mr. Walker folded his hands on his desk and his tone became more businesslike.

"So I understand you've selected a couple."

"I think so." Celia's voice was small, and her grip on Silas's hand actually hurt, but he didn't pull away.

"Great. Let's pull up their file."

Mr. Walker entered a password into the computer on the corner of his desk then turned the screen so all three of them could see it. A few clicks later, he had the file Celia had sent him opened.

"Jim and Denise from Twin Falls, Idaho. Ah, and they already have a daughter. They look like a nice family." Celia's nod was almost imperceptible. "We've prepared some paperwork for you to sign and then we'll notify the Jacobsons that they're about to be parents. I'm sure they'll be very happy."

Mr. Walker slid a small sheaf of papers across the desk. "These are the forms we talked about when we first visited in Dr. Vernon's office. You'll need to sign each of the places we've put a sticky note. The Jacobsons may want to visit with you, but of course you have the option of how much or how little contact you wish to have."

Celia's hands shook when she picked up the papers. She scanned the pages then slid forward and placed them on the desk. Mr. Walker handed her a pen. Celia took a deep breath and held her hand over the first signature line, but she didn't begin writing her name. The pen felt heavy in her hand and her mind felt muddled and numb.

After a minute, she looked at Silas, her hand still suspended over the paper, her eyes pleading. "I don't know if I can do it."

The room was silent for several seconds while Silas looked in her eyes. When he spoke, his voice was quiet but full of resolve. "Then don't."

Celia's face was a question, and Silas leaned forward in his seat, his eyes holding hers. He took the pen from her hand and set it on the stack of papers. "I love you." Celia nodded. "I love you and I love him."

Celia nodded. "I love you too."

"M-m-maybe you should choose us to be his p-parents."

"Do you mean it?"

"Do you think you can love the baby in spite of the way he was conceived?" Mr. Walker's voice startled Silas and Celia and they both turned toward him.

"I know I can. I already do." Celia slid the papers across the desk to Mr. Walker then turned to Silas, took his face in her hands, and kissed him. "Are you sure you're okay with this?"

"I think we'll make a good family." Silas wiped away the tear that slid down Celia's cheek. "We should get married."

Celia answered him with another kiss.

Mr. Walker was smiling when he interrupted them. "I hate to barge in on this romantic moment, but if you're sure about this, I think I should give you some legal advice."

Celia and Silas's joyful expressions turned serious.

"Don't worry," Mr. Walker said. "I think we should talk over some logistics."

Later that afternoon, when Silas and Celia told Nancy they were getting married, she clapped her hands and kissed them both on the cheek. "That's wonderful news. I'd be happy to take you to Portland to look for dresses."

Silas put his arm around Celia. "There won't b-be time for that. We're getting married next Monday."

Nancy looked surprised. "What's the rush? Don't you want to wait until you're not pregnant?"

"Mr. Walker said if we're already married when the baby comes, Silas's name can go on the birth certificate as the father."

"And if we're getting married anyway, we m-might as well let him b-be born to a father and mother."

Nancy looked from Celia to Silas and back to Celia again as she sorted through their words and realized what they were saying. "Are you keeping the baby?"

"Yes." Celia reached out and took Nancy's hand. "Are you okay? I'm sure this is a surprise."

"It will be hard to start your lives as a ready-made family."

"We've done hard b-before," Silas said.

Nancy took his hand with her free one. "I know you have. If this is what you want to do, of course I'm okay with it. It'll almost be like I'm a grandma."

Celia shook her head and hugged Nancy. "Not almost." Nancy squeezed her tightly.

"Well, what do we need to do to get ready?" Nancy looked like she might cry.

Silas grinned. "Nothing. We went straight to the courthouse and got a license. Now all we have to do is wait."

A look of concern passed over Nancy's face and she turned to Celia. "Is it going to be hard to keep the baby? You know, after what happened?"

Celia put her hand on her stomach. "At first I thought I could never keep it. It would remind me of him. But I love this baby. And honestly, he reminds me more of being here. This is where we were the whole time I knew I was pregnant. This is where I felt him move and watched his heart and felt his hiccups. I tried so hard to find him a different family and nothing felt right, but as soon as Silas said I should keep him, I felt joy."

"What about you?" Nancy asked Silas.

"It won't be hard at all. I have the chance to help Celia take something that was wrong and m-make it right. We'll do it together." He put his arm around Celia and kissed the top of her head and Celia wrapped her arms around his waist.

Nancy smiled at the two young people she loved. "Tomorrow should be a good day. We have much to be thankful for."

Chapter 44

After a gray and snowy Thanksgiving weekend, Celia was surprised when she woke to sunshine. It had to be a good omen that they would be married on a bright, yellow day. She smiled and turned onto her side. The gray dress and pink cardigan Nancy had bought on Saturday hung on the closet door. Celia was glad Nancy had insisted they go shopping. She had planned to wear the same dress she wore almost every week to church. It would be nice to have something special for the wedding.

Celia threw back the covers and pushed herself to a sitting position. She gasped and braced herself on the side of the bed. It felt like the baby had pinched the inside of her abdomen. Hard. The sensation was short, and when Celia stood, she felt a dampness between her legs. Was she wetting herself?

At the bathroom door, a rush of water ran down her legs and puddled on the floor.

"Nancy?" When Nancy didn't answer immediately, Celia called her again with more urgency. "Nancy?"

"Did you need me?" Nancy asked as she stepped into the hall. When she saw Celia gripping the door frame, she hurried to her. "What is it? What's wrong?"

"I'm pretty sure my water broke."

At first Celia was worried the baby was coming too soon, but the delivery nurse at St. Charles hospital assured her that two weeks early was fine. With the concern for her baby's safety calmed, her thoughts turned to the wedding that was supposed to happen. She wanted to ask Mr. Walker what would happen with the birth certificate since they wouldn't be married when the baby came. Whose name would be put down as the father? Why hadn't they asked more questions? Why had they been so careless as to presume the baby would wait for them to marry?

Celia was surprised at the intensity of the contractions. For several minutes she could talk and relax then an ache in her back would turn to a searing pain that felt like her entire midsection was being squeezed by a tourniquet of straight pins. Then the pressure would ease and all she was left with was the dull ache in her back. She was in the middle of one of these when Silas hurried into the room. He had gone to work that morning so he could make arrangements to get his job in order so he could take a few days off.

"Are you okay?" He sounded alarmed.

Celia, who clutched both bed rails, gave one quick nod while she blew out short, sharp breaths. When the pain subsided, she reached out her hand for Silas.

"My water broke. He's going to come before we get married." Before the words were out, tears spilled down her cheeks.

Silas held her hand, his thumb brushing over her knuckles. "It's okay. We'll still get married."

"But the birth certificate. What will they do?"

"I'm not sure."

"I don't want it left blank and I don't want his name on it." She fought to keep the panic out of her voice as she whispered. "I don't even know his last name."

"We'll work it out. Don't worry."

"Can you call Mr. Walker? Please? Ask him what will happen?"

"Of course." Silas leaned over the hospital bed and kissed Celia gently. "I'll go call him."

"I love you," Celia called as he left the room.

"You're doing great," the nurse said as she looked at the monitor beside Celia's bed. "It looks like you're about six minutes apart. How are you feeling?"

A fiery contraction seized Celia's back and abdomen and her knuckles turned white on the rails. After the pain eased, she answered the nurse. "I'm doing pretty good until that happens."

"Dr. Vernon said he's on his way."

"Where's Silas?" Celia asked Nancy when the nurse had left the room. "He's been gone more than an hour."

Nancy stroked Celia's arm. "Maybe he's having a hard

time getting through to Mr. Walker. I'm sure he'll be back soon." She reached under her chair for her purse. "I'll bet you'd feel better if we brushed through your hair." Celia leaned forward and Nancy gently lifted Celia's hair away from her back and brushed through it, smoothing out the tangles. Surprisingly, when she relaxed back onto the pillow, she did feel better, and she let her eyes close as she waited for the next wave of pain.

"That's it. Just rest for a few minutes while you can."

Celia slipped her arm under her back to try and ease the ache that wouldn't let up. A few minutes later, she heard Silas and Dr. Vernon talking. And then she heard another voice. It was familiar, but she couldn't quite place it.

She opened her eyes and looked questioningly at Nancy. "Who's with Silas?"

Nancy smiled, but before she could answer, Silas, Dr. Vernon and Pastor Davies entered the room. Silas walked to the bed, picked up her hand, and kissed the back of it. "Are you ready to get m-married?"

Celia turned to Nancy. "I'm sorry about the dress."

Nancy waved her off. "There will be plenty of time to wear that dress. The most imp—"

Celia didn't hear the rest of her words as a contraction tore through her midsection. She gripped Silas's hand and bit her lip until it gradually passed.

"I'd suggest if we're trying to beat this baby here that we don't waste another minute," Dr. Vernon said.

It wasn't the wedding most girls dream of. Celia wore a light blue gown with tiny, navy triangles scattered across it. There were no flowers or guests and the proceedings were accompanied by voices in the hall and the uneven shoosh-shoosh of the uterine monitor.

"Do you have the marriage license?" Pastor Davies asked

and Silas pulled it out of his shirt pocket.

The ceremony was short. Nancy and Dr. Vernon served as witnesses and Pastor Davies didn't even bother to ask if anyone opposed the marriage. Before the next contraction came, Celia Edwards had become Celia Toller, Silas and Celia had shared a passionate kiss, and the minister had signed the certificate.

Three and a half hours later, Jack Alexander Toller slipped into the world.

Epilogue

Pearl stepped into the parlor at the Halifax House Bed and Breakfast, her laptop tucked under her arm.

"I hope you're not planning to go anywhere," said a pink-cheeked girl as she straightened a few magazines on the coffee table. "We're expectin' a blizzard this afternoon."

"No, my dear. I plan to cozy up to this fire and check in on some old friends."

"Can I get you anything?"

"A cup of hot cocoa would be lovely, if you have some."

"Comin' right up."

Pearl took the seat closest to the fireplace and tucked a throw over her legs. Snow whirled outside the window and she was happy to be indoors.

It had still been dark outside when a glass-rattling wind had awakened her. As Pearl had stared into the darkness, two names had been come to her mind. Silas and Celia. Two nights ago, Pearl had seen Celia in a dream, and as she had suspected before she left Sisters, Celia had been pregnant.

Ten months had passed since Pearl had persuaded Silas

to drive her to Bend, almost ten months since she had arranged for Celia to board with Nancy.

Not every couple she matched stayed with her. Pearl knew some stories from the day they met until the time they died. Others she barely knew their names. Most often, Pearl worked her magic then moved on. There were so many who needed what she had to offer. But there had been something unusual about Silas and Celia, something so tragic in their pain and loneliness that it reminded her of her own losses, and she felt compelled to be sure they didn't carry the burden of those sorrows forever.

"I hope ya don't mind. I added a spoonful of marshmallow cream." The young lady handed Pearl a steaming mug.

"It smells wonderful. Thank you."

Pearl took a sip of the hot cocoa, carefully placed it on a coaster then opened the laptop. After a little searching, she found what she was looking for. In the *Central Oregon Bulletin* she found a birth announcement.

Delivered at St. Charles Hospital, Bend.

Silas and Celia Toller, a boy, Jack Alexander Toller, 7 pounds, 2 ounces, November 26.

Pearl closed the laptop, relaxed back in her chair, and took a sip of hot cocoa. She smiled. How many years would it be before she felt the urge to use her magic for little Jack Toller?

Author's Message

I have loved this project. I'm thrilled to have been able to collaborate with these amazing authors and I can't wait to see how they have Pearl meddle in the love lives of their characters. It should be a fun year!

I'd be an ungrateful jerk if I didn't thank you for taking time out of your busy lives to read this book. With so many books out there to choose from, it's a privilege for me to have shared Celia and Silas's story with you. Thank you.

I'd love to have you subscribe to my newsletter. I promise not to inundate you with silly stuff—just updates on my books.

As an author, I hope to have happy readers who spread the word about my books. If you'd be willing, I'd be so grateful for a review on Goodreads or Amazon or wherever else you might share your thoughts on books.

Happy Reading!

Karey

12 Novels by 12 bestselling authors in 12 months

Power of the Matchmaker

SERIES

November 2015... Power of the Matchmaker
(A prequel novella of the Matchmaker's story)

January 1, 2016

February 1, 2016

March 1, 2016

April 1, 2016

May 1, 2016

June 1, 2016

July 1, 2016

August 1, 2016

September 1, 2016

October 1, 2016

November 1, 2016

December 1, 2016

Acknowledgements

Several years ago, my family drove through Sisters, Oregon on our way to the coast. I fell in love a little bit and decided someday I'd like to live there. Since a move has become less and less likely, I decided to do the next best thing, and use it as a setting. Sisters was a perfect place for Celia to start over and heal. Yes, the Three Sisters mountains (Faith, Hope, and Charity) are real and they're beautiful. The whole town is. This past summer, my husband and I spent three days in Sisters talking to the locals, eating at the restaurants, and soaking in the small-town atmosphere. The quilt show is a real thing and if you feel inspired to attend, watch for me, because I fully intend to be there next summer (and maybe every summer after that). Thank you to all the kind people who shared their lovely town with me. Especially Suzy, from the Chamber of Commerce, who loaded my arms with literature, my mind with information, my heart with enthusiasm, and my imagination with ideas.

Thank you to Dad, Mom, and Lori, Rachael, Corinne, Stephanie, Kathy, Missy, and Amanda. Having early readers who are honest but encouraging is such a blessing. I'm so grateful for your input.

Thank you Natasha and Rachael for the beautiful cover.

A special thank you to Rachael, my dear author friend, who is always there to bounce ideas off of, to offer pep talks, and to share the ups and downs of the life of a writer.

Finally, huge props to my husband and kids, who support, encourage, and keep the edges of my life from fraying and coming apart. I love you guys!

www.ingramcontent.com/pod-product-compliance
Lightning Source LLC
Chambersburg PA
CBHW070656180626
46817CB00006B/2396

* 9 7 8 1 9 4 1 8 9 8 1 0 9 *